THE
KING

A DARK NOVEL

ERIS BELMONT

Copyright © 2023 by Eris Belmont

All rights reserved.

No part of this publication may be reproduced, distributed, or transmitted in any form or by any means, including photocopying, recording, or other electronic or mechanical methods, without the prior written permission of the publisher, except as permitted by U.S. copyright law. For permission requests, contact hisdark96@gmail.com.

The story, all names, characters, and incidents portrayed in this production are fictitious. No identification with actual persons (living or deceased), places, buildings, and products is intended or should be inferred.

Book Cover by Eris Belmont

Second edition [2024]

Content Warning

The journey you are about to embark on is intended for mature audiences. (18+) This is a dark novel meaning it will contain content not suitable for all ages. **Even if you are of age, this novel may not be for you.**

This will contain:

Violence

Physical/Mental Abuse

Strong Language

Non-Con/Descriptive Sexual situations

Intense Situations

If you feel any of these may be triggering to you, please do not continue past this page.

For my Readers. You helped me find the confidence and joy in writing something that the world isn't ready for. Thank you for making me Eris.

Prologue

CYRUS

For the first time in a long time, I feel pain. *Excruciating* pain. I slowly lift my head, looking around me at the surrounding faces. Faces of humans. I don't have to see their faces to know what they feel as they stare down at me. I can smell it coming from them in waves.

Fear.

I flinch in pain as another spiked chain digs its way deep into my flesh. I can't recall how I got into this situation. All I know is that I want more than anything to be out. My arms are tied and spread out in front of me. Chains are wrapped around my arms, chest, neck, and even face. Each is coated in an elixir to help the spikes dig into my flesh and do serious damage. They made sure to completely immobilize me for whatever it is they have planned.

I try to shift to my beast form, but I can't. Not like this. Whatever these spikes are putting into my body is making me unbearably weak. And I can tell by the hopeful expressions that this is just what they were counting on.

"The great prince, Cyrus. Son of King Magnus. What joy it brings me to see you like this."

I narrow my gaze as a man emerges from the shadows, a blade in one hand and a vile in the other. I jerk on my chains, ignoring the searing pain as they dig deeper into my flesh. I know this man. Alfred. He was once my father's advisor before we discovered his involvement with humans who were trying to start a war. It would make sense that he is behind this. No other human would be allowed to get close enough to me.

He smiles at my predicament.

"It's terrifying, isn't it? Being vulnerable. Helpless. At the mercy of others?" He chuckles, looking around the room before his flat gaze falls back on me, "Feeling human."

"What is the meaning of this?" I hiss. He laughs even harder, turning his back to me.

"This is retribution!"

Alfred looks out over the group of humans that are watching. I can see the excitement that radiates off of them at the sight of me. The sight of one of us being at their mercy. "For too long, they have ruled over us. For too long, they have acted as if the world is theirs and we only live in it. I say no more! Who gave them that right? Who told them we wanted to be ruled? Who told them they were better than us? They want us to treat them like they are superior beings? Like they are gods?"

Alfred turns to face me, crushing the vial onto the blade. I watch in rising anger as the blade absorbs the liquid, giving it the ability to slice through my flesh and kill me. I lock eyes with Alfred. I refuse to give him the satisfaction of any fear. He raises the blade, aiming the tip so that it is level with my gaze. A slow grin spreads across his face as he glares me down, the blade steady in his hands. I ignore the thundering of my heart and the twisting in my gut as I stare death in the face. This is it. This is the end. I am going to die at the hands of a human, no less. But I refuse to show any fear.

I pull on my chains, rising on my knees as I glare him in the eyes. I let all of the anger I can radiate off of me until I know he can feel it in his bones, ignoring the searing pain of the spikes digging deeper into my flesh.

"Do it," I growl. Alfred's eyes widen slightly, and he hesitates a split second before lunging with the blade, aiming straight for my heart. No sooner does the blade pierce the top layer of my skin do the doors to the chamber burst open. Screams rip through the room and echo off the walls as the humans take off, trying to find any exit available to them. But they can't. They won't reach any before we do. We're stronger and faster, and our senses are much more heightened.

We are naturally superior.

"Argh!" I cry out in pain as blood comes rushing up my throat and past my lips. The blade Alfred once held now protrudes from my chest. I look up at Alfred with a narrowed gaze, and he pushes it deeper, screaming his hatred as he prays for my death. Lucky for me, he's human and has managed to miss my heart.

Alfred continues to glare down at me with hatred of humanity, his eyes burning with rage. "This is only the beginning. We will rise from our places beneath you. We will fight until we can fight no more. We will not settle for your ways. Now, we will fight back! And now we have a chance—"

Alfred doesn't have time to register what's happening as a large figure lands behind him. His head is torn from his shoulders, and what's left of his body drops with a heavy thud. I stare at his lifeless body, trying my best to contain my anger. But the longer I look, the more hatred I feel festering within me for the human race.

"Cyrus." I recognize my father's voice as he begins to work on my bonds, his gaze filled with a mix of horror and anger.

"I'm so sorry," he says.

But I don't respond. I don't have to. My hatred is palpable. A bitter laugh escapes my lips as I glare at the lifeless bodies that now cover the room.

If it's war they want, then I will happily oblige.

Chapter One

ANNALISE

Growing up, my father always told me I was special. It's not unheard of for parents to tell their children how special they are. Of course, in your eyes, your child will always be perfect. Until forces out there make you face the harsh reality that they truly are not. And it isn't because they lack talent or ability. It's because there are creatures out there that are *truly* special.

Beasts are what we call them.

They are so special, in fact, that they outmatch us one hundred to one in strength and ability. And because we are human and they are beasts, the life we know has been one of complete fear. Fear of their power.

I've never seen a beast in person. My father says it's best that I never do. They're monsters. The life they have subjected us to is one that no one should ever have to endure, which is why humanity within their kingdom decided one day that enough was enough. They rose and began a war against beasts. Unfortunately, this war has lasted longer than the years I've been on this earth and has claimed the lives of more humans than beasts. I know nothing of the life my father left behind for this one. He never speaks of it. From the moment I was born, he left that world behind to live in a village outside of the beasts' kingdom. A village where humans that want no part in their war can live in hiding, protected by the surrounding forest.

Although we live away from it all, that doesn't exclude us from fear. One day, the war will find us and the beasts will discover us. It won't matter that we haven't taken a side. Because we don't live under the beasts' rule, we will be classified as the enemy and bludgeoned. We've seen the aftermath of the beasts' arrival, which is why my father is so set on living here. He knows the war against them is pointless.

"There's nothing we can do but submit. Submit to the higher power," he'd say.

Maybe he's right. Something in his past has made him believe no matter who wins, the war is pointless. I've always wondered what life would become if the war ever ended. If the beasts win, it may very well stay the same, if not grow worse. If humans win, life may grow to be better. My father doesn't seem like he will be satisfied no matter which way it goes. My father may have lost hope, but a small part of me hopes that humanity finds a way to end this war. I've lived hidden in this village my entire life. I would like the chance to be seen as an equal and live a life free of fear and hiding. I've heard stories of the beast empire from the passing soldiers.

They live like gods.

Their cities are clean with paved streets. Even the commoners live a more lavish life than I've grown up with. Part of me wants to live like the beasts. That part of me sympathizes with the human war efforts. If all humans want is to live as the beasts do, then what could be so wrong with that?

"Anna!" My father's booming voice pulls me out of my thoughts as he barrels toward me in irritation. The broth I was charged with watching boils over into the fire pit below, sending heavy smoke to the ceiling just as my father pushes me out of the way.

"What could possibly be running through your mind for you to watch the broth burn?" he hisses, shoving the wooden spoon into the giant metal pot.

"I'm sorry, Papa, I got distracted," I say sheepishly.

He huffs in irritation, keeping his back to me. A sense of guilt washes over me at his disgruntled mood. Tonight is a very important night. Although he's clarified that we take no sides, the soldiers have deemed our village a safe haven. For years, they have shown up on the moon's final phase, knowing they can expect a hot meal, a warm bed, and protection from the beasts. My father has made it very clear. We never turn our own away. Especially when they're in need.

That is our way of helping the war effort.

Over the years, my father has tried to instill in me that the fight against the beasts is useless. He doesn't want me or anyone who lives in this village involved in the least. But as I see the men and women that trudge through our village from the war, I can't help but feel bitter hatred towards the beasts and shame that my father expects me to stay out of the fight.

We shouldn't be subject to the beasts' rule. It's cruel and inhumane. We have every right and reason to fight for our freedom. But my father insists it won't end well. I assume it has something to do with my mother's death. He never speaks of her or how she passed. And asking never ends well. He's a mysterious man in more ways than one, his attitude toward this war stemming from whatever life he lived in the past.

I'm pulled out of my thoughts as my father continues to grumble about my lack of focus.

"Go check the bread," he says between complaints. I quickly back out of the kitchen and make my way to the brick oven to pull open the small iron door. The bread is still rising, but a golden crust has formed, meaning it should be ready in a short amount of time. I note my father has prepared a lot of loaves, garnering my curiosity. I close the iron door, looking back at the archway my father is in.

"Papa, are we expecting the army tonight or something?" I ask.

Silence greets me before my father exits the kitchen, wiping sweat from his face. I can tell he's thinking of something to say to me to drag my attention away from the abnormally large portions of bread, once again shielding me from the real world.

My father is a large man. In another life, he could have been a warrior with his wide frame and muscular build. But his cheeks always hold a rosy glow from constantly being in front of a flame. He has established himself as the village baker, providing strength and guidance not only through cooking but in the way he took it upon himself to care for those in need.

"Papa?" I call him again, urging an answer with my tone.

"No. We are not expecting the army. But you never know how many people may show up. The war is reaching even greater heights. You never know how many men will come through in need of their spirits being raised," he says.

I place my hands on my hips, eyeing him. "I thought you said we were not to take sides."

"We're not," he snaps at me.

I shake my head in disbelief. "Preparing a feast for wounded soldiers sounds like we're taking sides."

He looks out the window before looking back at me.

"These men are facing the monsters of our nightmares. We are not taking sides. But we are not turning our back on our fellow man. Especially when they are risking their lives," he says.

A few months ago, hunters came through the village trying to recruit for the war, but my father ran them out immediately without so much as a meal.

"But I want to do more. I want to join the war effort. I want to become a hunter—"

"No! You will never, ever join that pointless war or those corrupt hunters. Do you understand me?" My father's face turns even redder from anger as he looms over me. My eyes widen at his drastic change in tone and intimidating demeanor. My father rarely raises his voice at me. So I know that when he does, his patience has run out. Silence washes over us as my father thinks about his next words to me.

"Anna... I know it makes little sense, everything that I'm doing now. But everything I do, I do to keep everyone here safe. *Especially* you."

My father places his hand on my shoulder, and I raise my gaze to look at him.

"There is only one end to this war. I can't stress that enough to you. The hunters don't know what they're doing. They are only riling up the enemy. I just hope that you'll never have to witness the difference in power between us and the beasts," he says somberly.

A light knock sounds in the doorway, and we both turn to see Dimitri poking his head in with a smile on his lips. Dimitri is the son of the blacksmith. He's older than me by a few years and very handsome with his pale blonde hair and crystal blue eyes. I feel my excitement rising to the surface as I take him in.

"They've begun to arrive," he says to my father. My father makes his way to the oven, pulling it open.

"Lead them to the tables out back," he calls over his shoulder. Dimitri nods, making a move to leave when I call him.

"Wait! I'll come to help you," I say quickly. My feet are moving towards the door before my father can stop me and I step out into the open street just in time to see some men hobbling around the corner. My eyes widen as I take in their battered forms. They're in much worse shape than any of the soldiers I've seen in the past. My heart sinks for them as my father's words gain more meaning. Are they aware that the war they are fighting is a lost cause? Do they know that their deaths and injuries are in vain?

I feel a soft pull on my arm and look up to see Dimitri's bright blue gaze looking down at me. Dimitri has been a part of my life for as long as I can remember. He looks nothing like his father, so I can only assume he got his good looks from his mother, whom we've both never met. He's tall and exhibits soft features. His jaw is well-defined, his hair sandy blonde and his eyes are the color of the sky. Though I've always been fond of his good looks, ever since I became a "proper lady," another part of me has come alive at the sight of him.

He offers me a soft smile, revealing his dimples as he pulls me around the corner. Once we are good and hidden from view, he brings his lips to mine, pushing me against the brick wall. His lips are soft and comforting against my own, and I immediately feel safe. I wrap my arms around his neck, pulling him closer to me. My body grows warm from our close proximity, heat pooling between my legs when he deepens our kiss. I suddenly feel his hands around my waist as he pushes me away.

He has a strained look on his face as he fights for control, and I immediately reach out, placing my palm against his cheek.

"Are you alright? Did I do something wrong?" I ask.

Dimitri shakes his head, giving me a small smile.

"No, you did nothing wrong," he chuckles to himself.

His soft gaze meets mine, and he gently pushes a stray hair behind my ear.

"I missed you, is all," he adds, his eyes roaming over my face with genuine adoration. A smile forms on my lips as he takes me in. He makes me feel beautiful. I never met my mother, but my father says I have her eyes. My eyes are bright amber, yet my hair is black with loose waves in it. I've always hated the combination. I felt it wasn't as unique as Dimitri's. But when Dimitri looks at me, I feel like the most beautiful woman in the world.

I place my arms around his neck, offering him a soft smile.

"My father will be busy with the soldiers tonight. Maybe we can sneak away and... you know," I say, smiling.

Dimitri groans, stepping away from me.

"Annalise, you know I want you," he murmurs as he reaches for my face, "but I will not be with you in that way until you are mine. Completely."

"I respect you and your father too much to do what you're asking... before we are one," he says, smiling.

I take a moment to catch his double meaning. A squeal leaves my lips, my hands covering my mouth in excitement.

"You mean..."

Dimitri nods his head, grabbing my hands in his before placing a soft kiss across my knuckles.

"I will speak to your father soon. That is, if you'll have me?" he asks.

I nod my head vigorously before jumping into his arms.

"Yes, of course!" I shout, burying my head into his neck.

Happiness I haven't felt in a long time flows through me. Though life may be fleeting living this way, I've never been happier than at this moment.

At this moment, everything feels perfect.

"Anna!"

I jump when I hear my name coming from my father's lips across the field. I offer an apologetic smile to the soldier whose food I almost dropped before making my way over to my father. He has two pails and a carrying pole in his hands. I eye him in confusion.

"What's this?" I ask.

He looks out over the men enjoying their food before looking back at me.

"A soldier just informed me we're expecting much more. Much, *much* more. I don't have enough broth made, thanks to *someone* letting it burn and spill over, so I'm going to the river to get some more water. Can you hold down the fort until I get back?" he asks.

I give him my best smile, nodding my head when I catch Dimitri out of the corner of my eye. He's watching me with a knowing expression, and I can tell he's waiting to speak to my father. A brilliant plan forms in my head. My father has presented me with the perfect diversion.

"Actually, Papa... why don't I go get it?" I ask.

My father raises a brow at me. He knows my least favorite thing to do is make the trek to the river and back to the village with heavy water pails. But this seems like the only time he will be free to speak with Dimitri. Once I get back with the water, he'll be cooking and serving the rest of the night.

I motion for Dimitri to come to us, and he places his cup down, making his way to where we stand.

"It's my fault you're having to do this, anyway. The least I can do is get the water for you. I'm sure the men would love to see you when they enter the village to know they've made it," I say with a smile. My father doesn't seem to buy what it is I'm selling, but Dimitri reaches us just in time to pull my father's attention.

"At least take Dimitri with you—"

"No! Papa, I can do this on my own," I say in irritation. I try my best to hide the desperation in my voice as Dimitri stares at me with wide eyes. But my father doesn't seem to notice the desperation between us. His head tilts to the sky. The sun is only hours from setting, which makes the forests more dangerous. I can see him contemplating not letting me go.

"I know the trail like the back of my hand, and you know as well as I do that part of the river is deserted. Please, Papa. Let me do this," I say. He looks at me, then back to the sun, finally relenting.

"Fine. But take Adam with you. And be back before sundown, or I'm coming to look for you," he growls.

I smile, placing a soft kiss on his cheek before grabbing the pails.

"Of course! I'll be back before you notice I'm gone!" My gaze shifts to Dimitri, who is smiling at me. He offers me a wink before turning to follow my father. I watch them as they walk away, my heart giddy with excitement. When I come back, my life will be forever changed.

The trek to the river takes around thirty minutes, but it isn't so bad since Adam is capable of light conversation. The village is located far from the river. Rivers are a freshwater source that anyone could happen upon, man or beast. So, the trail to get to the river is winding and narrow. Only if you're from the village can you find the river. Anyone else would get lost if they tried.

As we approach the river's edge, I drop the pails, rubbing my shoulders as I take in the surroundings. Since we had extra hands, my father gave Adam a few pails as well, so we'll have plenty of broth when we return.

A bird flits overhead, catching my attention as it perches itself on a branch. The forest is beautiful at this time. The sun casts a pinkish-orange glow over the sky, painting a beautiful background for the changing leaves. We have plenty of time before the sun goes down. And with the extra hands, I'll be back in no time. I smile as I dip the bucket into fast-moving water, imagining my future.

I'll be a wife to Dimitri. I'll be able to wake up to him every morning, living a life with the man who has been by my side since I learned to walk. Maybe I'll even be a mother. Both Dimitri and I never met our mothers. I know nothing of her, as my father refuses to speak of her or her fate. I can only hope that this war won't strip my child of my presence. A soft smile forms on my lips as I imagine my and Dimitri's children together.

"What's got you so giddy, Anna? You've been smiling like a fool since we left the village," Adam says.

I laugh softly, trying to focus on my task. "I'm just happy, is all."

Adam scoffs.

"Could it be Dimitri?"

I whip my gaze around to Adam with wide eyes, and he's watching me with a grin.

"Don't act shocked, Anna. Everyone knows you and Dimitri have been eyeing each other since you were toddlers," he says, laughing.

"And it doesn't hurt that you're all he speaks about—" Adam's eyes widen as he spots something across the river. His smile drops immediately, his gaze narrowing as he reaches for his blade. I follow the direction of his gaze, every muscle in my body tensing just as my heart rate increases.

There's a man across the river, if I can call him that. He's too unique to be a man. His hands are submerged in the river. He brings the liquid to his face, splashing himself while using the water to push loose strands out of his eyes. His white hair is held out of his face in a ponytail that falls down his back. He's stunning to look at, if not terrifying. His jaw is sharp, his lips full and carved on his face by the gods themselves. His nose is straight, his entire face perfect in every way imaginable. He also has a muscular build that is easily decipherable because he isn't wearing a shirt. Only pants, his sinister-looking blade resting on the grass next to him. The longer I stare, the more I can make out the faint scars that adorn his chest, neck, and cross face. It doesn't look grotesque, though. It adds to his intimidation.

I slowly realize the predicament we're in. He must be one of them. There's no way he's human. My arms are screaming in pain as the water grows heavier and heavier in the bucket. I don't know what to do to not draw attention to us. But the longer I think about it, the more I realize we're dead.

"Anna." Adam's voice is low, but I keep my eyes focused on the beast.

He slowly runs his hands through his hair, his eyes roaming the surrounding land when he stops. He purses his lips before his gaze immediately shifts to meet mine. Crippling fear claws its way through me, wrapping around my throat like a vise as I take in those soulless eyes. All my father's warnings and stories are in my head, screaming at me that my death is near. The beast doesn't move—doesn't blink as he studies me. His emotionless gaze roams over my body and what feels like my soul.

My legs shake as he stands to his full height, grabbing his blade on the way up. His gaze never leaves mine as the corner of his mouth slightly upturns.

"Anna, run."

Those are the last words Adam speaks. The sound of his blade barely leaving its scabbard clips in the air, but he never fully unsheathes it. The looming presence of the beast suddenly appears behind me, and Adam's body drops next to me, lifeless, with blood pouring from his throat. I blink in shock, my eyes incapable of moving as fast as this beast. My gaze remains focused on where the beast once stood across the river, his looming presence now directly behind me. Tears spring into my eyes as different solutions run through my mind, all of which seem pointless as his terrifying voice fills the air.

"Where exactly did you come from, little human?"

Chapter Two

ANNALISE

My entire life, my father told me stories about the beasts. He said if I ever came into contact with one, I would know. At this very moment, I know. I feel the heat of his body behind me, yet my blood runs cold from the proximity of his presence. It's a strange thing, being terrified and enamored all at once.

A shaky gasp leaves my lips when I feel the warmth of him shift. He slowly circles me as a predator would its prey until he stands over me, his dark gaze studying me intensely. Now that he is this close, I can see the ripple of lean muscle that adorns his body. I can also see the healed scars that wrap around his chest and shoulders. They are much deeper than they looked from a distance. Whoever he is, he's been through literal hell. I can only hope it wasn't by humanity's hand. If that is the case, mercy will be the last thing on his mind.

His hand slowly comes to caress my cheek, and I squeeze my eyes shut, my body trembling in terror as my muscles gain a mind of their own. His touch is warm and oddly gentle as he strokes my cheek, using the pad of his thumb to test the texture of my skin. He gently pushes my hair out of my face, leaning in close to me, his nose hovering over the base of my throat as he inhales softly. My trembles grow violent as a low rumble emits from his chest.

"Please...," I whimper.

I'm met with a soft chuckle as he steps back, my gaze darting to Adam's lifeless body. His face is twisted into a permanent state of shock. My whimpers fill the air.

"Look at me." The beast's voice is low and gentle. The sound instantly soothes me as it caresses my ears, leaving a pleasant ring in its wake. I slowly open my eyes, my gaze rising to meet his. My legs shake as I look into the soulless depths that are his eyes. They are dark blue. A *very* dark blue. The color reminds me of the ocean. Not the shallow end, but where the land falls off, and you can see nothing but the dark abyss looking back at you. I can barely decipher the separation between his pupil and iris. But I can see the slight tremble of his pupil as it sharpens into the shape of a serpent's. Against my better judgment, more tears fall as I look death in the face.

The beast smiles at my reaction, revealing straight, white teeth. I half-expected fangs. His smile drops as he searches my face, and the terror I feel only rises.

"Answer me." His tone has changed in an instant. Now, it is cold and deadly. I open my mouth, willing myself to speak as I wrack my brain for a plausible lie. There's an army of wounded soldiers and a village of innocent people only miles from here. If I cave, they could be as good as dead. My gaze shifts to Adam's body, and I lunge for his sword. I pull it from its hilt, holding it out to the beast. But he's fast. His blade collides against mine, jarring my body violently. The force knocks the sword from my hands, and I cry out, my body buckling under the pressure. The beast isn't finished. He uses my body's momentum against me, stepping to the side as I fall forward. Sharp pain grazes across my back, forcing a scream from my lips. I collapse in the dirt, a pained moan escaping me, and when I open my eyes, the tip of the beast's sword is now aimed directly at my face. My shirt is now sliced open, allowing the once comforting breeze to touch the new wound.

It's excruciating.

My blood now drips from his blade, and he narrows his gaze slightly. I shiver as a smile crawls onto his face. "You are brave."

He makes his way to where I am in the grass, dragging the sword along with him. I try to move, but he sliced so deep into my back that my body can't hold itself up. I look up at him through strained vision. He's walking toward me without a care in the world, dragging the sword he just used to slice through my back. His smile slowly drops as he towers over me, kneeling to be at my level. He reaches for me, and I squeeze my eyes shut, waiting for death. I tense, feeling his hand as he caresses my cheek.

My eyes slowly open to see him watching me with a terrifying expression. I wish more than anything I could look away from his intimidating gaze, but I can't. It's swallowing me whole. His eyes finally leave mine but fall in the trail's direction we came from, the direction of the village. He focuses for a long time before a smile cracks his lips.

"Found you."

"No!" I squeak. It comes out small and pathetic, but he hears it nonetheless. He whips his deadly gaze in my direction.

"No?"

I don't know if he expects a response from me or is just shocked that I spoke out against him. I cower as he comes near me, snatching me up by my hair. He pulls my face inches from his, accepting my challenge.

"Let's just see where this scent leads, shall we?"

The sound of laughter assaults my ears, pulling me from my dazed state. I can hear the villagers from this distance, and the scent of freshly baked bread hangs in the air. Usually, the sound would bring me comfort and joy. But I only feel horror in the wake of what this means.

He found them.

Using my scent, the beast tracked down the village. He never needed me to tell him where it was. I groan in pain as he steps over a rock, causing my body to jar against his. The taste of blood lingers in my mouth from my split lip. And he easily carries me like a sack of flour under his arm. I slowly lift my head to take in my surroundings. We are at the edge of the village where the trees meet the entrance.

My stomach lurches as he drops me into the dirt, causing me to moan in pain. When I look up, the beast is watching me in irritation. I slowly sit up, trying my best to stand, but failing miserably. I drop to my knee, gritting my teeth in pain.

"What... do you... want... from me," I manage.

His face morphs from a blank canvas to a slight raise of his brow. Slowly, his lips curve into that smile as he pulls his blade from its sheath. My back throbs in pain as I imagine what he is about to do with it. He places the tip of the blade in the center of my chest, and I flinch from the small pinch of it, biting my skin.

His emotionless eyes slink past me to the village beyond.

"This is your village, is it not?" he asks.

I don't know how to respond. He's already clarified he knows I came from here. But I fear the consequence of admitting I lied to him. More tears spill over as I squeeze my eyes shut, trying to stay brave.

I nod my head slowly.

"Yes," I whisper.

I open my eyes when he removes his blade. He's watching me with an amused grin.

"So what do we do now, do you suppose?" he asks. I hate that he's toying with me like this. He's holding not only my life but everyone beyond these trees lives in his hands as he drags it out for his twisted pleasure. His smile drops, and his eyes take on that murderous gleam.

"Answer me," he growls.

I sob, shaking my head. "I don't know."

"Look at me, human," he commands. I slowly lift my gaze, meeting his. If I live through this, his gaze will haunt me for the rest of my life. The beast tilts his chin, studying me deeper.

"Go," he says.

Confusion washes over me as we both stand across from one another. His sudden change in mood is worrying.

"I said go. Before I change my mind."

I slowly take a step back, and he continues to watch me, his gaze never wavering. He's taking me in as if memorizing my physicality, tilting his head slightly before a small smile graces his lips. It's so small I almost miss it. And in an instant, he vanishes. I gasp in shock, taking in the now-empty area. He did the same thing at the river's edge. I inhale deeply as I realize what this means before turning to limp into the village at the best speed that I can.

I make my way through the familiar houses and alleyways, all of which will be a ruin in history within the hour. Villagers and soldiers are all centered at my father's bakery enjoying the feast. They have no idea what's about to happen to them. The louder the laughs, the heavier the weight in my chest feels. A whimper of pain leaves my lips, my struggles pitiful in the face of reality. I need to warn them. I have to.

I finally round the corner, my father coming into view. It isn't hard since he's a large man. He's smiling at a soldier, their laughter once again ringing out in the air. My chest aches as I take in his smile. It is something I haven't seen from him in a while.

"Anna!" I turn just in time to see Dimitri coming toward me. As he gets closer and his eyes adjust to the condition of my body, his joy slowly morphs into horror. He reaches me just in time and I collapse in his arms.

"Anna, what the hell happened to you? Where's Adam?" he asks. I can hear the worry in his voice. A small part of me wishes the worry would stay this insignificant. I'm sure he thinks I fell or got lost in the trail. But with a few words, his entire existence will shatter. And his world will never be the same.

"Adam's dead. It—the beast—"

Dimitri doesn't hear me as he places his hands under my legs, hoisting me up. I immediately look around, trying my best to find signs of the beast, but he's nowhere in sight. I even look toward the woods for good measure but still don't see him. I grab hold of Dimitri's shirt, trying to get his attention.

"Take me to my father," I whimper.

Dimitri looks at me in shock before shaking his head. "Anna, we need to get you to the doctor—"

"Dimitri! They're here... you need to take me to my father," I whisper.

His eyes widen as he studies me. I know he can see the fear in my eyes and the way my fingers tremble against him. He moves in the opposite direction, quickly maneuvering through the crowd to get me to my father.

"Paul!" Dimitri shouts over the crowd. My father looks in our direction and sees me in Dimitri's arms. He rises quickly, making his way to us.

"Anna? What happened? I thought you said you knew the trail! Where the hell is Adam?" My father reaches out, taking me from Dimitri, already walking toward our house.

"It wasn't the trail. They're here. We have to warn everyone," I sob.

My father pauses mid-step, looking down at me with wide eyes. "Who, Anna?"

His eyes are wide and filled with desperation for me to tell him. But he already knows the answer before I confirm it for him.

"The Beasts."

Once the words leave my lips, the entire mood of the night shifts. I tense as the air shifts and a chill travels on the wind. I know everyone else can feel it, too. Gasps and murmurs fill the air as all eyes fall in one direction. I follow the direction of everyone's gaze and feel my heart sputter in my chest. It's him. All alone. Walking toward us with a deadly expression.

I let out an audible gasp as fear wracks my soul, my body shaking in my father's arms. My fingers clutch at his shirt as sheer terror fills me.

"Papa..."

I feel my father stepping backward slowly as the beast opens his mouth to address the crowd.

"This is where you pathetic weasels run to lick your wounds, then?" His gaze roams over the humans in attendance, and he wrinkles his nose in disgust.

"Rejoice. The Kingdom is in need of more slaves. If you do not die this night, you will have further purpose." He accompanies his words with a chilling smile as he pulls his blade from its resting place. The same blade he used to cut my back open. The air is eerily still. No one dares speak, let alone move. Being a slave is a fate worse than death. You suffer and starve in unsuitable conditions. The stories that have made their way out of the kingdom are terrifying.

A guard near us slams his fist on the table, laughing. He pulls his sword out as well, dropping it on the table.

"You come in here alone, beast, and expect us to surrender our freedom to the likes of you?" he shouts to the beast. More men stand in agreement, but the beast doesn't seem worried in the least. He's amused. It adds to my uneasiness. It's obvious from his confidence that he is a powerful beast especially if he came into a village full of soldiers offering the option of surrender.

But the soldiers don't see it that way.

"We are trained hunters of the king. Our last battle against your king was a victory! It is our people who now have yours in captivity! Do you think we came here to recover? We came to celebrate! Your king's reign is ending! This will be our world as it once was. And we will die before we let you take that away from us, beast!" The men all stand and cheer, roars of excitement echoing across the field. I look around at the faces of the villagers. Their faces hold hope. But when I look at my father, I see no hope there. I see desperation.

"You will die today, beast. And no one will be left to mourn you!" the soldier says, raising his weapon. The men all cheer, grabbing their swords as they charge toward the beast. To my shock, he doesn't look frightened at all. He smiles. It isn't the same smile he wore previously.

It's sinister.

Dimitri moves next to us, but my father grabs him roughly around the collar. "No, Dimitri! Don't be foolish!"

Dimitri looks at him in shock, but my father drags him away from the upending battle along with me. My father is moving fast on his feet, making his way to our home. He barges in the door, placing me on the cushions before running to the center of the room. Dimitri silently kneels next to me.

"Are you okay?" he asks. I nod my head grimly, looking toward the window—the silhouettes of villagers running flit across the glass.

"It was him. He did this to me," I say.

Dimitri gently squeezes my hand, but both of our attention is pulled when my father rips up the floorboards with his bare hands. I watch in shock as he reaches into the hole in the floor, pulling out a chest, followed by a sword. He swiftly opens the chest and begins rummaging through it, a look of desperation on his face. I finally pull myself out of my shock and question him.

"Papa, what are you doing?" I ask, trying to hobble from the cushion. He tosses a small bag out, reaching in to pull out a necklace. He makes his way to me with a determined look on his face as he fastens it around my neck, looking at Dimitri.

"Take her into the woods. Stay away from the streams. Make sure you escape to the East," he hisses.

Dimitri shakes his head in confusion. "What do you mean? The King's army is out there right now fighting—"

"They are useless! Did you not listen to me when I told you? There is a reason they call these things beasts! Listen!" my father hisses. We quiet down, and that's when I hear it—the screams.

"Oh my God," I whisper.

One beast. Just one is causing all of this turmoil.

"Those men won't keep him busy for long. He is powerful. Soon, he'll turn on the town." My father grabs the bags, shoving them in Dimitri's hands.

"There's money in there. Go somewhere far from here. Make a life for yourselves. Never look back," he growls.

My father's gaze is focused on Dimitri. "Remember what we talked about. I'm trusting you."

Dimitri grabs me, lifting me from the cushions, but I look at my father with wide eyes.

"Wait, Papa. You're coming with us, right?" I ask.

"No. I'm afraid this is where our journey ends, Anna." He places a soft kiss on my forehead, pulling away to look me in the face. He silently looks over me, tears forming in his own eyes as he studies me for what will probably be the last time.

"I'm sorry. For so much and for what I kept from you. Always remember everything I did was to protect you." His gaze dips to the necklace he gave me. "Never take that off. It is your protection. Only you are meant to wear it."

My father looks at me one last time before focusing his attention on Dimitri.

"Go."

Dimitri and my father move in opposite directions, and I watch in horror as my father picks up the blade he had hidden and walks back to the front door.

"No... No! No, Dimitri, we can't just leave him, no! Papa!"

I scream and beg, but my father keeps his back to me as we run out of the house. The screams are more prominent out here as everyone else runs into the forest to get away from the bloodbath. Some villagers are covered in blood with looks of terror etched onto their features. I look over Dimitri's shoulder, taking in the last remnants of the village, my eyes widening when I see a massive black cloud seem to take over the night sky.

I immediately bury my face in Dimitri's chest, letting him carry me away from certain death and the screams that will haunt me forever.

Chapter Three

ANNALISE

I tense, the pain unbearable, as a healer gently dabs my back with a medicine-soaked cloth. Dimitri and I have been traveling for days. We've been lucky enough to find a village on our way to the docks, and my father left us enough money to buy provisions and pay for a doctor. We found one just in time. Sweat and grime began infecting my back so heavily that I was afraid the skin would begin to rot.

"Who on Earth could have done something so gruesome to such a delicate young woman?" the healer murmurs to herself over my body. Bitter tears brim my eyes, forcing me to drop my head in my arms as sobs wrack my body. It's hell knowing that everyone in the village is dead or enslaved now because of me. I led the beast directly to the village. And my father paid the ultimate price.

I hear her shuffling around before she presses salve into my wound. "You should consider yourself lucky to be a refugee. I feel for the ones that the beast empire has enslaved."

I flinch when I feel the sharp tip of a needle pushing through my skin as she stitches the wound closed.

"Lots of travelers have come through here and told stories of the lives of slaves in that kingdom. The rumors claim the beast king despises humans. They captured him during the very first uprising and disfigured him terribly when he was just the prince. Rumors claim he goes through ten slaves a day, most of them dying by his hand," she says softly. Her words do little to help my mood, but it does give me solace, knowing my father is more than likely dead rather than enslaved.

"The beast king is cruel. He does unspeakable things to slaves. And for him to consistently go through them makes me wonder if we've even made a difference in this war," she adds, making me think of the beast's words as he addressed the village.

"The kingdom is in need of more slaves."

If one beast can do what he did to a village full of humans, it's no wonder the palace is in constant supply of slaves. And it sheds light on our lack of footing in this war.

The healer releases a bitter sigh, pulling my attention.

"There is no comparison, humans versus beasts. They are much stronger. Our 'king' is nothing more than a fool who has been brainwashed by his forefathers to think we are great. He has had a losing battle passed to him and now fights this belligerent war out of sheer pride. We are humans. They are beasts. That is all," she grumbles hopelessly.

"But surely you don't think we should just submit to living under their thumb?" I ask.

She shrugs, chuckling aloud. "You say that as if we have a choice in the matter. This isn't a war. It's a nuisance. And I pray

I never see the day the beast king joins the battlefield. He will make us pay for annoying his way of life."

The healer uses a blade to cut the stitching and wraps the now-closed wound with a fresh cloth.

"There. All set. I wouldn't stay here too long. The people here don't care for refugees. They've chosen their side in this war, and it isn't to sympathize with the lot of you," she says as she moves away to begin putting the discarded medicines up. I lift from the table, pulling what's left of my shirt over my head.

"Thank you," I say softly.

Dimitri is waiting for me as I exit the hut, a worried expression on his face.

"How are you feeling?" he asks.

I give him a sad smile. "Much better. So what's the plan now?"

"Now, we keep going East. If the beasts found our village, that means the war has shifted outside of their kingdom. None of this is safe. We have to get as far away as possible from the war," he says.

We continue our trek through the village, giving me time to study Dimitri. He lost his family as well, but it seems as if he is fine. I'm curious if he is trying to be strong for both of us. I gently place my hand on his arm, intending to ask when I realize we're heading toward the Inn.

"Dimitri, where are we going?"

"We need to get a good night's rest before we can make a trip across the river. It'll be hazardous and deadly," he says.

"The doctor said we shouldn't stay here. These people turn new faces in," I say as my gaze travels over the village. It's larger than ours, and the people here keep to themselves. They refuse to look in our direction, but I know they are aware of our arrival.

Dimitri takes a deep breath, looking at me with a raised brow. His gaze shifts, falling on the dense forest we should be heading through. He studies it intensely for a full minute before shaking his head. "We can't worry about what *might* happen right now. All that matters is survival. I will not hike into the woods as the sun goes down when we're on the run from beasts because of a rumor you heard from an old woman. We'll be much safer once we're rested and the sun is high in the sky."

He gently pushes my hair out of my face, giving me a smile.

"Besides, you're in no condition to travel."

I barely recognize myself as I stare in the mirror. The woman reflected at me looks as tired as I feel. My eyes are dull, sunken, and red from crying. My hair is wild and ratty, and my skin is raw and bruised. The swelling of my bottom lip has finally gone down, I notice. I gently press my lip, immediately thinking of the beast that put the bruise there. He was relentless in his attacks, amusement plastered on his terrifying face. There was no remorse, no mercy.

It makes me wonder why he let me live. Who was he to be so far away from the kingdom and without an army? Was he a scouting soldier looking for slaves for his king? Will he stop at our village or continue to the next one? He had to be someone stronger than a simple soldier to take out a large group of trained men. I release a breath, looking behind me at Dimitri. He's looking at a map he bought, his brow furrowed in frustration.

I make my way across the room, wrapping my arms around his shoulders before placing a soft kiss on his cheek. The warmth from his body is comforting. He has always been warmer than the average human, the heat giving me a sense of comfort when I'm in his arms.

"What's this?" I ask, looking down at the map.

"This is our ticket to freedom. There's a port just south of here. It's a three-day trip, but I think we can make it in two if we minimize rest stops. We can hop on the next ship out of this hell and head across the ocean," he says. I never thought about sailing across the ocean. No one knows for sure what lies on the other side. But there are ports that lead to the destination for humans, meaning there cannot be beasts. And since the war has expanded this far outside of the beasts' kingdom, it may be our only option.

"Are you prepared for that? To leave everything we know behind?" I ask.

Dimitri looks at me, placing his hand along my jaw. He gently runs his thumb over my skin in comfort as he smiles. "As long as I have you with me, I'm ready for anything. You're my home now, Annalise."

I smile, leaning in to kiss him. His lips are soft. And as I kiss him, I realize just how alone we are. We only have each other to rely on in this war. Tears spill over my cheeks as I deepen the kiss, wrapping my arms around his neck. Dimitri has been by my side for as long as I can remember, our future laid out plainly in front of us. But now it looks bleak and uncertain. I wrap my legs around his waist, pressing myself against him as the ache between my legs grows. The desire to feel something other than this overwhelming loss is taking over my senses. But the moment I feel Dimitri's erection pressing against me, he pulls away from the kiss.

His deep blue gaze studies me.

"Anna—"

I force the best smile I can, wiping my tears. "It's okay, I want this," I say desperately.

"No. Not like this," he urges.

I frown.

"Why not?"

He gives me a sad smile, wiping my tears as he speaks. "You're injured. And we're both emotional from losing everything we ever knew. Is this really how you want to remember your first time?"

"I—"

"Shh," Dimitri hisses, his grip around my arms tightening as his gaze whips to the door. His eyes narrow, and he moves quickly to the chair, grabbing his blade. I watch with wide eyes as he looks at me, placing his finger over his lips.

Quiet.

Suddenly, the door is ripped off its hinges as men enter the room with weapons. Dimitri immediately attacks, fighting them off, but there are too many. They are on us in seconds, snatching me off the bed as a group of them attack Dimitri, ripping his weapon away from him.

"Dimitri!" I scream his name as I'm dragged out of the Inn, and no one does anything to help. My struggles become annoying to the man carrying me, and I cry out in pain as he strikes me across the face. The world spins, and I vaguely make out Dimitri's screams as the world blurs.

The men take us into the very forest we were going to escape into, roughly dropping me into the dirt. Pain ripples up my back as they irritate the wound. A pained groan escapes me as I try to rub myself to staunch the pain. It takes a moment to realize my hands have been bound. My screams fill the forest as I try to free myself, to no avail. And in the darkness, I make out Dimitri's limp form. He's unconscious, with a nasty wound on his head.

My gaze shifts over the clearing desperately. Any hope I was feeling disappears in an instant when beasts emerge from the shadows. The flame of the torch slowly illuminates their terrifying form, solidifying my defeat. I've only ever seen a beast days ago. And now I am seeing two more clad in armor. Their sheer presence forces the human brain to comprehend that they aren't human. Something about them is off. And although they have human features, those eyes are haunting.

Their dark eyes roam over the both of us, stopping when they take in Dimitri.

"What happened to this one? Is he dead?"

My heart explodes in my chest from his words, forcing my struggles. Their gazes shift to that of irritation as they take me in before our captor roughly shakes me.

"Shut up! Or I'll slice his throat."

I instantly stop my struggles, not wanting to do anything that could risk Dimitri's life.

"He was stronger than we thought he'd be. We had to make sure we could get him out without a struggle. Took five of us to get him down."

One beast approaches Dimitri's unconscious form, lifting his head to inspect him. "You say they escaped from the village west of here?"

Our captor nods.

"We'll take them. The king will be pleased with this one's condition. We don't bring in too many in good shape."

"No, you can't do this! We are one of you! How can you turn in one of your own!" I screech.

My words, however, have no effect on the men. They turn their backs to me even when I continue to scream as they take us into custody. I scream even when a gag is placed over my mouth, struggling like a maniac before the butt of a sword comes hurtling toward my face, and darkness envelopes me.

The sounds of life slowly enter my headspace. Uneven footsteps sound, the light chatter of conversation, and the giggles of children. I am greeted by the pink streaks of the sky as I crack my eyes open, the jostle of the wagon jarring me awake.

It's afternoon.

The surrounding architecture is foreign to me. The buildings are tall and covered in a clean material that makes them shine. The streets are paved, and the trees are in full bloom, covering the area. The jangle of chains accompanies the laughter of children and the giggles of women as I sit up. A soft gasp escapes me as I touch the collar locked around my throat. My wrists are attached to the same chain.

"Anna! Thank God you're okay!" My body feels like it's trapped in a daze as I follow the sound of Dimitri's voice. He's attached to the back of the cart, his chains mimicking mine.

"W-what happened?" My voice sounds scratchy from the lack of use. I study Dimitri to make sure he's okay, my gaze lingering on the blood crusted in his hair.

"They caught us. And we're in their kingdom now, Annalise," he says grimly.

My eyes widen. This is the beasts' kingdom. I look around in awe-filled terror. They live starkly different, the war not seeming to have affected their way of life in the least. I slowly turn to take in the looming palace that sits ahead of us. It's surrounded by a powerful waterfall and a bridge connecting the street to the entrance of the palace. The white stone shines brightly, with some parts topped with glass ceilings. The palace is so large more bridges that overlook the water connect the other buildings. I've never seen anything like it.

It forces the dark reality of just how fucked we are.

The beasts live in a completely separate world from our own. We are out of our depth. I face Dimitri, our gazes locking. We both have nothing to say nor do we have a way out of this. We were so close to our freedom, and they brutally ripped it from us in an instant.

Looks of disgust are shot our way as the kingdom's inhabitants notice us. But I'm focused on the vast array of beasts. Some have black hair, while others have red. Some have pale skin, and others are tan. Growing up in our village, I've never seen such a variety of beings.

The trip to the palace takes another thirty minutes. The cart comes to a halt in front of the palace, leaving me in complete awe. It's much larger now that we are in front of it. I look at Dimitri with wide eyes as the beasts converse. But he's as lost as I am. After a moment, a beast comes to the back of the cart for Dimitri. Fear is replaced with desperation as I launch from my place on the cart, only to be held back by my chains.

"No!" I scream. I watch helplessly as they pull Dimitri away from me. But he doesn't fight.

"Everything is going to be fine, Annalise." His voice is broken as he offers me a sad smile.

We both know it won't be fine. We both know that this will be the last time we see each other. I am going to die in this kingdom. I drop my head in defeat, tears streaming down my face.

"What is this?" I tense at the sound of a chillingly familiar voice. It's a voice I thought I would never hear again. My gaze whips up, landing on the owner of that voice.

It's the beast from the woods.

He looks different now. He's wearing robes that are a mix of whites, grays, and blacks. His hair is neatly pulled from his face and held in a tight bun atop his head. He doesn't look ready to kill an entire village. He looks regal and relaxed. In fact, other than the scars that were already there, he seems to have gained none from his battle with our entire village days ago.

His dark eyes roam over the scene before him, stopping when he spots me. His gaze is intense as it settles, studying me with purpose. A chill grips my spine as the corner of his mouth twitches ever so slightly.

Every beast in the vicinity bends to their knees, bowing before this beast.

"Your Majesty."

My mouth drops slightly as the words ring in the air, revealing how important he is. He wasn't a random soldier on a mission.

He's the king.

Chapter Four

ANNALISE

The King.

He's the *King*.

A million questions are running through my mind at the moment, but I don't have the time to address any of them as he moves around the cart toward Dimitri. All of my fear disappears as I once again pull at my chains in frustration.

"Get away from him!" I cry.

The king ignores me, his malicious gaze shifting to the soldier who holds Dimitri.

"What. Is. This?" Irritation drips from his words as he repeats himself.

"A valuable slave, Your Majesty. He has a strong muscle build and stamina. We found him in a village a little further west. We think he will be a good addition to the war unit," the soldier says, visibly intimidated by the beast circling him.

The king's eyes fall on Dimitri as he grasps Dimitri's face between his fingers. He shifts Dimitri's head from side to side, inspecting him like cattle, and Dimitri holds his gaze, pulling his head out of the king's grasp.

"I see. Send him to Rowan. I'm sure he could use the extra hands," he says.

The king's eyes drift to me as they hoist Dimitri up. "What about this one?"

"That one is going to the auctions."

My stomach drops from the guard's words. The auctions are where the worst of the worst go to purchase their unwilling slaves. No one that goes to the auctions lives past a week.

No one.

Dimitri's struggles fill the air at the revelation, desperation clear on his face as he tries to break free. His struggles pull the king's attention, his eyes narrowing in irritation. His gaze slowly drifts back to me as he slowly realizes the gravity of our situation, a vicious smile forming on his lips. The king approaches me, his fingers wrapping around the chains. With a swift movement, he pulls me from the cart. Since they chained my wrists to the center of the collar, I cannot catch myself, and I collapse in the dirt beneath him. He bends to my height, placing his finger under my chin as he forces our gazes to meet.

My heart beats faster in my chest as he studies me. His eyes are deep blue, the pupil trembles slightly, sharpening like a serpent, and he smiles. "I'll take this one."

Dimitri's reaction is immediate.

"No!" He lunges for the king, but the guard roughly rips him back. My eyes widen as Dimitri's grunts turn almost animalistic as he tries to attack us. The guard quickly uses the butt of his sword to knock Dimitri unconscious, his body falling limp before us. I'm pulled away from Dimitri before I can reach for him. I hold my fingers out, tears forming as I try to pull against the chains.

"Dimitri," I whisper his name, but he doesn't stir. And the king of the beasts himself pulls me away from him without allowing me one last look. Or one last touch. Nothing. We're both pulled apart by the beasts, and I find the will to fight. I turn to the king, digging my heels into the ground.

Dimitri is my life. And without him, I have nothing. I am nothing.

"You will have to kill me before I ever willingly become a slave," I growl.

The king halts, turning to face me. He wears an emotionless expression as he studies me, deliberating how he will end my life. He doesn't move. Doesn't blink. I can't tell if he's breathing. But he finally moves, slowly standing over me. The closer he gets, the more I am forced to crane my neck to look him in the eyes. I can't breathe as he stares into what feels like my soul.

A small smile forms on his lips as he looks over my shoulder. "The slaves that belong to the sword smith have it easier than most. They perform hard labor, so we need them strong enough to do a good job. We feed them, clothe them, and try not to beat them too much."

His smile disappears as he roughly grips my chin, earning a gasp from me.

"One word from me, and that future disappears for your lover. Any future disappears. Do you understand?" he says in a terrifying tone. His eyes search mine, and I can't bring myself to form a coherent thought, let alone a sentence.

"Your Majesty!"

The king is still searching my face as footsteps belonging to the perky voice approach us. He stands to his full height, facing the voice. Judging from the expensive gown and intricate jewelry she adorns, I assume she is noble. She's a beautiful beast, her light brown hair pulled into an updo to show off her features. Her eyes, however, are that haunting blue that all beasts share.

Her gaze shifts to me, and a visible frown forms on her lips.

"I thought you were going for a walk?" she asks.

"I was," the king pulls on my chains, causing me to stumble forward, "but the guards brought me a new slave."

The female beast steps away from her servants, approaching me. I drop my eyes out of fear as she stands over me.

"I can take her. I am short of slaves at the moment," she says. My gaze slips past her to the servants that belong to her. They're dressed in fine silks, the colors coinciding with hers. But they are not human. The humans are the slaves at the back, dressed in dull garments, with sunken eyes and bruised faces.

"How dare you look at me without permission!" I don't have the visual speed to register her hand coming near my face. Luckily, I don't have to. The king catches her hand inches from my cheek, the small breeze forcing my hair to lift slightly. I watch them both with wide eyes as the king moves inches from her face, his amusement gone.

"Do not overstep, Marzia. I did not say you could have this one," he says with a warning in his tone. Fear flashes behind her gaze before the king roughly releases her, pulling on my chains. It makes me wonder what kind of relationship they have. As I take in this female beast's expression, the healer's warnings about the beast king come to mind. I recall what the healer said about his reputation and the beast that he is. I see the dynamic clearly.

Beasts fear him as well.

A cruel smile forms on the king's lips as he takes in her expression, a wicked gleam in his eyes. "Will you be joining me tonight?"

The beast, Marzia, trembles at the mention of his invitation.

"No, Your Majesty, I only came to visit," she says shakily.

He chuckles softly, placing a kiss along her cheek, but I notice her visibly pale at the action. Who she is at this moment compared to who she was moments ago is starkly different.

"That's too bad," he says. He doesn't spare her a glance as he pulls me along to enter the palace, leaving the trembling beast behind.

"You are all here because your life has no other purpose. Your purpose now until you die is to serve. You are slaves. Nothing more. So do what you are told, or you will face death much quicker than you would like."

I look around the room filled with new slaves, hoping to recognize anyone from my village, but there is no one. All the humans here are strangers. I tense when a girl beside me sobs from the beast's pep talk.

The king brought me to servants who had me washed and dressed with the rest of the incoming slaves. They then brought us to the lower level of the palace where the beast in charge of the slaves now gives us our new life meaning. He calls himself the "Overseer". He's an older beast with graying hair around the edges. His dark eyes roam over us in disgust. There are about twenty of us here that are new. The rest of the slaves were dismissed when we arrived. I could see from the lifeless looks in their eyes that none of them know which day will be their last.

I shudder to think about which will be mine.

"There are rules within the palace that you are to follow at all times. If you are seen straying from these rules, you will be put to death. We do not tolerate disobedience here, so I suggest you all listen very carefully. You are not to look your superiors in the eyes. You are not to speak to anyone within the palace walls. You are nothing more than furniture—living, breathing furniture here to serve. You are never to be in the palace halls at night unless you have been given specific instructions. And we will know if you have permission. Do not test this. You will die," the Overseer continues as he eyes us in disgust.

Once he's satisfied with the amount of fear on our faces, he opens up a journal and begins separating us into groups. He walks within the lines, his eyes roaming over each of us individually to mentally decide where it is each of us belongs. Once the groups are separated, he goes individually to each, giving them their assignments. I look around at the people that were placed in my group. Three other girls that look older than me are staring lifelessly at the ground.

I can't help but wonder where in the kingdom they came from. How recently was their village destroyed? It's depressing to see how many of us a day are brought in to become slaves. It's even more depressing to think of how many were given death instead. I think back to my father. He sacrificed himself for us to get away, and we failed him. I lower my eyes to the ground, letting my tears fall. There's been no time to mourn, and I know once the Overseer comes around to give us our assigned tasks, I will no longer be able to think about the fate of Dimitri and my father. I will only be able to focus on surviving.

I hear footsteps and keep my eyes trained on the floor.

"You three are being assigned to the king's division. You will report to the kitchen immediately for work. Beatrice will show you the way."

The Overseer meant what he said. We are nothing more than furniture. Secret corridors have been placed within the palace for slaves to move about without being seen.

We are a hindrance to the eyes of the beasts.

The kitchen is busy once we arrive. The servants prepare dinner while the slaves clean, wash, and sort. I step into the kitchen with the other two women, lightly pulling at my dress. It's an unflattering brown dress with long sleeves that reaches my ankles. Some unlucky soul has clearly worn it before. The material is worn, and there are tears around the sleeves and within the skirt. Lucky for me, the collar is high enough to keep my father's necklace hidden.

The blonde next to me is still crying about the fate she's been given, and I can see why. As I look around, I notice some slaves have hideous bruises and scars on their bodies. If this is what our future has in store, I would have been better off dead.

"Are you the new slaves, then?" A female beast approaches, her dark gaze roaming over the three of us. She's a tall beast with sharp cheekbones and an even sharper blade in her hands as she looks at us. She clicks her tongue in disappointment.

"The slaves are in worse shape each time they send you," she says aloud.

She looks at the crying blonde in irritation. "Stop that now. You won't be here for much longer. Slaves don't last a week in the king's division. He'll end up killing you for a stupid mistake, and the next set will replace you." She plasters on a sarcastic smile. "Rejoice. Your suffering will only be as long as the week," she adds.

I feel my heart beating as the urge to cry comes over me, but I fight it. Unfortunately, the blonde next to me cries even harder, her loud sobs pulling the attention of beasts in the vicinity. My eyes widen as a beast approaches us with a look of irritation on her face. She pushes through us with ease, grabbing the blonde. I watch in horror as she pulls the blonde in close, using a blade to slice her throat.

A scream leaves my lips along with the other girl who came in with me as the blonde collapses, clutching her throat. Blood pours from the wound as she gurgles on the floor, but no one seems to care. The beast who stabbed the blonde holds her blade inches from my face to prove a point.

"The king doesn't give a damn about any of you. If you hinder us from doing our jobs, you will lose your life by our hands as well. Do not forget that. You have no rights. You are the property of the kingdom. If you are going to be useless, you have outlived your purpose here," she snaps.

The door to the far wall opens, and in comes more servants.

"I need the king's dinner!"

The beast with her knife in my face narrows her gaze.

"Come with me," she snaps before looking at the other slave. "Clean this up."

I feel numb as the beasts shout their orders at me, shoving plates in my hands. I follow them silently, holding back the tears and the emotions threatening to bubble to the front. We are considered the lowest of the low here. The Overseer said it himself hours ago: we are living furniture. Our lives mean so little that a servant can take it if it suits them at the moment. The king's wrath is only another possibility.

We can die at any second.

I feel a rough snag on the collar of my dress as a beast shoves me to the back of the group.

"Slaves at the back," she hisses.

I keep my head down as we leave the kitchen, making our way to the king's quarters. The doors are tall and seem to be made of gold. There's also a tree engraved on the material. A servant steps forward, knocking on the door before stepping back to wait. After a long pause, the door is opened to reveal a female beast. She's dressed in transparent clothing, her breasts visible to all of us. None of the beasts seem to be shocked by the display.

"Your Majesty, your dinner has arrived," she says softly over her shoulder.

After a moment, three more beasts exit the chamber with panicked expressions, wild hair, and unfastened dresses. Then, the king himself emerges in all his naked glory. Only a robe hangs from his shoulders as he takes in the group of servants before him, a terrifying look on his face.

"Enter."

I lower my gaze, remembering the rules as we make our way into the king's chambers. The servants quickly set up the food at the table, roughly yanking the plates out of my hands. They take a while to set everything up, and once they finish, we all bow to leave. I wait until all the servants are at the doors before I walk with them, remembering the rule to stay at the back.

I'm almost out the door when I feel a rough yank on the collar of my dress.

"Not you."

I shiver as the king's voice washes over me. He pulls me into the room, and I stumble backward from the force. I watch in horror as the last servant pulls the doors closed, locking me in the room with the king of the beasts.

Chapter Five

ANNALISE

My eyes remain trained on the floor as I clasp my hands in front of me. It's all I can do to stop the trembling as the king of the beasts steps away from me. I'm alone with the beast that wiped out my village all on his own. The silence is deafening, forcing me to take a deep breath.

"Come here." His voice carries across the room to where I stand. It takes all my mental power as I force my legs to take me to where he's seated. I feel his gaze on me as I approach, keeping my eyes down for fear of what could happen.

"You can look at me." His voice is gentle, but I don't miss the mocking tone.

I lift my gaze, almost breathing a sigh of relief when I see his eyes focused on the spread in front of him. He's sitting at the small table with food laid out before him, giving me an opportunity to study him. His hair is free, the long tresses tumbling down his back. My gaze shifts to the bed that is completely askew, and I think of the three beasts that ran out of here when we arrived. I can't even begin to imagine what kind of beast this is.

As if sensing my thoughts, he looks up, causing my breathing to hitch as our eyes meet. Looking into his gaze takes more out of me than the hike to the river. Our close proximity doesn't help the frantic beat of my heart as he studies me, and he knows it. He smiles at my reaction, making me realize just how much I hate his smile. It's something that will give me nightmares, right next to the soulless depth of his gaze.

"You were so vocal at the entrance of the palace," he says with an amused grin.

He continues to watch me, reveling in my silence. "Are you hungry?"

Confusion strikes me. I don't know why the king of the beasts would care whether I eat or starve to death, especially since he is the reason I'm here in the first place.

"You have an issue with answering questions," he says. His expression has lost amusement, morphing into irritation as he studies me. It reminds me of the first time I laid eyes on him across the river. He was asking questions then that I refused to answer.

"I'm sorry," I whisper, no longer able to hold his gaze, "I am hungry."

Silence washes over the room before he stands. "Look at me."

I slowly raise my gaze, looking into his. They're the eeriest eyes I've ever seen.

"You can eat." His gaze dips to my chest and he slowly raises his hand, his fingers trailing along my collarbone until they find the chain of the necklace my father gave me. I tense as he pulls it from its hidden place. "If you tell me where you got this from."

He pulls it up enough that it rests between us. My heart hammers against my chest at the closeness of this beast. He carries such an intimidating confidence. It's no wonder he is the king.

"It's a family heirloom," I whisper. I don't know how he noticed the necklace when it was hidden, but I hope he won't take it when he hears how important it is to me. I recall my father's words as he handed it to me in a panic.

"Never take off. It is your protection. Only you are meant to wear it."

The king's expression is unreadable as he studies the necklace with an intensity I don't understand.

"A family heirloom...," he murmurs.

He continues to study it, his brow furrowing slightly.

"How did your family come into possession of this?" he asks.

"I don't know." My response pulls his attention, his gaze once again meeting mine. He narrows his gaze slightly before stepping aside, letting go of it.

"Eat," he says. My stomach clenches in pain as I take in the abundance of food on the table. I don't know when I last ate a proper meal, but I don't trust him. I take a small step back, shaking my head.

"It isn't my place," I murmur, hoping he'll let me leave, but it doesn't seem to be on his mind as he slowly circles my body, inspecting me as he does so.

"Your Majesty," he says.

I look at him in confusion. "Wha—Ah!"

The king roughly grips my chin, raising my gaze to his.

"You have the manners of a three-year-old. When addressing me, you say 'Your Majesty'. As it is your place," he growls.

I'm quick to recover.

"Yes, Your Majesty."

The king chuckles, releasing me. "So you aren't *completely* dull."

He once again falls silent as he studies me.

"Turn around," he says. I slowly will my legs to move, turning so that my back is facing him. The heat his body emits is intense as he steps closer to me. His fingers pull at the strings of my dress until it falls loosely around my shoulders, forcing tears to spring into my vision. Heat washes over me as his fingers lightly brush the wound he caused, forcing me to release a trembling breath.

He senses my fear.

"Calm down, human. I won't touch you in that way to sully my reputation. You are a slave, and I am the king. You're no better than the dirt beneath my feet," he says in amusement. I hate to admit it, but his words sting. I was raised around men who adored me and felt I was the light of their lives. To hear I am nothing more than dirt chips away at my barely stable mental state.

I tense when I feel his fingers brushing over my wound, playing with the stitching.

"I was wondering how you were still alive," he murmurs. He presses his palm against my back, pushing into the wound. Suddenly, a wave of warmth trickles over me, all heading in one direction. I cry out from the pain that instantly turns into a pleasurable warmth.

In an instant, the feeling is gone.

I stumble forward, out of breath, turning to face the king in confusion. His eyes are dark as he looks at me. He's studying me. But he won't reveal his thoughts. Finally, he turns away from me, making himself comfortable at the table, and I take that as my cue to pull my dress over my shoulders. He silently watches as I do so, popping a piece of fruit into his mouth as he drops the thread from my wound to the ground.

"What is your name, slave?"

"Annalise, Your Majesty."

He smiles at my use of his title, repeating my name to himself softly. "Annalise."

My name rolls off his tongue with familiarity.

"I am assuming you were assigned to the kitchens?" he asks without looking at me.

"Yes, Your Majesty."

"Hm," is all he says before returning to his food. Time passes as he silently eats in front of me. I keep my eyes down and my mind clear, trying not to think of the painful hunger that's constricting my stomach. My mind wanders to how Dimitri is doing. I hope he can hold on. I don't know where humans are in the war, but maybe we'll be saved. Maybe someone will come through for us.

"Annalise." The king is looking at me with a blank expression.

"Tell me about your village," he says.

I blink in confusion, trying to decipher the situation. He clearly knows something that I don't. He's been interrogating me on things that I don't have the slightest clue about. But he's also been very vague in his questioning.

"What about it, Your Majesty?"

He picks up the glass of wine and takes a small sip.

"Why was a small village that stayed out of the war housing and feeding soldiers?" he asks.

"We would never turn our back on our own," I whisper, repeating my father's motto. The king smiles, taking a sip of his wine before setting it back down on the table. He looks at me for a moment, standing.

"Your village was an enemy of the empire. Not only were you aiding soldiers, but you were also housing weapons that were meant for beasts' destruction," he says, approaching me. I'm shocked to hear that bit of news. My father always said we were a peaceful village. We wanted no part in the war. My eyes widen as the king approaches.

"I don't—"

"Of course you don't. I see now that you're just a naive girl who knows nothing of the war or the people around you. It's very clear to me you are no threat," he says.

He hesitates, looking at me.

"Though I can't say the same for the man that raised you," he adds.

I perk up at his words, earning a smile from him.

"Am I correct in assuming he gave you that 'heirloom'?" he asks.

It's difficult to find my voice as he glares at me. "Yes, Your Majesty."

"He was among the few hiding in that village under the guise of being naïve villagers." The king watches me carefully as he speaks, and I know he's watching for a reaction. But I'm shocked. He fought my father? I never even knew my father was a fighter, let alone able to hold his own against a beast.

"How do you know the man you fought was my father?" I ask. This earns a smile from him. He brings himself closer to me, his nose hovering over my throat.

"His scent lingers on your necklace," he murmurs. Tears spring into my eyes, and I take a step back from him. His smile is gone as he towers over me, studying me in confusion. "But not on you."

Before I can think of what his words mean, he's pointing to my necklace.

"Take that off," he commands.

His voice is cold and threatening. A sob escapes my lips as I reach up with trembling fingers, clasping the necklace.

"Please... it's the last thing he gave me," I manage.

My pleas don't phase him, though. His eyes flash as the same darkness I saw when he was fighting the army in our village appears. I think about my father's words to me and squeeze it tighter. It will either protect me, or I will get myself killed trying to protect it.

The king's gaze narrows, and I've clearly pushed him to the end of his rope. His hand is around my arm, pulling me flush against him in an instant. I don't have time to register what's happening as he rips it from my throat and shoves me back. His strength is so hard I can't catch my footing and hit the ground in a heap. When I look at him, he's studying it with vicious intensity, his hate-filled gaze focusing on me. My body freezes as fear overcomes me. I want to reach for the necklace or at least fight for it, but I've seen what this beast can do. And he's been more than generous with my lack of compliance.

"Get out," he snaps. I stand, rubbing my throat in pain. I try to speed for the door when there is a rough pull on my hair, forcing my body back and into the chest of the beast.

"Bow before leaving your superiors, slave," he growls into my ear.

He releases me swiftly, and I don't waste time bowing to him before scurrying from the room.

Chapter Six

ANNALISE

The King is a vicious and cruel beast. The rumors are nothing compared to the horrors I've witnessed. I grab hold of the legs of what's left of the body, hoisting it up and into the cart. Out of all the slaves that arrived with me that day, I am the only one left. And I can only assume it is because I have not come into contact with the king since the day he took my necklace. And that was weeks ago.

Since arriving, I have lived a tortured hell. The food, if I can call it that, is barely edible. A slave is the closest thing to a rat. And they won't waste food on rats. The bread is molded and stale; the gruel is sour and old. And we are too low in their hierarchy to be given meat. They beat us for everything. The bruises that I saw on the slaves when I first arrived have now appeared on my skin as well. I have no hope. All I can do is wait for a servant to slip and end up killing me if the king doesn't do so first.

I'm pulled from my thoughts as a servant rushes behind me, shoving me roughly in the process.

"What are you doing standing around? The king is waiting to be served!" she hisses at me. I look around in confusion, trying to find the right words.

"I'm not among the slaves that serve the king," I whisper.

She whips around, and I barely have time to register her fist coming toward my face. Pain explodes in my cheek as blood fills my mouth.

"How dare you talk back to me," she hisses.

She yanks me up by my throat and begins squeezing. And I slowly realize I can't breathe. I don't fight, though. I wait. I wait for the air to leave my lungs and my brain to shut down. My vision clouds as my brain panics from the lack of oxygen, but I force my instinct to fight down. I want this more than anything. And just when I think my wish has been granted, I'm released. I fall to the ground, coughing and gulping in as much air as I can. When I look up, the Overseer is speaking to the servant who was choking me only seconds ago.

"Apologies, sir," she mumbles with her head down.

The Overseer looks down at me in disgust.

"It's your lucky night, slave. We are short of staff, so you will have to fill in until the new shipment of slaves arrives," he says.

He tilts his chin, studying my face before he speaks again.

"Have her cleaned and prepared for dinner. The king is expecting guests, and I won't have a single mark on his reputation because of a filthy slave."

I stand in the grand dining hall with a crystal pitcher in my hands. I've been given the task of refilling the wine. Why they would trust me with such a hands-on task, I do not know. My head is throbbing from the beating I received only hours ago, and I can feel my cheek swelling as well.

I can only hope my disheveled appearance doesn't anger anyone else.

The doors open and in comes the nobles. They all walk in with their heads held high, beautiful gowns, and expensive jewelry, something I will never experience in this life. They file around the table, standing behind their seats as they patiently wait for someone. Seconds later, the doors are opened, and the king's arrival is announced. My eyes widen slightly at his appearance. He's wearing royal attire that has been fitted for his frame, and his hair has been released around him, with his crown holding it out of his face.

Everyone in the room bows.

"Your Majesty."

He nods in acknowledgment, gesturing to the table.

"Please," he says politely. The surrounding beasts take this as their cue and sit, digging into the meal. My stomach tightens in hunger as the smell of cooked meat wafts over my nose. I've been starving for weeks now, never coming close to having a full belly. I keep my gaze trained on the glasses of wine as the dinner progresses, but so far, no one's cup has run low.

A noble pipes up in the silence, beginning the conversation for the night.

"If I may, Your Majesty, how much longer do you think this war will last against the hunters?" he asks.

The king looks up at this, taking a small sip of his drink.

"War?" he repeats, chuckling at the word.

"If that's how we want to describe this massacre of the human race, I'll play along," he says, rolling his eyes. Everyone at the table laughs at his retort, but it only makes my chest ache at how little of a threat he sees this as.

"I don't think it's a war anymore, especially at this rate. The humans have their resolve and their battles and ambushes, but it does nothing to affect the empire. If anything, it just helps us to exterminate them quicker and easier," he says as he takes another sip.

"And what of the recent raid you led on that village? The one that was harboring weapons? Do you feel that is cause for concern?" someone asks.

The question doesn't faze the king. He only shrugs.

"I do not. The humans have their weapons, but that is all they can do is generate weapons. We are stronger, faster, more capable. I don't feel the human race is a threat at all. I feel as soon as I discover the location of this... king they love to bring up before their deaths, the sooner this will all be over with," he says with a smirk on his lips.

The king downs the rest of his glass, looking in the direction of the serving staff. His eyes land on me immediately, and I take note that his demeanor shifts. Something flashes behind those eyes as he takes me in, and the corner of his mouth twitches in amusement. I quickly bow my head, making my way to his side to do the job assigned to me. I feel his eyes on me as if they're burning into my soul as I fill his glass. My stomach takes this moment to release a growl. And I know he hears it because I hear his soft chuckle before he turns away from me and continues the conversation with the rest of the room.

Even though he speaks to his people, the king keeps his eyes on me the entire night. Sometimes, he just glances, and sometimes, he stares at me in the corner. I especially hate it when I have to refill someone's cup. His gaze is closer than I'd like.

I'm refilling another glass when a splitting headache rips through my head. The pain is sharp and sudden enough to cause me to flinch, hitting the glass that I was filling and knocking it over. I gasp aloud, trying my best to catch it. Instead, I manage to drop the crystal pitcher on the ground, causing it to crash into a million little pieces.

Silence plagues the room as everyone looks to the king, waiting for his wrath to descend on me. And even though it is against the rules, I look too. He's staring down at the broken glass with a blank expression.

I immediately drop to my knees, pressing my forehead into the ground as I beg.

"I apologize, your majesty. Please forgive my mistake," I say as quickly as I can. I hear footsteps, and I know it's him coming toward me. I can feel the malice as he descends upon me to pass judgment. But the Overseer rushes to his side in an attempt to placate the king.

"Your Majesty! She is the last one we have—we're short-staffed, please—"

"James. Can I see your sword?" The king interrupts the overseer, and I'm trembling as the sound of a weapon being handed over fills the air.

"Slave. Hold out your hand," the king's voice is strangely soft as he speaks the command. My body shakes as I try to appeal to him one last time.

"...Please," I whisper, with tears falling down my face.

"Hold. Out. Your. Hand. I will not say it again."

I slowly move my hand out in front of me, leaving it flat on the ground. The king doesn't hesitate. I feel a sharp pain in my palm as he drives the blade through my hand and through the floor, anchoring it to the ground. I open my mouth, letting out a scream, and suddenly, he is kneeling in front of me, his hand still on the blade.

"You will sit here and think about your insolence. And you will not make another sound," he hisses.

"Someone clean this up," he calls to the remaining servants.

I lower my head, trying to silence my sobs as the king walks away from me, leaving the sword protruding from the ground. I remain with my hand anchored to the floor by the blade, even when the nobles make their exit. And when the servants start cleaning the table, I still remain. I can feel their stares as they go about their business, probably praying that they don't end up like me.

The hour is late when the sound of the door opening pulls my attention. I look up, expecting to see the Overseer, but to my shock, it's the king. Everyone bows as he enters, no longer dressed in his regal attire. He's clad in his robe, with his hair pulled back in a low ponytail. His gaze slowly drifts over the room.

"Leave us." The command is finite, causing everyone to scurry for the doors, but the king doesn't acknowledge them as he stands over me. My eyes remain trained on the ground as I try to silence the sobs threatening to leave my lips.

"Time here has not been kind to you, I see." The king's voice is laced with amusement as his hand wraps around the hilt of the blade. Pain ripples through my hand as he pulls it from the ground, blood pooling with it. I cradle my hand to my chest, remaining in my position.

"Look at me, Annalise." I hate the way he says my name with such taunting cruelty. But I look up, once again sucked into the emotionless depths of his gaze. He's able to elicit fear without speaking a word.

"I should have cut your hand off. You should be grateful this was your punishment instead," he says.

"Thank you for your mercy, Your Majesty," I whisper.

He laughs, the sound ringing from the walls.

"It seems you have learned since arriving here..." He trails off mid-sentence as his eyes detect something on my face. His movements are sudden as he comes toward me, grabbing my face between his hands. I flinch but remain steady as he gently brushes his knuckles over my bruised cheek.

"Who did this?" he asks.

I look away, suddenly unable to hold his gaze.

"A servant, Your Majesty. It was my fault for talking back. I earned a just punishment for my thoughtless outbu—"

His grip on my face tightens as he pulls me inches away from his. "I do not need an attitude from a slave that should have been dead an hour ago. Understand?"

My breathing is shallow as I hold his gaze. Because of his tight grip on my cheeks, I can only nod. I expect him to release me, but he doesn't. He remains close, his gaze sweeping over my face. Once he's pleased with himself, he releases me.

The sound of fabric ripping pulls my attention, and when I look toward the sound, I see he's ripped a piece of fabric from his expensive robe. The material of the robe is thick, but he rips it apart as if it were a piece of paper, demonstrating the stark contrast of strength between humans and beasts.

"Give me your hand," he says softly. I slowly hold my hand out to him, earning a smile when he sees how much I'm trembling. He firmly grips my palm, steadying me. To my shock, he brings my bloodied palm to his lips, pressing a soft kiss to the injured area. His eyes travel up to mine as he licks the wound, forcing a chill to come over me. He then wraps the wound with the fabric from his robe, tying it tightly around my palm.

"Keep it on for one day. It will be healed by tomorrow."

He releases my hand, moving to the doors to leave.

"Goodnight, slave."

Chapter Seven

ANNALISE

I jolt awake as the doors bang open, and the sounds of screaming slaves assault my ears. I'm immediately on high alert, my eyes scanning the dirty cavern for the threat.

"Shut up, all of you!" The overseer's irritated voice cuts through the commotion. I clamor from my bed in an attempt to reach for my clothes when I'm roughly pulled away by a guard.

"What's happening?" I ask.

I get no response as I'm dragged from the dank chambers along with the other slaves that have been chosen as well. I can see that none of us had the time to pull on our clothes. We're all clad in our dirty nightgowns. Mine was given to me upon arrival, and I could immediately tell it belonged to several slaves before me, slaves whose deaths still stain the dingy material.

We're dragged from the slave's quarters in chains. Each chain is interconnected, attaching us to one another in a straight line. There are ten of us in total; the rest left to return to sleep, I assume. I shiver violently as the chill of the secret passageways nips at my skin. Since this passage is used for slaves to move in and out unseen, there are no torches or fireplaces to keep them warm. And the chill of autumn is growing colder by the day. Meaning winter is coming soon.

A guard pushes open a hidden door, leading us into the warmly lit hall. I want to breathe in relief when the warm air envelopes me, but I know wherever they are taking us is not cause for celebration. We continue to walk through the palace until the foreign sounds greet us. As we get closer to our destination, I decipher the sound of other beasts. Light conversation and music are pouring from the archway that cascades light into the hall. The scent of food and wine also hits my nose, once again taunting me.

It doesn't take a genius to understand what awaits us in the presence of the beasts. The king is entertaining, and he's ordered slaves that aren't even fully dressed. I can say with confidence we will not be making it through the night.

We're all going to die.

My eyes widen as we round the corner to reveal the beasts' party. The room is large, with male and female beasts standing on platforms in each corner. They're dressed explicitly as their fingers run over their bodies sensually, their dark eyes filled with lust. I recognize most of the beasts from the noble class seated in the center of the room in large cushions. And among them sits the king. He's speaking to a stern-looking beast seated next to him. The beast says something that makes the king laugh, and my eyes widen in shock as a genuine smile appears on his lips, one that isn't filled with malice or the promise of pain.

The king's hair isn't pulled out of his face, and his shirt is open to reveal his chest that a beast is rubbing her hands over intimately. The beast that made the king laugh is a stunning beast as well. He has a look of indifference on his face as he looks over the room of people, but his eyes hold darkness to them I don't want to understand.

My gaze shifts swiftly over the beasts in attendance, and I pause when I see someone I thought I would never see again. My heart stops as I take in Dimitri. He doesn't look as awful as the palace slaves. Physically, he looks healthy. His body is lean, and he doesn't seem to be starved or beaten. But I don't miss the haunted look in his eyes. Whatever he has gone through, he will never be able to recover from.

Tears form in my eyes as I take him in. The last time I saw him, I was being dragged away from him, unable to touch him one last time. The world falls away, my legs moving before I can stop them. My fingers itch to touch him. I just need to know that he's okay. His name falls from my lips as I move.

"Ah!" I cry out as a guard slaps me across the face hard. My body collapses from the brute strength, blood already welling past my lips as the world spins around me. The guard doesn't allow me to recover from his attack. He pulls me up roughly, jostling my body so much that I cannot focus.

"Guard." The room falls silent as the king's voice carries his command across the room. The guard doesn't release me but turns to face the king, bowing slightly.

"Your Majesty."

The king's footsteps come in our direction as he crosses the room, irritation prominent on his face. "Do not ruin the entertainment before my guests have had their chance."

The guard immediately drops me, stepping back. "My apologies, Your Majesty."

"Entertainment? Cyrus, is this truly your idea of entertainment?" A new voice washes over the room. It's the beast the king was speaking to earlier. I notice Dimitri is standing behind this beast. Not only has this beast spoken to the king on a familiar level, but he's given me a name.

Cyrus.

Cyrus smiles, looking over all of us, and I immediately remember to lower my gaze.

"Yes. I find them very entertaining," Cyrus muses.

I hear a girl scream, followed by the jangle of the chains as he yanks her out of the lineup.

"If you beat them long enough, they make for very entertaining subjects," he says.

My body trembles, the fear setting in from his words. My earlier hunch was right. We are going to die.

"Strip her. Tie her up," he says before moving on to the rest of us.

I may not have been here for long, but you don't have to be to learn the tendencies of the king. Rumors spread fast among the slaves and servants. No one survives his beatings. And I've helped dispose of enough human carcasses to see his handiwork firsthand. He whips his victims hard enough to strip meat from their flesh. Only then will he allow you to bleed out and feed your body to the birds. And that's a happy ending. If he is in an "entertaining" mood, he'll demonstrate his precision with a whip and break your bones, shattering them with one strike.

The king continues to pick slaves out of the lineup. Some men and some women. They all whimper as the reality of what's about to happen sets in. I keep my gaze lowered, but that doesn't stop me from trembling the closer he gets. His feet stop in front of me, and instinctually, more tears pour down my face. His finger gently presses under my chin, lifting my gaze to meet his. His soulless gaze pours into my own, making me want nothing more than to die in this instant.

Cyrus scoffs lightly, pointing to the man next to me. "And you."

His gaze lingers on mine for a moment before finally turning away as the guard unlocks the man beside me.

"The rest of you are to serve," he calls over his shoulder.

I watch him as he walks away, relief blooming in my chest until my eyes fall on Dimitri. Horror is etched into his features as his gaze roams over my battered form. My sniffles only grow as he continues to look at what's left of me. But both of our attentions are pulled to the front of the room as the "entertainment" begins.

I flinch as another scream echoes through the chamber. I don't want to look. I can't. But I do. And the sight that greets me is gruesome. The bones of the man the king is beating jut from his body. The woman next to him is lying in a pool of her own blood, already dead.

This is torture in its purest form.

To my horror, the beasts are watching in pure fascination, light applause erupting as the king steps away from his victim, a wicked smile on his lips.

"Your skill never ceases to amaze me, Your Majesty," the king's friend calls to him.

Cyrus chuckles, responding to his friend. "You flatter me, Felix."

My eyes remain trained on the slave, who is no longer conscious as the king makes his way toward me. In my terror, I don't notice him approach until he stands directly over me, his fingers reaching for me. I flinch, earning a laugh from him as he continues to reach for the fruit on the tray I'm holding. He pops a grape into his mouth, his gaze remaining focused on me before speaking.

"Come this way, slave. I don't want to reach to eat."

The king makes his way back to the cushions, sitting next to the beast he referred to as Felix. Felix eyes me curiously, and I immediately lower my gaze as I approach, standing near the king.

"Where did this slave come from?" he asks. I note Dimitri remains standing behind the beast named Felix. His eyes hold terror, but his lips refuse to move as he takes me in.

"She is from the village I caught harboring weapons. I picked her up at the front of the palace, causing quite a scene," Cyrus smiles as he leans back in his seat.

His gaze shifts past Felix to Dimitri, cruelty spreading in his smile. "She came from the same village as your new slave."

Now Felix is intrigued. He sits up taller in his seat, eyeing me with interest.

"Oh?" A wicked smile graces his lips as well. He slowly turns to face Dimitri, and the room suddenly feels frigid as he speaks.

"Dimitri, do you know this slave?" he asks.

Dimitri's skin turns pale as he studies me, his shaky reply barely audible.

"No, sir."

Cyrus's smile widens as he looks between the two of us. He knows the truth, and he's playing with us for his sick and twisted amusement.

"You dare lie in my presence, slave?" Cyrus stands along with Felix, irritation prominent in his gaze. I always saw Dimitri as tall. He was taller than me, so it didn't matter. But this beast dwarfs him. He looks small, not only in height but in size as well.

"Do you want to be punished? Answer the king," Felix growls. Dimitri's gaze shifts between all of us, his eyes filled with the most fear when he settles on Felix. This beast terrifies him to the point of lying in front of the king. He's seconds from hyperventilating.

"Dimitri!"

"Yes... I know her," he whispers.

Felix's interest grows with each passing second as he studies Dimitri. "How?"

Dimitri is visibly shaking now, his eyes focused on Felix.

"She's... just a girl from my village. We grew up together. She is no one important," he says desperately.

I don't refute his words, either. I know he's lying for a good reason, especially from the fear evident on his face.

"Annalise," Cyrus speaks my name, forcing my heart to pound harder in my chest. I think for sure he is going to ask me the same line of questioning or hurt me to prove a point to Dimitri, but he doesn't.

He looks beyond me.

"Theresa," he calls. A beast immediately stands, a sensual smile on her lips as she approaches us. The king wraps his arms around her waist, nuzzling her hair as he speaks.

"I am retiring for the night. Join me."

Her face lights up, and she immediately nods, a seductive giggle leaving her lips.

"Of course, Your Majesty," she says.

Cyrus looks at me, his amusement replaced with disgust. "You shall come along. I will be hungry after the night's activities."

The king doesn't wait for a response as he turns to exit the ballroom with Theresa. I shift my gaze slightly to take in Dimitri one last time, but he is already focused on his master. His body vibrates as Felix glowers at him. I slowly begin to walk away when I notice something.

Felix watches Dimitri with not only anger but... lust?

He grips Dimitri's chin, pulling him in close to say something in his ear, something that brings a tear to Dimitri's eye.

"Slave!"

I jump, turning to follow Cyrus and his bedmate for the night into the hall of the king. There's nothing I can do. I can't see Dimitri, I can't ask him if he's okay, I can't even give him words of encouragement. I'm here at the mercy of the king, just as he is at the mercy of his new master.

This is our new life.

Chapter Eight

ANNALISE

I feel numb. Each time I blink and close my eyes, I see Dimitri's tortured expression. The way Felix looked at him and the way he touched him, I can't imagine the horrors Dimitri must be going through. I recall Cyrus telling me he would never touch me in that way to stain his reputation. That mentality extends to all the nobles, right? Is Felix so careless about his reputation that he would do such things to Dimitri?

I hold back tears threatening to spill from my eyes as I imagine that beast violating the man I love. I've never seen Dimitri so terrified. He's always been strong, forward, and brave. Even when faced with the king when we first arrived, he fought for me. But his expression in that chamber was one I had never seen before.

He was paralyzed with fear.

I push my thoughts away as I follow the king and Theresa through the empty halls. He has his arm around her, pressing kisses into her neck and cheek, and she continues to giggle as he does so. I can no longer hold back my tears as I think of the times Dimitri and I would kiss and hug. That chance has forever been ripped away from both of us.

We reach the king's chambers, and the guards pull the doors open for the both of them. I keep my gaze down, continuing to walk, when a guard places his sword in my way, roughly shoving me back.

"Where do you think you're going, slave?" he hisses.

"Do you not see the tray of food the slave carries? Let it through." I hear Cyrus's voice cutting through the door, and the guard reluctantly lets me pass. Bitterness seeps through me at his referral to me as "it." No beast misses the opportunity to make me feel less than alive. And as I walk into the chamber, I feel less than small. Theresa wears a beautiful silk gown that hugs her features and reveals her healthy body. In contrast, I am in a used, dirty, crusted gown with matted hair and dirty skin.

I am nothing.

I slowly lift my gaze as I enter the king's chamber. He and Theresa are already on each other as she pulls at his clothes. He looks at me, a wicked smile on his lips.

"In the corner, slave."

He turns away from me, his hands roaming over the body of the beast. I quickly move to the corner, keeping my eyes down. Theresa giggles as he touches her in the most intimate of places. I couldn't imagine being with a beast like the king. It took me years of seeing Dimitri to even work up the courage to express my feelings for him—especially my sexual feelings.

"You aren't really going to let the slave stay and watch, are you?" I'm pulled out of my thoughts as Theresa expresses her disdain for me being in attendance.

My gaze shifts in their direction, and I instantly wish I had kept my eyes down. The king is shirtless, his pants hanging dangerously low on his hips. His face is dark, and his eyes are void of emotion as he glares down at Theresa. He slowly steps closer to her, placing his hands on the shoulders of her silk gown. In one swift movement, he rips it from her shoulders, exposing her breasts. He roughly shoves her onto the bed, and a gasp escapes her lips. Her eyes widen and her excitement has been replaced with fear.

"If that is a problem for you, leave." Cyrus's amusement has evaporated in an instant. He looks deadly as he glares down at the beast. I can almost feel the fear she releases as she gazes up at him, and I clutch the tray even tighter, trying to anchor myself to something as I watch this horror unfold before me.

"N-no, Your Majesty, I didn't mean to offend—" He cuts her off as he crawls over her, placing his hand over her throat. His eyes visibly darken, and the room suddenly feels heavy. He roughly pushes her deeper into the bed.

"Shut up." I shiver from the chill in his voice. He doesn't speak again as he unfastens his pants.

I lower my eyes, focusing on the ground, but I can still hear them. The sound of him gripping her tightly as he holds her down accompanies her gasps. To my shock, her gasps morph into moans. I squeeze my eyes shut as the rhythmic colliding of their bodies fills the room. Her loud cries suddenly sound muffled, pulling my gaze. I look up, thinking he's strangling her, but what he's actually doing frightens me further.

He's pressing her face into the mattress, his fingers intertwined with her hair. Her back is arched as the king enters her roughly from behind, each thrust forcing a loud moan from her lips. The king's attention is focused on the beast, but his eyes slowly rise, finding me in the corner. I'm locked in his gaze as a wicked smile slowly crawls over his face. His free hand snakes around her front, squeezing her breast before he wraps it around her throat, lifting her and exposing them both completely. He keeps his eyes focused on mine, but I can see everything. I can see her voluptuous breast and beaded nipples jar with each violent thrust. I can see the way her back is arched as the king holds one of her hands down while the other squeezes her throat.

Her mouth is open, her eyes wide as she glares at the ceiling. It's all she can do. He has her completely immobile.

"Ah, My King, I-I'm cumming!" she screams. As soon as the words leave her lips, her entire body seizes up as she convulses. My eyes widen in fear as I study her. She looks like she's having a seizure. Her eyes roll back as she spasms ever so slightly each second, yet she continues to moan through it.

The king's smile widens as he takes in my reaction. I can only imagine the horror etched on my face. He gives her three more hard thrusts before he finally lets go of her, and she collapses on the mattress in front of him.

I gasp softly.

Did he kill her?

I immediately lower my eyes, not wanting to see the king completely naked. I fear that if I do, he will kill me where I stand for gazing upon his body when I am only a slave. Slaves have been killed for much less. But my body is trembling even more so at this point. I don't really know what just happened.

I tense when I hear a deep breath. It's her, Theresa. She's alive.

"Get dressed. Get out. And if you value your life, never question me again." The king's voice rips through the chamber colder than ice.

"I-I'm sorry, My King. Please forgive me... It will never happen again," she whispers.

"Good. Leave."

I hear the frantic rustling of clothes and the light patter of footsteps as she takes off out of the room, the sound of the doors closing behind her echoing off the walls. I don't know if she put her clothes back on or if she even could, seeing as he ripped her dress off. I bite my tongue to calm the whimpers threatening to leave me. I'm all alone with the king.

"Come, slave. I'm hungry."

I will my feet to move, keeping my gaze down as I approach. Once I'm standing before him, his soft chuckle fills the room.

"You can look at me," he says.

I keep my eyes down. I've never gazed upon a man naked. And I don't want the first time I do to be of a beast. The king especially.

"Annalise."

I tense when he uses my name. I hate it when he uses my name. I slowly lift my gaze, looking at his face. He doesn't look tired at all, even though he just used a lot of energy with the beast. He gestures to the area next to his bed. I quickly move around, holding the tray out so that he can easily reach it. He grabs another piece of fruit and places it in his mouth.

"Did you enjoy the show?" he asks.

I feel my cheeks redden as images of what just happened flash through my mind. So, I choose not to respond. He takes in my silence, laughing.

"You grow so bashful at the mention of sex as if you—Ohh h…" He trails off as he puts the clues together, and I hate it. His loud chuckle fills the room.

"Look at me." His tone leaves no room for argument. So I do. I look him in his eyes, and it chills me to the bone. His dark gaze roams over my body, coming to a rest on my face.

"You have never been touched by a man, have you?" he asks.

I open my mouth to respond.

"No, your majesty," I whisper.

"Odd since you and your lover fought so hard for each other. He never deflowered you?" he asks.

I feel more shame. He speaks about my personal life and business as if he has every right to it. I hate it.

"No, Your Majesty," I murmur. He's silent for a moment before pulling the tray from my hands. I gasp, looking up in shock, but he's watching me intensely, forcing me to drop my hands by my side.

"No wonder you look so frightened at the sight of sex," he chuckles.

I narrow my gaze at him.

"That wasn't sex," I say.

He seems to be in a good mood and indulges me, his smile widening. "Oh? Then what is sex, *slave*?"

He's toying with me—something he loves to do.

"Sex is when you give yourself to the one you love. It's passionate and caring... and you create life from it—" The king interrupts me in a fit of laughter. My eyes widen slightly at the sight of his smile as he tosses his head back in amusement.

"Is that what your lover told you?" he says between laughs.

I drop my eyes.

"No," I mumble.

"Strange you've never had a cock in that virgin pussy, yet you drawl on about the passions of sex."

My cheeks burn from his vulgar use of language, and he notices, placing his fingers under my chin. He forces my gaze up to meet his amusement, twinkling in that dark gaze.

"Sex is about power. It's about taking your partner and controlling their every whim. Their pleasure. *Causing* that pleasure and controlling it. *Allowing* them to have release. Allowing their body to react to your touch. If you control sex, you control their mind." He watches me intensely, finally releasing my face with a chuckle. He continues to hold my gaze, taking a bite of an apple.

"If your lover never told you or even tried to deflower you, it's best he didn't fondle around between your legs. You should rejoice. You never had to give yourself to him. It would have been a waste. Especially where he is now." Amusement plasters his features as he slowly tears my reality down. Silence washes over us, and he suddenly moves, grabbing hold of my hand. I ignore the heat that spreads through my palm at his touch. His eyes focus on the inside of my palm as he runs his fingers over the smooth skin.

"I see you followed my directions. What did you do with my robe?" Curiosity laces his tone.

"I hid it, your majesty." My words capture his attention, and he's looking at me again with that terrifying gaze.

"Hid it? Where?"

I gently pull my hand from his grasp, my mouth suddenly dry as I reach with shaky hands for my leg. I slowly reach under the dingy dress, untying the fabric from around my thigh. I fold it before holding it out to him, and he eyes it with interest.

He actually looks impressed.

"You are very clever indeed," he says softly as he takes the fabric from me.

"I was curious if you would be foolish enough to keep it visible. They would have killed you if they caught you with this." He rises from the bed, making his way across the room. I catch a glimpse of his naked, muscular ass flexing as he walks, forcing me to look away. He shuffles around before coming back, and I breathe a sigh of relief when I see he's wearing a robe. The corner of his mouth upturns slightly as he observes my reaction.

"Take that off," he says.

My eyes widen, and I step back. "Please, Your Majesty, I—"

"You reek. That dress is filthy. Take it off and wear this in my company," he says as he drops another robe in front of me.

My eyes widen slightly as I take it in.

"I told you. I will not touch a slave. But I cannot stand you in my presence with such filthy clothes and smell," he says. I feel my cheek burn as a wave of embarrassment washes over me. It isn't my fault the conditions we're forced to live within the palace. I have never been this filthy in my life. The king turns away from me, and I use the moment to hastily pull the dress off and place the oversized robe on, using my hands to hold it closed.

When I look up, the king is watching me with an unreadable expression. He finally moves, laying back on his massive bed.

"Tell me about your lover, Annalise," he says lazily.

I raise my brow in confusion. I don't know why he would ask me about Dimitri unless he's planning to kill him.

"He's harmless, Your Majesty. He won't do any—"

The king laughs, looking at me.

"I know he's harmless. I want to know what man fights as he did for you, carried you out of harm's way, but never claimed you as his own," he says.

I blink in confusion. "He wanted to wait until marriage."

I feel my stomach drop as this information genuinely piques the king's interest. He slowly rises in the bed, looking at me, his smile dropping.

"You were engaged to this man?" he asks.

I slowly nod, forgetting all the etiquette they have taught me since arriving here. The king's sudden change in demeanor disturbs me.

A scoff leaves his lips. "Whatever future you envisioned with him will never come to be. It's best you forget he ever existed. I promise you, he will never look at you in that way again."

I drop my gaze, letting the tears fall.

"Yes, Your Majesty."

Silence overcomes us, and he comes towards me, dropping the tray of fruit at my feet.

"Eat. You only have a few hours before the sun comes up."

Chapter Nine

ANNALISE

Each night, it's the same thing. Somehow, the king finds an excuse for me to be present in his chambers when he ravishes women. Each night is a different experience. Some nights, he only has one, and other nights, he has three. He does all kinds of unspeakable acts to their bodies, things I never even knew were possible. And each night, he forces me to stand in the corner with a different form of refreshment.

I tense from the scream of his newest partner. She is on top of the king, her body facing me with legs sprawled as he holds her arms behind her back while another female beast licks between her legs. The king's thrusts are vigorous as he pushes her hair aside and begins suckling on her throat. Then, his eyes meet mine, and a mischievous grin appears on his lips. He thrusts even harder, causing the woman to groan. She tosses her head back, her cries growing silent as her body convulses, meaning the night is ending, I've noticed. I immediately lower my eyes, focusing on the ground. The sounds of kisses and moans still resonate in the air as he moves on to the next woman, pleasuring her as well.

It's another hour before the king finally dismisses the beasts. He gets up along with them, walking them to the door. He mumbles something to the guards on the other side before closing it, once again leaving me alone with him.

"Come here, Anna." I tense when he uses the nickname my family once used. It's the same name Dimitri called me out of affection. But I force my feet to move, regardless of my feelings. I silently make my way to my usual spot next to his bed, holding the tray of food for him. Instead of reaching for the food, however, his hands come to my face, grabbing my cheeks between his fingers.

His dark eyes study me intensely. "Did you enjoy the show?"

I slowly shake my head, causing him to laugh.

"You stand here each night with such a look of horror on your face, Anna. It may look vulgar, but it is quite pleasurable," he says.

I try to move my face out of his hand, but his grip tightens.

"You've never even touched yourself, have you?"

I don't have to answer because he knows. He's toying with me the way he always does. His eyes dip to my chest before returning to rest on my face.

"Or another man, for that matter." His voice takes on a sultry tone as he speaks, and I notice that he's still completely naked. Although he just finished with two beasts, his cock is still somewhat erect, glistening from the night's conquests.

"How long were you planning to marry that boy?" he asks. I hate it when he brings up Dimitri. He asks personal questions, making me more distraught about our situation each time he brings him up.

"He was asking my father for my hand the day you arrived in my village," I whisper.

This causes his smile to widen, his interest fully captured as he looks at me. I don't like the way he looks at me like he wants to ravish me as well. All I can do is count on his words when I first arrived. He would never touch me, not to sully his reputation.

To my relief, he releases my face, his hand drifting to my throat.

"I imagine he has it much better than you and the slaves that live in the palace. Why do you seem so distraught whenever he is mentioned? Did I not tell you to forget about him?" he asks.

I slowly nod my head, looking away in fear.

"I'm sorry, Your Majesty..." I trail off when his hand drifts even lower to the small opening of my gown. His hand presses against my collarbone, his eyes taking on a deranged shade as he stares. So I keep talking, hoping to distract him.

"It's hard to forget someone you love. You care about their well-being and health even after they're gone from your immediate life," I whisper.

He chuckles softly, his eyes finally pulling away from my chest.

"Love. Is that what you think you felt for him?" His gaze is like a black pit, swallowing me whole.

"You've barely scratched the surface of your short life. You do not know what love is, slave." The king holds my gaze, forcing my fear to climb higher the longer he remains so still. After what feels like an eternity, he blinks, his terrifying demeanor melting away as he does so. His eyes silently roam my face, lingering on my cheeks.

"What did you get into today? You are filthy," he asks. My eyes widen at his sudden shift in conversation.

"I helped dispose of bodies today, Your Majesty." I tense as he chuckles softly, waiting for the slew of insults I know are coming. The king hates the way I smell, the way I dress, and that I am human. The sheer amount of death and torture I see in the palace daily makes me believe it even more. We are useless. This war seems all but pointless.

"And how does that make you feel? Seeing the bodies of those so much like you, yet somehow you evade death daily?" he asks.

"I feel..." I trail off as tears blur my vision. The king smiles, turning away from me. He enjoys my reaction. I watch as he crosses the room, returning with the robe he forces me to wear in his presence.

"Change," he says, holding out the robe to me. I quickly change, trying my best to do it before he turns around and sees me naked. It's a small victory for me, though I know it means nothing to him.

"You have yet to answer my question, Anna," he calls to me.

I drop my eyes, quickly wrapping the robe around my naked skin. "I wish I could die along with them, Your Majesty."

I hear his footsteps approaching, tensing when I feel his hand under my chin. He lifts my gaze once again, forcing me to look into his eyes.

"You wish you could die alongside a group of slaves you've never even met?" he asks.

I slowly nod my head.

"The way we are treated is inhumane," I say.

He studies my face before laughing and stepping away.

"You are very amusing, Anna. Why do you think humans deserve better than the treatment they already have?" he asks, sitting on his bed, crossing his arms as he looks at me.

So, I attempt a response.

"Because everyone deserves a right to li—"

"The strong deserve to live. The weak deserve whatever happens to them. And when the weak aren't happy with the lives they've been allowed by the strong, they must accept their fate or perish," he says irritatedly.

I drop my gaze. "Yes, Your Majesty."

He's silent before standing. "Eat and take the tray back to the kitchens. I have no more use for you tonight."

I don't eat. I never do. It's another small victory I gain especially since it allows me to leave immediately. So I quickly make my way through the halls and into the kitchen to put the uneaten food away, even though my stomach is pinched with unbearable hunger.

I grunt from all the effort it takes to toss the dead body onto the pile. I know this woman. I was lying next to her only hours ago. She left the kitchens this morning, not knowing it would be the last thing she ever did. I wipe the light sheen of sweat from my brow as I stand up straight, looking at all the dead bodies. There's more than usual. I don't know what got into the king after he dismissed me from his chambers, but he took it out on these poor souls. I shudder at the looks of horror still etched into their features.

"The Overseer has arrived!"

We all tense as the announcement comes over the field. We line up, bowing our heads as the beast who owns each of us walks among us, inspecting our condition. He's a cruel beast. I've seen him frequently take and kill one of us just for whimpering. He says our actions reflect his work, and he won't have his work marred by a lack of obedience.

His footsteps continue to move along the lines and, to my horror, he stops in front of me. I close my eyes, saying a silent prayer that my death will be swift. I can't think of anything I've done to deserve death, but within the palace, breathing can get you killed. He roughly grabs hold of my cheeks, lifting my face to meet his. I force myself to hold in the whimper threatening to escape me as I stare into his eyes. His gaze roams over my face, and he wrinkles his nose in disgust.

"Bring this one. The rest of you, back to work."

I cry out in fear as a guard grabs me around my arms, roughly dragging me away. My screams are ignored as I'm dragged through the palace to a small room. The guards roughly shove me against the wall using a hooked spear to pull my clothing from my skin.

"What's happening?" My voice comes out shaky.

"Wipe your eyes, slave. Today is your lucky day." The Overseer approaches me with a narrowed gaze just as female servants enter behind him with buckets and scrubbers. The Overseer gestures to me, and the servants splash me with cold water. I cry out as my muscles tense and my skin stings from the frigid shock. The water also has soap in it, burning my eyes just as rough hands grab me and scrub my skin. I'm sure the rough bristles are tearing away the dirt and the top layer of skin.

"I don't know how you did it, but the king has placed you at his personal disposal," the Overseer calls over the sound of scrubbing. I grit my teeth in pain as the bristles dig into my flesh without mercy, and more cold water is thrown on me. I fall to my knees, coughing and spitting up water, my fingers digging into the tile as the Overseer stands over me.

"Make no mistake, you are a slave. Nothing more. Do not anger the king in any way, or I will personally see to your torture and immediate execution. Your actions reflect on me. And I will not let a degenerate human ruin my reputation. Understood?" he snaps.

"Yes, sir," I manage.

"Good. Get her dressed and sent to the king for approval."

The guards escort me silently to the king's study. The doors are solid wood, and they push them open to reveal the surrounding upper balcony. My eyes immediately fall to the chandelier in the center. It seems to glow on its own, releasing the perfect amount of light. As we descend the spiraled staircase, the king's voice grows more prominent.

The study is massive. There are books on shelves that stretch higher than the stairs we are descending. The windows are large as well, showing the east side of the palace, which is made up of the surrounding mountains and waterfalls. The windows also allow beautiful natural light to filter in, lighting the magnificent study. We finally reach the bottom of the stairs, and I see who it is the king is speaking to.

Felix.

My heart drops in my chest as I take him in. He looks much more menacing today. His stature is rigid, his face blank of emotion. He's pointing to the map that's laid out on the king's desk as he speaks. "I can have a small battalion ready in a few weeks. The trip will take a few days at most. I will lead it myself."

The king's eyes are downcast on the map, but he looks up as we approach. My heart beats against my chest as his eyes roam over me. I don't have the slightest clue as to why he would summon me to be by his side, nor does his expression give away his internal thoughts. His face is completely blank of emotion as we approach. Felix straightens up as well, his gaze roaming over us. His eyes linger on me, narrowing in disdain.

"Leave us," Cyrus speaks, pulling me out of my fear-ridden trance.

"See how long it will take to prepare the attack. I will accompany you as well." Cyrus keeps his eyes focused on me as he speaks to Felix.

"Yes, Your Majesty." Felix bows slightly before exiting the room with guards in tow, leaving me alone with the king. Silence stretches over us, and Cyrus rises from his seat.

"How different you look when you're not covered in blood, dirt, and piss," he says nonchalantly.

My cheeks burn in embarrassment, but I brush off the insult.

"Look at me," he says.

I slowly raise my gaze to meet his.

"Rejoice. You are the first slave ever to wear a servant's uniform," he says.

Cyrus turns away from me, reaching for a plate of food next to his desk. There's actual food on it, not just fruit. "Eat. Or you will not like what happens. I know you don't eat when I tell you to. And don't even think about forfeiting your life. I will go after your betrothed if you do so. As you can see, I have easy access to him," he says, leaving no room for argument.

My eyes widen at his threat, but I obey nonetheless. I silently approach his desk, reaching for the meat. I bring it to my lips, almost moaning in pleasure as I taste something other than mold and sour food for the first time in months. When I open my eyes, the king is studying me with an unreadable expression. He cocks his head slightly, examining me like I am prey.

"I have moved you to my personal slave. Which means you are to stay by my side all hours of the day. No one has ever been given this privilege. I suggest you learn quickly and efficiently how to do your new job," he says.

I finish chewing and look at him. "And what have I done to earn such an honor, Your Majesty?"

He chuckles at my sarcasm, but his smile disappears in an instant.

"Absolutely nothing yet, slave."

Chapter Ten

ANNALISE

The king's wrath has not improved since I became his personal slave. I still don't know the reason he would give me such a position in the palace. It hasn't made my life any easier. If anything, it makes it much more difficult. I am with him from the crack of dawn until he falls asleep at night. Then, I must sneak back to the slaves' quarters and wait until the next day. I am beaten by the servants excessively as well. They hate I've been given a position so close to the king. There is significant bruising under this dress.

The king himself seems more vicious now that I spend my entire day by his side. He tortures and kills religiously and indiscriminately. And if there's one thing I've come to understand while being at his side, he *hates* humans with a burning passion. Sometimes, I even notice him glaring at me. I fear the day he acts on whatever impulse is running through his mind.

"Slave!"

I cry out in pain as the whip in his hands rips through the thin fabric of my sleeve, licking the top layer of flesh away from my skin. I look at the king in terror, but he is livid, his dark eyes carrying not an ounce of regret.

"I said to come here!" he shouts. I immediately make my way over to him with the tray that holds his drink. While he grabs it from me, I make the mistake of looking over to what's left of the mangled body he's been interrogating. His victim's back is stripped open, the flesh torn to ribbons. I feel vomit threatening to escape my lips when I see him move, and I immediately look away, keeping my gaze down. Cyrus chuckles in amusement at my reaction, placing the drink back on the tray.

"You will be pleased to know he came from a village in the same region as yours, Annalise." Cyrus steps away from me, running his fingers over the bloodied whip.

"When we checked the houses, guess what we found?" His eyes meet mine, and I feel a chill sweep through the room. "Weapons."

His amusement is gone as he glares at me. He extends the whip, holding my gaze.

"What do you know about the necklace your father gave you?" he asks.

I'm taken aback by his question. My father gave it to me in his last moments with no explanation. Yet Cyrus thinks I knew about everything in my village. Even the weapons my father pulled from the floorboards were a shock to me.

"I know nothing, Your Majesty," I say quickly. I notice his jaw twitch before a loud crack ripples through the room, and the man is screaming in pain again. Nausea washes over me when I realize the crack came from the bone now protruding from his back. Cyrus was able to force a broken bone with the strike of a whip.

"Don't lie to me, Anna. What do you know?" he snaps.

I shake my head, looking at him, pleading with my eyes.

"I know nothing!" I shriek.

He shakes his head in anger, striking the whip again.

The man screeches.

"You know something!" He comes towards me with a quick stride, grabbing me around the throat. I drop everything I am holding as he raises me off the ground with ease. His grip tightens around my throat as my feet dangle uselessly beneath me. I struggle for breath, but none comes. My hands claw at his own, but he doesn't flinch. A chill ripples up my spine when I see a smile slowly appearing on his lips.

"Is that it? That's all the fight you have in you?" he asks, taunting me further.

He slowly lowers me toward him, his voice washing over my body. "Is your life worth anything to you, Annalise?"

My vision becomes clouded as my consciousness wanes. Cyrus releases me at the last second, and I fall to the ground, coughing and choking, sucking in as much air as I can. I cry out in shock as the whip strikes the ground inches from my face, scurrying back in fear. Cyrus grabs the blade nearest him, making his way over to the man. I let out a squeal as he runs his blade through the man. But he doesn't kill him. He keeps his blade inserted as the man screams in agony, dragging it through him and cutting him apart from the inside.

Vomit rushes past my lips onto the floor from the display, my screams mingling with the man as we both endure different forms of torture. I finally realize his screaming has stopped, and when I look up, the king is watching me with a wicked gleam in his gaze as he rips the blade from the man's lifeless body.

"You will be next if I find out you're lying to me."

The room is warm. It's especially fascinating as well. The walls are golden, and the floors are smooth. Textured coverings exude light in the most beautiful of ways, casting a warm glow over the area. I would be in complete awe if I weren't terrified for my life.

I'm on my knees, shaking as the king sits in the pool of steaming water, his eyes focused on me. Two beasts have joined him in the water, and servants stand silently to the side holding oils and scents, ready to pour them in if requested. I am not alone with the king, yet I feel more terrified than ever. His threat from earlier lingers in my mind, and now that he has placed me by his side, my death could come at any second.

My eyes remain focused on my knees. It's the only thing I can do to keep from falling over. My throat is throbbing from his grip, and I know it's probably already forming a bruise. My arm hurts as well from where he tore the dress with only a whip. Each time I close my eyes, I can see the way he killed the man in front of me.

I'm pulled out of my thoughts when the trickle of water grows louder. It takes me a moment to realize the beasts in the water with him are trying to get him aroused, their giggles and moans filling the room. My cheeks burn from once again being in such close quarters with something so vulgar.

"Everyone out."

I'm shocked that he isn't following up on the night's promise, rising myself as I try to follow the women and servants out.

"Not. You." I shiver from his tone but slowly sink to my knees again as I listen to the doors close.

"Look at me, Anna," he calls to me. I lift my gaze, making it a point to focus on his face, even though it terrifies me. His hair is free of its usual updo, and it's in the water floating around him. His dark gaze is suffocating as he studies me, forcing me to tremble in his presence.

"Why are you shaking?"

I squeeze my eyes closed, trying to rein in my fear.

"I'm sorry, Your Majesty," I whisper.

He chuckles at my words. "I know you are. Come this way."

I slowly rise, moving toward the edge of the water. The weight of his gaze follows me until I am kneeling in front of him.

"I think back to that day I saw you standing by the water, and I wonder, what were you doing in the forest by yourself with someone who could barely defend himself?"

I look away, not wanting to answer. It will only lead to a discussion I don't want to have. But I know I cannot refuse the king's questions, or I will be punished severely for it.

"My father was going to make the trip to the river, but I volunteered because Dimitri was going to ask for my father's permission to marry me. So he sent someone he trusted to protect me if it became dangerous." I finish my sentence, finally looking at Cyrus. He's watching me with an unreadable expression.

"Grab those oils and pour them in," he says as he gestures to the tray holding the colorful oils the servants left behind. I grab them with shaky hands, pouring them into the water, Cyrus's gaze on me as I do so. Once the vials are empty, I move to put them back on the tray when I feel a hand around my arm. I cry out in shock when I'm pulled into the water, my entire body submerging in the warm pool.

I immediately rise to the surface, gasping for air, when I feel a warm body pressing me against the ledge. My breath hitches in my throat as I look into the eyes of the king. His eyes roam over my face, his hand reaching for the tight bun that holds my hair up. He doesn't speak as he pulls it out, freeing my hair from its hold. His gaze shifts to my hair as it falls around me in waves.

"Do you still think of him? Of what could have been?" he murmurs.

"No, your majesty," I whisper shakily.

His eyes continue to roam over my face until they drop to the base of my throat. His hand reaches for my neck, tracing the bruises, no doubt.

"Anna... you're lying," he murmurs.

My eyes widen as his hand continues to trail down the front of my dress, dipping under the water. He keeps his eyes lined to mine as he moves under my dress, his fingers brushing against the flimsy material of the panties I wear.

I release a soft gasp, trying to move, but he uses his body to pin me to the ledge.

"Y-your majesty—"

"Shhh," he murmurs, studying my face closely.

"I don't know why it bothers me so much. Every time you mention that boy, I want to kill him," he says.

A knock sounds at the door, and I jump in fear, but he doesn't move. He doesn't even flinch. His eyes continue to roam over my face before he answers. "What?"

"Your Majesty, the Duchess of Emat has arrived." The timid voice comes out from the other side of the door. Cyrus smiles, letting go of me. I immediately scurry against the edge of the bath, trying to put as much distance between us as possible.

"Have her wait for me in the throne room," he calls to the servant.

He looks back at me, his eyes shifting slightly as he takes in my soaked body.

"Get out."

I watch as the servants finish the last-minute fastening of the king's clothing, tying the strings, and adjusting the fabric correctly. I am not allowed to do such a thing. I'm not allowed to look at the king, let alone touch him. Yet he allows me by his side. And as of an hour ago, touches me in secret.

My heart beats even faster as I think of what could've happened just moments ago if a servant hadn't interrupted. Was he going to touch me the way he touches those women? He even said he wanted to kill Dimitri every time I mentioned him, even though he's the one who asks about my plans with Dimitri.

The servants finally finish with the king, and he studies himself in the mirror before turning to me. His expression is back to the same one I'm used to. He approaches me silently, his dark eyes peering into my soul. But I don't know what could be running through his mind as he looks down at me. He's a constant puzzle I don't understand in the slightest. When he's pleased with my reaction, he smiles and walks past me to the doors.

"Let's not keep the duchess waiting."

Chapter Eleven

ANNALISE

The throne room is beautiful, just like every other room in the palace. Its extravagance and wide range of elegance are a stark contrast to the home I grew up in. It doesn't seem like the war that has been going on for years has affected the beast empire in the least, especially when the throne room comprises walls made of polished marble.

I peek from under my lashes behind Cyrus as he enters with his head held high, an aura of intimidation coming from him in waves. As we approach, I realize I recognize the duchess. It's Marzia, the beast from the first day here. The one that tried to hit me. She immediately rises when she sees him enter, bowing in greeting. She's just as fearful today as she was the day the king brought me into the palace. It makes me wonder why she would willingly visit the king when he frightens her.

"Marzia, what brings you to my palace unannounced?"

The king sits on his throne, and I stand silently near the floor as directed when the king does business. Marzia lifts her gaze to look at the king. Her dark eyes are shaped like almonds, framed by thick lashes. She's a strikingly beautiful beast, as are they all.

Even her hair is styled in an updo to show off her delicate neck, with jewels once again adorning her.

"I haven't heard from you in weeks, Cyrus. I thought spending an afternoon together would do us some good," she says. I hide my shock from her open use of the king's name. Whoever they are to each other is closer than the average beast. I've only ever heard one other beast use the king's name. Even the women he has in his chambers refer to him as "Your Majesty." I've never seen this beast in his chambers at night, yet she refers to him with familiarity.

The king's expression shifts to one of irritation as he speaks. "You thought? That's new."

She lowers her gaze once again, doing a terrible job of hiding her fear of him. Silence fills the air as the king decides his next move.

"Leave us," he calls out. Every beast in attendance bows and scurries from the room. I follow suit, facing the king to bow. His eyes fall on me, and he doesn't have to speak a word for me to know what he's thinking.

Not you.

He must be pleased with my quick understanding of his unspoken command. A small smirk appears on his lips as he turns back to the frightened duchess.

"We are only betrothed, Marzia. I have not followed through with the engagement yet. There is no need for you to come here under the guise of spending time with me. I know your father put you up to this," he says.

My eyes widen in shock at the revelation. He's betrothed to this beast?

Marzia's gaze meets Cyrus's.

"I know you hate this decision, Cyrus. I am doing my best to meet you halfway through this. This wasn't my decision either." Her voice is stronger as she speaks, bitterness seeping into her tone.

Cyrus releases a loud laugh. "Your decision." The sound of Cyrus rising from his seat to descend the steps fills the air.

"Our betrothal was my father's choice, not mine. And your father has milked that decision since my father was taken in battle. And now that he sees the war continue and his position is threatened, he sends his daughter adorned in jewels and silks to remind me of just how stunning my future could be." The king stands in front of Marzia, his fingers gently dipping under the pearl necklace she wears. He roughly pulls it, breaking it in an instant as he tosses it from her throat.

"But I do not see a future with you. I see a woman willing to do anything her father tells her if it means she will be queen someday. And that makes you no better than a whore," he seethes. Goosebumps break out across my skin as I imagine the cruel decision he has already made for Marzia. He places his hand along her shoulder, her eyes widening as she comprehends his unspoken command.

"Cyrus—"

He gently grabs her hand.

"Marzia. Are you a whore, or aren't you?" he asks. She trembles slightly as she kneels before him. I watch in horror as her shaking hands shift to his pants, unfastening them. Her gaze shifts behind him, meeting mine for an instant, and I look away, wanting to spare her some dignity. The sounds that I've become accustomed to in his chambers fill the throne room. I squeeze my eyes tighter as the sounds of her choking on him fill the air. I don't know how long it lasts, but I almost breathe a sigh of relief when I hear her collapse onto the ground.

"Slave." I tense when I hear the king's voice. I look up, meeting his gaze.

"Yes, Your Majesty?"

He motions for me to come to him, so I force my legs to do so, trembling all the while. I notice the corner of his lips twitch in amusement as I approach until I stand before him. He grabs the skirt of my dress, keeping his eyes lined to mine. Excitement fills his eyes at the situation. He rips the bottom of my dress, handing a piece of the tattered fabric to me.

"Help the Duchess." His voice is cruel. I bow slightly, reigning in my terror, and quickly move to help her. Her eyes are downcast, the corner of her face covered in the king's semen. I bend, moving the fabric to her lips to wipe it away when her gaze meets mine, swallowing me whole. She immediately yanks the fabric from my hands, shoving me hard.

"Get away from me, slave," she snaps. I land hard on my ass, the force of her shove propelling me further than I had expected.

I hiss in pain as my skin burns from being dragged across the floor with such force.

The king's chuckle fills the air as I try to stand up. He puts himself away, bending to where she kneels. His hand dips under her chin, using his thumb to smear his cum on her face. "I suppose you need something to tell your father when you return from your visit. Come to my chambers later."

He doesn't wait for her response as he turns to leave.

"And if I refuse?" Marzia calls after him. Her eyes are still focused on the ground as she speaks. But the threat doesn't faze Cyrus. He laughs loud enough for it to echo off the wall, not sparing her a glance.

"Then someone else will be."

I tense as the horns sound, signifying the beginning of the hunt. This hunt is to honor the king before he leaves to fight another battle against the enemies of the beast empire. I fear for the village that is about to be destroyed by the king and his army. I doubt it takes all of them to even take down this village. It only took the king himself to ruin mine.

I see him a small distance away, speaking with nobles—one of which I recognize.

Felix.

He's dressed up for this event, a warrior's blade resting on his hip as he speaks to the king. He has a look of disinterest on his face, though he always seems distant whenever I see him. But his dark eyes give off a terror I can only imagine. I breathe a sigh of relief when I realize Dimitri isn't here. A small part of me worries, though. If Dimitri isn't here, it could mean Felix hurt him. But I have to keep those kinds of thoughts out of my head, especially if I want to remain sane today.

I also look around for the king's betrothed, but she is nowhere to be seen. For the first time in a while, the king didn't require my presence in his chambers last night. I imagine it's because his betrothed was occupying the room. But I also wonder how badly he injured her for her to be absent from such an important event.

"Slave." I look up to see the king fastening a quiver around his chest. Once he finishes adjusting it, a servant hands him the large bow, and he walks toward me with an unreadable expression.

"We are joining the hunt," he says, walking past me.

I fail to hide the shock on my features, stepping forward to protest.

"We, your majesty? I am not prepared, nor have I trained for—"

He whips around, his murderous expression silencing me.

"If I send you into this forest to hide and hunt you down like the animals we seek, will it have been worth it to question your king?"

I slowly shake my head. "No, Your Majesty."

His expression slightly calms and a small smile appears on his lips. "Then come."

No servants follow us into the thick brush. My heart beats faster as the extent of the situation dawns on me. I'm heading into the forest with the king alone. I keep my eyes trained on his back. He has broad shoulders and a muscular form. His white hair is pulled into its usual updo as well. He's a cruel and terrifying beast hiding under the guise of a beautiful creature. The longer I study him, the more I wonder why he has features so different from the rest of his people.

We walk for a while before the king stops near a creek. He quietly bends, placing his hands in the water, and I take the time to look around at the greenery. It's beautiful and abundant. This forest makes me question the one I grew up in. I look up toward the sun shining high in the sky. I haven't felt or seen the sun since my capture. I disappear from this moment, just focusing on the warmth the sun gives me.

I miss this.

I open my eyes, looking down at the king, who splashes water on his face. His eyes are focused on the river, his face lax of emotion.

"Did you have a restful night, Anna?" His eyes remain focused on the river, so it takes me a moment to register he's speaking to me.

"Yes, Your Majesty."

He chuckles softly, standing. At his full height, I only come to his chest, so I keep my eyes focused on his chest as he stands uncomfortably close.

"Look at me, Anna."

I obey him, slowly lifting my gaze to meet his. His dark eyes roam over my features, and he suddenly reaches for my face, causing me to flinch instinctually. He chuckles softly, but his hand only brushes my cheek.

"I missed your presence in my chambers." His thumb rubs lightly over my cheek as he speaks.

"Marzia is an eyesore and a terrible lay. At least, with you in attendance, I would have had some amusement. Seeing the horror in your eyes always lifts my spirits," he smiles.

"I wish you could've seen what I did to her last night. You would have been absolutely mortified," he trails off as his eyes roam over me. My heart doubles in speed as I take in his eyes. The darkness of his pupils expands, sharpening into a serpent-like form as he studies me. I know he can smell my fear as the reality of my situation washes over me. I'm alone in the forest with the king, completely at his mercy.

"I—" I close my mouth, not knowing what to say to divert the king's sudden interest.

"Your Majesty, the hunt," I try.

He laughs, his hand roaming to the collar of my dress. "The hunt will proceed whether or not I take part. I don't need the entire day to hunt down the beast. I can smell it from here," he trails off, his nose hovering over my throat, "the same way I can smell you, slave."

I shudder as his tongue lightly licks over my pulse.

"The scent of your fear is almost tangible. Like the prey that surrounds us, you are no different. It calls to me." His hands dip under the collar of my dress, grasping my breast. I gasp, pressing my hands against him, but he moves me with ease, pinning me against a tree.

"Your Majesty—"

"Shh. I don't know what it is about you, but the longer I fucked her, the more I wanted it to be you writhing under me. Why would I feel that way for a human? Much worse, a slave?" he mumbles. His lips press against my throat, suckling the skin there, and the foreign feeling sends a ripple of adrenaline through me.

"Maybe I've grown bored with the upper class. Maybe my desire has reached an unspeakable place. Maybe I should just indulge in the one thing I am forbidden to touch," he says.

"Wait, please—" He cuts me off as he presses his lips over mine. His kiss is searing, sending heat through me that settles in the pit of my stomach. I immediately struggle, pressing my hands against his chest, but he's much stronger than me. He pulls away, his eyes filled with lust as he looks over me with a mixture of confusion and arousal. I'm trembling against him as he brushes his thumb over my swollen lips, his hand resting at the base of my throat.

"Please, Your Majesty, don't do this. I am just a slave. I am nothing. You can't ruin your reputation for the likes of me—Agh!" I'm cut off as his hands tighten around my throat. His lust disappears in an instant, replaced with irritation as he looks at me.

"Do not tell me what I can and can't do, slave."

I try to respond, but it's no use. There's no air left for me. Just when I think I'm going to pass out, he releases me. I drop in the dirt, gulping as much air as possible. When I look up, he glares down at me in confusion before swiftly covering it up, stepping over me as he snatches his bow up.

"Come. Let's hunt."

Chapter Twelve

ANNALISE

The King has left the palace.

It's been a little over a week since the king departed with his men to the edge of the forest to seek more villages like mine. Villages that are harboring weapons made to kill beasts. It's interesting the king's absence has placed a calm over the palace. The servants don't beat us as often, and slaves themselves have gained personalities. Among the slaves, conversation happens more often, but I try to keep my distance, especially seeing as any of us could be dead within days of the king's return. I don't want to deal with the sadness of loss any longer.

Today, I've been assigned to the king's chambers. The Overseer monitors me from a distance, keeping me away from tasks that could get me killed. The king may be gone, but even the Overseer has noticed he favors me. I silently make my way through the laundry rooms, avoiding the glares that I get. The king was right about me being the only slave to wear a servant's uniform.

I am the only slave permitted to do the tasks I've been assigned. I pull the warm sheets from the line, stuffing them into the basket as my thoughts take over. I can't get the king's words out of my head. Lucky for me, he takes his war seriously and left before he could act on his confession. Does he plan to act on it once he returns? How could he go back on his word and do something that would taint his name?

Whatever's going through his mind, I hope his time away from the palace deters his lustful need for me. I've seen him do unspeakable acts with all kinds of women. The last thing I want is for him to perform those acts on me. I can't begin to think of what awaits me upon his return. He disregarded me as he departed, not even glancing in my direction. But with each passing day, I feel more and more heavy-hearted.

I keep my eyes down as I lift the basket full of linens, making my way through the halls and to the king's chambers.

The day is spent deep cleaning the king's chambers. Word has reached that he is returning to the palace after a successful battle.

"Straighten out those sheets, slave." A servant brushes by me in irritation as I carefully make the bed. I keep my back to her so she doesn't see my tears. It saddens me to think of how many humans have been killed by the king. I hastily wipe my eyes, blinking back my tears to focus on my task.

The king's sheets are extremely soft. In the slave's quarters, our beds are stone, and sheets are itchy leftover material. The king's bed and sheets are made from materials I've never seen before, not even during my days of freedom. It's just another reminder of how useless this war is.

I turn away from the bed, tossing the old sheets into the basket. A soft gasp pulls my attention to the corner where the king's liquor sits. The servants that are supposed to be cleaning with me found the decanter that holds his wine. My eyes widen as they open it, giggling with one another.

"My salary would never let me taste anything like this," she murmurs to her friend as they pour themselves a glass.

I silently pick up the basket. I can do nothing. I am not a servant; I am a human. I can't even scold them. It's shocking watching them giggle with glee among each other as if they wouldn't be killed for doing something so bold. I turn away from them, grabbing the basket of old sheets to leave the room, when I feel a rough pull on the collar of my dress.

"Where do you think you're going, slave?"

I cry out as I'm thrown to the ground, the sheets spilling from the basket. The servants stand over me with disgust in their eyes as they take me in.

"I was taking the sheets to the laundry," I murmur.

The blonde servant steps around me, closing the door to the king's chambers. My stomach dips in horror as I realize what's about to happen.

"You will not leave until we say you can," the blonde growls, stepping around me. "Go sit in the corner."

I keep my eyes down, gathering the sheets once more before making my way to the corner. The servants not only find their way into the king's liquor, but his wardrobe as well. They pull his robes from their place in the armoire, holding them up in awe.

"Have you ever seen such fine silk?" The brown-haired beast smiles at the blonde, pulling the robe around her shoulders.

"You look good in the king's robes. Maybe you should find your way into his bed, Elisa," the blonde giggles. Both beasts return to the decanter, drinking the wine as if they don't have a care in the world. I continue to focus on the door, but I know I can't leave without them getting to me first. I'm trapped until they've had their fill. But the longer I sit, the clearer their intentions with me become.

My gaze shifts to the window. The sun is setting, meaning the Overseer will come by at any minute to inspect the chambers. Unfortunately, the decanter has reached its lower limit. The king is bound to notice someone has been drinking out of it. Both of the beasts realize it all too late, but just as I suspected, they have a plan.

"Come here, slave," the blonde calls to me.

My stomach coils. They're going to blame me. I slide from my seat, stepping away from them.

"No," I whisper.

Elisa's gaze narrows as she stares at me.

"No?" She doesn't give me a chance to fight back as she crosses the room instantly, her hand colliding with my face. I cry out in pain, the room spinning around me. Before I can reorient myself, I feel my arms and legs being dragged away from the doors and to the corner of the room. They roughly shove me in the chair, yanking me by the hair.

"Let go of me!" I open my mouth, screaming, but they use it as an opportunity to force the wine down my throat. I cough and choke on the wine, clenching my teeth, but the women are relentless. They hold my nose, waiting for me to open my mouth so they can force more liquid down my throat. I don't know how long I struggle this way, but soon, my thoughts are no longer tethered to my mind, and my body feels like it's floating.

I try to find my footing, but the room is spinning. All I can do is stumble drunkenly into the walls, using them for support. After many attempts, I fall to the floor, rolling onto my back as the beasts giggle across the room at my predicament. Pretty soon, the Overseer will arrive, and I will be so far gone he will have no choice but to execute me himself.

My mind drifts all over the place as I now cannot control my thoughts or keep them at bay. I think of my father, Dimitri, and my village. Just thinking about them brings an ache that seems incurable in my chest in this state. Tears pour down my cheeks, my sobs filling the room as I think of the fate given to my father.

I roll to my knees, trying to stand as my body suddenly feels too heavy to hold up. I angle my gaze, taking in the beasts that forced this state on me. They still sit at the king's table, sipping from the crystal. They're enjoying themselves and will continue to do so once this night ends. I will take the blame for drinking the king's wine and going through his wardrobe.

A bitter chuckle escapes me as I struggle to my feet, stumbling to the door. They have actually done me a favor. I only hope death will come swiftly for me and before the king's return. I continue to stumble, my feet falling one over the other until I trip completely, smashing into a solid wall of muscle. Strong hands steady me, pulling me away from the body, and when I look up, my blood runs cold.

The king watches me with a terrifying expression, his eyes drifting past me to the servants. "What is this?"

He's back early, dressed in royal attire. My gaze shifts from his face to the blade that rests on his hip. It's the same blade he used the day he found me at the river. The same blade he killed my father with.

I pull away from the king, shocking him as I stumble back onto my ass.

"Your Majesty!" Both servants fall to the ground, pressing their heads into the floor.

"We left her to clean, and when we returned, she had gotten into your wine. We don't—"

"Stop," he snaps.

He walks past all of us, pulling his blade from his hip to rest it on the table. He remains silent as he moves to stand over the servants. "Get out."

They immediately stand, making their way to the doors. I try to stand as well, but my body is too heavy, and I can barely rise on my knees before a groan leaves my lips.

"Not you." The king pulls his remaining armor off, including his shirt, until he is left in nothing but a pair of pants. My eyes widen as I take in his muscular form. His skin is flawless other than the faint scars that wrap around his torso from something horrible in his past. Other than those, I see no remnants of fresh wounds from the battle this week.

Once he's comfortable, he turns to face me, his dark eyes roaming over me in interest. He's silent as he closes the distance between us, bending to where I kneel on the ground. His face is smooth with no emotion. No hint of what he's feeling. He reaches toward me, and I flinch, but he only runs his thumb along my cheek, and I can no longer remain silent.

"They forced me. I tried to leave," I slur out.

He chuckles softly. "Of course they did."

"After the week I had, I wanted to come back to my palace and have a good night's rest. Instead, the slave I so loathe is in my chambers, drunk off her ass on my wine," he says. He walks to his bed, plopping down on the sheets I just spent an hour making.

I try to stand, wobbling to my feet as I look for the door. "I will go, Your Majesty, Goodnight."

I don't know if he understands me, but he doesn't let me stumble far.

"Come here, slave," he calls to me.

I breathe deep before making my way to where the king sits, amusement twinkling in his eyes as he studies me.

"You are responsible for keeping me awake. Now, you must help me fall asleep. Tell me about your week without me. If you can." He's grinning as he speaks, but my mind is on high alert.

"I... started with laundry..." I try to lower my gaze as I speak, but he stops me.

"Look at me, Annalise," he says.

I raise my eyes, looking into his as I speak, and relay my week to him. The longer I talk, the less I'm convinced he's paying attention. His eyes rest on my lips as I speak. And he moves while I'm explaining cleaning the stalls. His hand drifts to my hair, where he pulls the pins holding my bun in place so that it falls in waves around my shoulders.

Silence overcomes the room as he studies me, the darkness in his eyes shifting.

"Your Majesty—"

He isn't interested in what I say. He stands, making his way to the doors. He remains in front of them for a moment, thinking before the sound of the lock clicking into place echoes over the room.

My breathing is heavy as he turns to face me, his expression blank.

"Your Majesty—"

"Tell me about your future," he says as he approaches me, each muscle flexing as he does so. It's interesting he would ask about my future, knowing he has taken it from me. And I think that's precisely why he asks—so that I completely understand it in this vulnerable state. Tears form in my eyes but don't spill as we look at one another.

I gently shake my head, caught in his trance.

"I have none," I whisper.

He smiles, reaching for me, his fingers curling around the collar of the dress. My mind flips into panic mode, and I step back, feeling the edge of his bed against my legs.

"No," I hiss.

Cyrus laughs, standing at his full height. He towers over me with his powerful frame, and I suddenly feel smaller than I ever have. He reaches for a stray strand, studying it as he twirls it between his fingers.

"We can do this the easy way or the hard way. Regardless, I will be buried in your virgin pussy tonight." His voice is smooth as he speaks the words, sending a chill across my skin.

Dimitri flashes in my mind at this moment. His smile, his bright eyes, his always positive attitude. His proposal and unconditional love. He's the man I was supposed to give my body to.

A man.

Not a beast.

But as Cyrus stands over me, it becomes painfully clear that will not be happening. It's as he made me admit only seconds ago. I have no future. But I can't bring myself to embrace that.

I shake my head, trembling. "Please…"

Cyrus's eyes darken at my pleading, and he vanishes in an instant. I gasp when he is in front of me, a loud tear echoing through the room as he rips my dress from my shoulders. I don't have time to register what's happening as he's on me, and it doesn't help that the wine is running through my veins. I stumble back, tripping over the tatters of my dress and the edge of the bed, crying out as my world flips. But Cyrus is fast. He catches me, his hands tightly wrapping around my waist as he pulls me down with him to the bed.

I scream and kick, but it all falls on deaf ears. Cyrus easily pins my hands above my head, his free hand trailing between my legs as he plays knowingly between my folds. I let out a gasp as a sensation I've never felt before sweeps over me. The heat from the liquor combined with this strange new sensation is too much, and I find myself squirming underneath him as liquid pools between my legs.

"No," I moan as he inserts a finger.

The feeling is foreign, and yet I want more. I arch my back, trying to move away from him, and he uses the opportunity to latch onto my nipple with a mastery he gained from the many women in this position before me.

"Stop, please," I moan.

Cyrus laughs, his tongue laving over my nipple as he looks at me. "So *you* say, but your body wants me to continue."

He inserts another finger, spreading my inner walls further. A moan leaves my lips as pleasure spreads within me. I've never been touched in such a way, the king of the beasts the first to do so. His lips cover mine, swallowing my moans, and I use the opportunity to bite down on his lip. He pulls away from me before I can react, the room is spinning and stars explode across my vision as he strikes me hard. I look up at him, trying to regain my consciousness, and he's wiping the blood from his lip. He looks at the blood on his hand, then at me, but instead of rage, I see amusement.

"Do you think you can stop me from taking what I want? I am the king of the beasts. I rule all. You will not keep me from what I have claimed."

He uses his hands to push my legs apart as he frees himself from the restraints of his pants. My eyes widen as I take in his size. I knew from all the nights standing in the corner that his cock was large. But seeing it from this angle as he's about to penetrate me makes things completely different. I try to roll away, but his hands wrap around my waist as he positions himself at my entrance. He doesn't miss a beat as he pushes inside of me. I cry out in pain, screaming from the sudden intrusion. He pulls out slightly before shoving back in two more times until he fully sheathes himself inside of me.

I sob beneath him as he keeps my arms pinned above my head. The pleasure I felt from his fingers is gone, replaced with hot pain as he stretches me impossibly to fit himself. To my relief, he releases my hands, and I press them against his naked chest, the heat from his skin standing out at this moment.

"Look at me, Annalise."

I slowly open my eyes, shifting my gaze to look at him. The king of the beasts. The beast that has taken what I had saved for someone else effortlessly. I can feel him lodged inside of me as I look into his eyes. He leans over me, placing a soft kiss on my cheeks. Then he covers my lips with his. His kiss is gentle as he slowly pulls out, only to thrust again. My nails dig into his skin, steadying me as he finds a rhythm.

I hate myself as a moan escapes my lips. Pleasure ebbs its way back into me at this moment as he strokes me gently, stretching me with each thrust to fit him. He threads his fingers through my hair, pulling tight to expose my throat as he suckles on my neck. I cry out in pleasure as my body climbs to even higher heights, reaching for something. I spread my legs wider for him, his thrusts growing more urgent as he stretches me impossibly, bringing me closer to the release I seek. My eyes widen as panic washes over me. My body takes on a mind of its own.

"Wait, wait, Ahh!"

A new sensation washes over me as my body seizes up, my inner walls spasming on his thrusting length. I toss my head back as pleasure rockets through me, my guttural groans echoing through the room. Cyrus's mouth covers mine, and he swallows my moans, his tongue dipping into my mouth as he adds to my pleasure.

I finally come down from my pleasure-filled high, my body limp and weak. My nails are digging into Cyrus's back; to my horror, he's still hard inside me.

I tense when he places a soft kiss along my throat, his lips next to my ear.

"The wine that beasts drink is far too strong for your kind. I doubt you will remember this in the morning. And I plan on enjoying you like this... completely at my mercy."

Chapter Thirteen

CYRUS

What is it about her that has me so enamored? It must be her beauty. As I stare at her sleeping form, I am lost as to what it is. Nothing about her is spectacular. Other than her background, she is human. She is talentless, weak, and part of the filthy breed that exists at our reluctance. Yet I find myself drawn to her. Her raven hair and amber eyes call to me like a siren. The innocence that pours from her begs for me to steal it away and claim it as mine.

I hoped last night would sate me of that desire. Each time I watched her stare in utter horror at the sights in front of her every night, it only made me want her more. It made me want to show her what the pleasures of sex can be. To give her the same sensation I give each woman in my chambers at night. And each time she would admit to her fantasies of giving herself to that boy Felix fucks, it made me want her even more.

She's an obsession. Plain and simple.

Last night did nothing but burn my desire even hotter.

Annalise stirs lightly in her sleep, her cheeks still holding a small blush on them from the amount of alcohol she consumed. Those servants could have killed her by forcing her to drink that wine. I make a mental note to have them executed for doing something so careless. Though I should thank them, I never would have claimed her body as my own otherwise.

I only wanted to toy with her as I usually do, but the longer I watched her speak with eyes so wide and innocent and cheeks blushing, calling out to be touched, I couldn't help myself. I couldn't stop myself, not even after three times, nor when she was begging me to stop from exhaustion. I ravaged her until *I* was sated. And now, the sun is slowly making its ascent into the morning sky. And she still lies naked in my bed, her blood staining my sheets.

I laugh softly.

It was a fun night. But it can never happen again. I am the king of the beasts. If anyone caught wind that I was messing around with a human, there would be hell to pay. But she won't remember, and I won't speak of it. I can only hope I can control myself now that I've had a taste.

I get out of bed, gently picking her up with me to avoid jostling her. I must sneak her back to the slave's quarters before she awakens.

Annalise

I'm in pain.

And I don't know why.

I slowly lace up the corset of my dress, trying not to tie it too tight for fear of it squeezing the parts of me that are hurting.

The king has returned, and in honor of his victory, the palace is hosting a ball at the end of the week. This means all the slaves and servants will be busy preparing the palace for the arrival of nobles during this time. For me, it only signifies the worst. The war we are fighting is a losing battle. We are laughably outmatched. No one is coming to save us, and I will die in this palace.

"You." I look up as a guard enters the slaves' quarters. His dead eyes fall on me with disdain as he turns his nose up in disgust.

"The king has summoned you."

I watch him with wide eyes as he turns to leave. I wipe my suddenly sweaty palms against the dress as I try to think of what he could want with me so early. I remember little from last night after the servants forced the wine down my throat. But when I awoke this morning, I was back in my bed and sore all over.

I silently make my way through the hidden halls in the direction of the king's chambers. I can only assume we weren't caught, and I somehow made it safely to my bed. I've had wine before. My father would let me drink it on special occasions. I've even had drunken nights with Dimitri. But this wine was nothing like what I had tasted over the years. This wine was powerful, and I remember nothing past falling to the floor.

I flinch from the bright sunlight as I step into the main hall of the palace. The wine was much too strong, the effects of it worse than any I've had in the past. I round the corner, approaching the king's doors. The guards eye me silently but don't say a word as they knock twice before pushing the doors open to reveal the king.

He's standing near the window, shirtless, with his back to me. His hair is down as well, the strange color catching my attention. He turns to face me upon my entrance, his eyes roaming over my body. His gaze lingers, undressing me, and to my horror, my body reacts the way it did with Dimitri. And he notices. The corner of his mouth twitches slightly before he raises a brow at me, and it dawns on me that I've been staring instead of greeting him.

I bow, lowering my gaze.

"Good morning, Your Majesty. I'm glad to see you've returned victorious from battle."

He chuckles softly, walking past me to a chair. I can still feel his eyes on me as he takes a seat.

"Are you?" he asks.

I turn to face him, and he's watching me with a strange expression.

"Are you glad that I've returned?" A vicious smile forms on his lips as he studies me.

"Yes," I say softly. My gaze shifts past him to the bed. There's blood on the rumpled sheets. I look back at Cyrus, but he has no visible wounds.

"Annalise." His voice pulls me out of my wanderings.

"What are you looking at?" he asks, angling his head.

It's a curious thing to see him do something so human when I know he is far from it. The soldiers that came through our village told stories of the beasts and their true nature. After observing it up close for the past few months, the stories didn't do them justice.

"I was told you summoned me, Your Majesty. I was only trying to see what needed to be cleaned," I say softly.

Cyrus scoffs at me. "Nothing needs your attention. But I need you to answer a question for me."

My eyes widen as he reaches under the table, pulling the half-empty decanter from its place. My heart slams against my chest as he places it atop the table, perfectly in view. I don't know how to react, nor if I should. But my body has already betrayed me.

He smiles the moment he hears my heartbeat increase.

"Your Majesty—" I take a small step back, flinching in pain as the soreness between my legs flares up from my movement. He notices the actions, his smile deepening.

"Are you in pain, Anna?" He's toying with me again, but I don't know why. I shake my head, unable to find any words. He stands quickly, approaching me with intent. The closer he gets, the more terror floods through me. I keep my eyes trained on his chest as he stands over me, pushing a stray curl from my face.

He leans in close to me, his lips inches from my ear. "I asked you a question."

I breathe a sigh of relief when a knock sounds at the door, interrupting his teasing. Though he doesn't at all seem annoyed at the interruption. If anything, he seems more excited.

"Enter."

The doors open just as he steps away from me and my eyes widen in horror as the servants from last night enter. Their arms are tied in front of them, their faces bloodied. Seconds after stepping into the room, their eyes fall on me, anger appearing in their expressions. Cyrus stands tall behind me, his words like ice as they fill the air.

"Have you forgotten your manners in the hours from last night until now?" he growls. Both beasts drop to their knees, greeting the king. Their voices tremble as he stands over them, glaring at them in contempt. I keep my gaze focused on Cyrus as he speaks. The tone he uses is one I haven't heard since the night I served the beasts in the dining hall.

"It would seem manners aren't the only thing you have forgotten," he says, glaring down at them. My eyes widen as their whimpers grow louder. We didn't get away with it. Someone caught us. It must have been the Overseer, or I wouldn't be here to witness this situation.

"Rejoice. You will be an example for your fellow servants of what happens when you overstep. You do not touch what belongs to the king."

The women cry and beg, but it all falls on deaf ears.

"Whose idea was it?" Cyrus asks.

Silence fills the air as they consider their answers, but the blonde is the first to speak. "It was all her, your majesty! The slave! She stole the wine and rummaged through your clothing. We scolded her but—"

She's cut off as Cyrus places his hand on her shoulder. His touch is gentle, his expression blank.

"Rise," he says. She stands, and the brown-haired beast remains kneeling with her face pressed into the floor. Cyrus circles her, coming to a halt when he's directly behind her. His eyes meet mine as he presses a soft kiss where her neck and shoulders meet. It's something I've seen him do before he fucks women. Only he doesn't strip her. His hands come up to hold her head steady as he bites down, his teeth piercing her flesh.

His eyes remain focused on mine as blood spills from the wound, and her screams fill the room. Her bound hands reach up, trying to push him away, but the moment her hands meet his skin, his grip tightens, and he twists. A loud crack resonates off the walls, and her lifeless body collapses, her neck bent at an unnatural angle. I watch in horror as she dies, Cyrus glaring at her lifeless body in disgust. He wipes her blood from his lips, spitting on the floor.

"I assume she was the one in charge," he says as he kneels to the brown-haired beast's height, lifting her chin with his bloodied fingers. He doesn't give her an opportunity to speak, his hand snatching her around the throat. He doesn't choke her like I expect him to. He squeezes. Terror fills my veins as he continues to squeeze, blood pooling around his fingertips.

I look away just as the crunch of him crushing her throat and spine sounds.

When I finally find the courage to look his way again, his gaze is already focused on mine. My hands are covering my mouth, holding in my sobs. Cyrus scoffs, standing to make his way in my direction. The closer he gets, the more violently I tremble. I'm next. I am looking death in the face.

I keep my eyes trained on his chest when he's standing directly in front of me. "Annalise. Look at me."

I try. I really do, but my body is paralyzed. He roughly grabs my cheeks, blood oozing between his fingers and my face. I whimper in fear as he forces my gaze to meet his. His eyes are murderous.

"You will be flogged. Fifteen lashes," he snaps.

Cyrus walks away from me, gesturing to the lifeless bodies.

"Clean up the blood." He makes his way near the bed, a smirk finding its way onto his lips as he takes in the sheets. He looks at me, his eyes holding knowledge I don't understand.

"*All* of the blood."

Chapter Fourteen

ANNALISE

"Ah!" I hiss in pain as the servant lightly dabs my back and arms. She clicks her tongue in irritation.

"Hush. You should count yourself lucky. Offenders don't usually survive the lashings, let alone slaves. You should be grateful you're being treated at all." She roughly presses the cloth into my open wounds, forcing me to bite my lip so as not to cry out in pain. Servants look for any excuse to punish or kill slaves. This one is no different, especially from the way she scrubs my back.

"Those two servants were foolish to offend the king. Yet you walked out alive," she chuckles bitterly, once again digging the cloth into my back. I bite my lip harder, the taste of blood filling my mouth from trying not to cry out.

"He should just kill you. The village you came from was a dangerous one. You're a risk to us all. You probably bewitched him. Maybe I should do him the favor of breaking the spell—"

"Brigida." The servant steps away from me, bowing slightly as the Overseer steps into the room. His eyes roam over me in disdain, and he looks back at her in irritation.

"The king is here," he says.

I flinch, looking away as he strikes her across the face. "Don't be so foolish as to think you are above his rule. I will not have another of you overstepping."

Brigida holds her face in pain. "I'm sorry, forgive me."

Silence washes over us, but he finally relents.

"Get out," he growls.

I hear her footsteps scurry away, and the Overseer walks to the door without another word, pushing it open.

"Your Majesty."

I hear Cyrus entering, his footsteps coming in my direction.

"Leave us." His voice echoes across the chamber, and the Overseer slowly bows before backing out of the room, leaving me alone with the king. Cyrus is silent as he looks over my back. I flinch when I feel his fingers lightly tracing the gashed wounds.

"You are lucky," he says. I want to scream at him, but I know I can't. I cannot offend the king. Each time I close my eyes, I think of the horrid death that awaited that servant. The gruesome brutality of it all was incomprehensible.

"Tell me what happened," he says.

His fingers are still roaming over my back.

"I don't understand—"

"Why were you drunk in my chambers with servants?" His voice is strangely soft.

"They offered me—" He chuckles out loud. Grabbing my hand in his, he slowly helps me up to a sitting position, and I have to hold the torn blanket over my naked chest. His eyes visibly dilate as he watches me, but he pauses, a frown appearing on his lips. His eyes are focused on my lips, and he reaches for me.

I flinch, closing my eyes, but feel his thumb rubbing lightly over my bottom lip. When I open my eyes, he's looking at the blood on my mouth with a strange expression.

"Your Majesty?" I call to him.

He finally looks back at me. "Anna. I know you didn't drink that of your own free will. There's no use in lying to me. Those servants have paid for their mistakes with their lives. And you have paid with your flesh. So make it easy on yourself and answer me truthfully."

I keep my eyes trained down, and he gently places his finger under my chin to lift my gaze.

"Look at me." His dark eyes swallow me whole. I clench the blanket closer to my chest. His gaze is intimidating and demanding all at the same time, and I can't stop the words from coming out of my mouth.

"They... wanted to try the wine... I was doing my assigned task, cleaning the chambers, and they decided to use me as the scapegoat if they got caught because I would be killed for it once you discovered the wine missing and a drunken slave."

His eyes roam over my face. "That wine could have killed you, Anna."

My lips are moving before my brain can stop it.

"Why do you care? I'm only a slave. I should have been dead months ago," I say bitterly.

Cyrus's entire demeanor shifts at my outburst. If anything, his eyes grow darker than I've ever seen. In an instant, his hand is around my throat, instantly cutting off my air supply. I immediately reach for his hands, trying to pry them away, but I can't. I can even feel the pressure of my bones threatening to crack underneath his hands. He doesn't say a word. He only glares at me, watching me fight for my life. A small smile creeps onto his lips as he watches. My world dims, and my fingers grow cold. And just when I think he's going to end it, he releases me.

I lean forward, coughing, trying my best to breathe and soothe my throat at the same time. His hands roughly thread through my hair as he yanks me up.

"I can still have you around with your tongue cut out, slave. Do not mistake my amusement of you for kindness. Do not forget that I am, first and foremost, your king."

Once he feels his words are heard, he releases me, storming out of the room.

The king is back to his old ways.

I stand in the room's corner, a tray of food in my hands as he pleasures himself with yet another woman. She is on her hands and knees as he thrusts roughly in and out of her, her moans of pleasure filling the room. I wonder who these women are to be so readily available to have sex with the king. The king who has a fiancée. It makes me even more curious about the beast society. It seems all of his subjects are terrified of him.

The sound of choked gurgles fills the room, and I look up to see the king has his hand around her throat. He's choking her. Her eyes are wide and full of fear as she tries to pull his hand away from her throat. Irritation is prominent on his face as he looks at her, and his eyes slowly rise, meeting mine across the room. His grip tightens around her throat, and it's silent. Only the sound of Cyrus fucking her body can be heard, and she's slowly growing unconscious. I don't know if I should say anything or let him be.

"Your Majesty," I murmur.

I take a small step forward. His eyes remain focused on me. He seems to be in a trance.

"Your Majesty," I say louder. "You're killing her."

He chuckles softly, his eyes moving away from me as he leans down, placing a kiss on her cheek.

"Am I?" He glares at me, waiting for me to respond, but I don't. I know I've angered him. I drop my head, stepping back. He finally releases her throat, and she collapses, unconscious. I let out a soft gasp as the king gets up, not sparing her a glance as he pulls his robe around his shoulders, making his way to the doors.

"Come."

I move to follow him as we step out of his chambers and quip his command to the nearest guard.

"Have the palace doctor take a look at her once she awakens."

"Anna, you look frightened." I look up from my corner in the steaming room to see Cyrus smiling at me with an amused grin. Tonight, he decided he wanted a bath. A late one that requires no one but me present since half the staff is asleep at this hour. I enjoy the warmth swirling around the room from the heat of the water. It helps soothe my nerves.

"She's alive if that's what you're worried about," he says.

"Yes, your majesty," I whisper. I still have the bruises from him choking me earlier, and he didn't do it until I passed out. I can't imagine how she's going to feel when she awakens. I slowly look up at Cyrus. He's still watching me with that strange expression. It's the same expression he's had since he came back, and I don't understand it.

Or him.

"How is your body?" He smiles as he says it. I don't sense genuine concern coming from him, which means his words come with a double meaning that I miss.

"It's fine, your majesty. Thank you for your concern," I say.

He chuckles. "Come. Join me."

My eyes widen at his command. He knows I'm about to refuse because he interrupts me.

"Now."

I slowly move towards the bath, placing the tray on the ground next to it.

"Remove your clothes," he says as his eyes never leave mine.

I take a deep breath.

"Your Majesty, please—"

"Now, Annalise."

I shakily reach behind me, unlacing the dress. It grows slack around my shoulders, and I hold it there, not wanting it to fall any lower. Cyrus's eyes dilate to that terrifying hue as he watches me. He rises from the water, standing at the edge of the pool.

"Anna. If I have to take that off of you, you will have nothing to wear. And how will you explain your nudity to the Overseer?" he says teasingly.

I slowly remove my hands, letting the dress fall.

"Now, come here," he says.

"Your Majesty, my back is bloody. I will surely—"

"Annalise," he snaps.

I shut up, making my way to the water. It's hot but feels soothing against my aching body. Cyrus watches me with an unreadable expression.

"You are so shy of such a body," he says in amusement. His eyes roam over me, taking in my naked form. Something that I only ever wanted Dimitri to see.

"Were you planning to be this bashful with your lover?" he asks.

I squeeze my eyes shut, letting the tears fall, earning a hearty laugh from Cyrus.

"Tell me, Anna. Do you think he wants your virginity at this point in his life?" He uses his hands to guide me so my back faces him. I flinch when he traces my wounds with his fingers.

"Answer me," he says when I don't respond.

"I have no dreams of him anymore, Your Majesty. I don't envision any future with him," I say. He places his flat palm against my back, and a second later, warmth spreads over me. My wounds tingle for a moment, and the aching pain I've felt since my lashings suddenly vanish. Cyrus runs his palm over my back, but there's no pain. I turn around, facing him.

"What did you do?" I ask in confusion.

He doesn't respond, only moves to sit again, submerging his body.

"What do you envision, then?" He ignores my question, poising his own.

"Nothing," I whisper.

His eyes roam over my face, taking in my answer and he holds his hand out for me, issuing a silent command. I will my legs to move through the water. He reaches for my hand once I am close enough to him, pulling me closer. I gasp, but he doesn't release me. He keeps his eyes trained on mine as he pulls my hand lower and lower. Fear rocks me as he puts my hand over his erection. I try to pull away, but he holds me tight.

"Your majesty—"

"Feel me, Anna. Do you see what you caused? I didn't finish earlier because of your concerns." He has a sinister look in his eyes as he speaks, and it terrifies me.

"You haven't the slightest clue, the trouble you cause Anna.... or what has already taken place in this palace." He pulls me in closer to him, his hand brushing over my breast, coming to rest around my waist. A whimper escapes me, but I try to compose myself. I am the only one at the mercy of his wrath tonight.

"If you ever interrupt me while I'm with another woman..." His grip tightens so much that I feel a small pop in my wrist. I cry out in pain, but he still doesn't let go. "You will be her replacement until I am sated. Remember these words, Anna. My patience has run out."

Chapter Fifteen

ANNALISE

The palace is hosting a royal ball. The ball is in five days, and the royal tailor is doing last-minute touches on the king's suit. I stare silently at the old man as he pushes another pin into the expensive fabric. His dark eyes don't hold the same darkness as the king. He seems kind, unlike the beasts of the palace. My father once told me beasts are very hierarchical. Rank is extremely important among the beasts. Not only is the king the most powerful of the beasts, but there is no one out there that matches his strength. The beasts believe the strong flourish and built their society on that terrifying belief.

"This will be my best work yet, Your Majesty." The tailor smiles as he pulls the coat from Cyrus's arms, handing it to his servants. He must be a rich beast himself to have servants. But then again, why else would he handle the king's clothing unless he was that talented?

"I can't wait to see it, Cedric. Send my regards to your wife. I hope to see you both at the celebration." Cyrus smiles at the man, the sight taking me by surprise. The tailor leaves the chamber, closing the door behind him once again, leaving me alone with the king. Something that keeps me on edge. Cyrus hasn't touched me since that night in the bath. He hasn't so much as teased me like he loves to do. But he's always watching me with that strange expression. I don't know if he's planning something, especially since he's barely voiced his inner thoughts.

Cyrus walks to the desk in his study, grabbing his shirt. He pulls it over his head with ease, looking at me expectantly. I make my way over to him, grabbing the loose strings to tie. His eyes roam over my face, and it makes me just as nervous this time as it does every other time. Silence washes over us as I complete my task, Cyrus's gaze fully focused on me. I dip slightly, stepping back, but he reaches out, grabbing my injured wrist.

I release a gasp, looking at him with fear in my eyes, but he isn't looking at me. He's looking at my wrist. After studying it, he finally speaks. "Does it hurt?"

The skin has already turned a hideous purple, the bone still swelling grotesquely. It's sore, for sure, but I won't tell him that.

"No, Your Majesty," I say.

Cyrus chuckles softly, stepping around me without another word, and I release a breath of relief. His words from the other night ring in my ears, constantly placing me on high alert.

"You haven't the slightest clue, the trouble you cause Anna.... or what has already taken place in this palace."

I slowly turn to face him. His back is to me as he leans over his desk, eyeing whatever contents are strewn over it.

"Have you ever been to a ball, Anna?" he asks.

His back remains to me as I respond. "No, Your Majesty."

Cyrus laughs, turning to face me with a raised brow.

"Really? The king your people fawn over never invited his subjects to enjoy a night of celebration for at least one of his fabled victories?" he asks.

"No, Your Majesty. I knew nothing of the king or his war," I say.

"What about the man that raised you? He never mentioned the king, at least?" Cyrus's tone pulls my attention, and I look up. He's watching me with a curious expression, as if he knows something about my father that I don't.

"You mean my father, Your Majesty?" I ask.

Cyrus makes a face, studying me intensely.

"Sure."

"No. My father never spoke of the king. May I ask why you want to know about my father, Your Majesty?" I ask. He glares at me for a moment before shrugging and going back to pulling on the rest of his clothing.

"I am curious about your upbringing. And why it was so far from the protection of your king."

The room is silent as Cyrus thinks of his own answers for my upbringing. He finally drops the conversation, making his way to the door.

"Come. For now, we have a meeting to attend."

The meeting differs from usual. No nobles are in attendance, only what I assume are military heads. I've seen them in passing at dinners or meetings Cyrus doesn't allow me to attend. But now they are all gathered in one place. I stand silently behind Cyrus as the leaders file into the room individually, each congratulating Cyrus on his latest victory. I still have yet to hear any details about the battle, but judging from how these beasts react, it must have been an important one.

Nine beasts enter the room, each with a servant standing near them. I am the only human in attendance. Each beast that approaches the king in greeting has an intimidating aura that swallows me whole, their gaze avoiding me as they greet their king. It must be a war meeting. The king just returned victorious and only beasts that are part of his military are in attendance. The only question is, why am I here? Surely, Cyrus doesn't trust me this much.

I'm pulled out of my thoughts as the last official arrives. My eyes widen slightly as the intimidating beast steps into the room, his gaze once again holding an indifference to the world around him.

Felix.

He's a terrifying beast. Not only is he tall, but he's extremely well-built. His muscular form shows easily through the fabric of his clothing. His dark hair is pushed back to reveal the sharp contours of his face. He's as terrifying as he is beautiful. His gaze slips over the room, commanding the same level of respect that Cyrus receives. The beasts even bow to him in greeting.

My heart slams to a standstill when Felix's servant enters behind him. Dimitri has his eyes trained down as he steps into the room. His eyes once held so much light and joy within them; now they hold misery. My nails dig into the palm of my hand, my chest squeezing tighter as Dimitri's eyes shift, immediately falling to where I stand.

Instantly, the room falls away. It's as if only he and I exist at this moment. My fingers itch to touch him, to play in his blonde hair, or even have him laugh at one of my jokes. I want to feel him in my arms and embrace his warmth, feel his kiss, anything.

Anything at all.

My eyes widen slightly when I notice his eyes are glassy. He's holding back tears as he looks at me. And to my horror, my own tears spill down my cheeks. Cyrus turns to face me, his gaze deadly.

"Go fetch the wine and fill my guests' glasses," he growls.

I keep my eyes down, bowing, but Cyrus snatches my arm, holding me close. "Do not take advantage of my leniency, Annalise. Swallow your tears before I do something you'll regret."

He roughly shoves me toward the decanters as he faces the room.

"My friends. Please, take a seat," he says to everyone in attendance. I hastily wipe my eyes, pulling myself out of my trance. I can't afford to let my feelings show, especially now in front of what appears to be his war council.

As the meeting stretches on, I feel more hopeless than before. My assumptions were correct about the battle being important.

It was the last of the human settlements being used to distribute weapons to the hunter army. As Cyrus speaks, beasts are infiltrating villages important to the war. It's only a matter of time before they discover the hunter's camps or, worse, the human king's stronghold.

Cyrus is too focused on the meeting to notice if I steal a glance in Dimitri's direction. So, I take the time to memorize his features. His bright blue eyes always reminded me of the sky. The intensity of the blue, however, was always something that stood out to me. My gaze lowers to the soft pout of his lips. And when I look at his face, I notice a light pink scar running up the side of it. I also notice his hair has gotten longer in his time in captivity. But the more I watch him and Felix, the less I think he's a captive. He seems to enjoy freedoms I don't.

"The hunters have masked themselves in these villages as well. They pose as regular villagers. I didn't want to speak of it until I was certain, but it has become clear with this last week's raid." I silently fill Cyrus's glass before stepping back, studying the map as he speaks.

He points to the regions.

"They have spread to the east. This explains the weapons in the villages and why our usual raids weren't effective. Not only were they hiding to pick us off in villages, but they have been planning ambushes, using all of their manpower to capture one beast at a time. Lately, it has been the strongest," Cyrus says, causing murmurs to erupt.

"Are you certain of this, Your Majesty?" One of the beasts speaks up.

Cyrus nods grimly, and another beast speaks. "Why are they ambushing only to capture one of the strongest instead of trying to kill us off?"

Cyrus releases a deep breath. "I thought it was just bad luck when my father went missing. But in the past few months, I've noticed a pattern. Powerful beasts that go missing are near villages that aren't on our maps, or routes that are near these villages we discovered to have weapons."

Cyrus pulls something out of his pocket, holding it up for the room to see. My eyes widen. I recognize it as the necklace my father gave me.

"We all know what this is. But upon closer inspection, I found this one contains my father's blood. I discovered it recently on a slave entering my palace from a village harboring weapons," he explains. The silence in the air is palpable as Cyrus looks at the necklace.

"The hunters must have realized long ago that this war was a losing battle. They began looking for ways to harness the power they used to fight us. They put that power into these trinkets. Unfortunately for them, the best they could do to give a human a fraction of our power is breed a halfling whose blood they could use in these trinkets. But to use a full-blooded beats blood, they learned they had to breed children strong enough to withstand the strain. They are breeding weapons," Cyrus says.

A beast stands from his seat, his fists clenched in rage as he glares at the king.

"Are you certain of this?" he asks.

Cyrus studies him intensely, his gaze shifting to me. He keeps his eyes focused on me, making an internal decision.

"Come here, slave." All eyes of the room fall on me, forcing me to clutch the decanter tighter to my chest in fear. Cyrus's gaze remains level with mine, issuing a silent challenge. I slowly place the decanter on the table, clasping my hands in front of me as I make my way across the room. I keep my eyes level with his chest, my body trembling.

"Face the room." His voice is strangely gentle as he speaks to me. I try to wrack my brain for a solution out of this. I don't know why he would bring me to the front of the room to prove a point. Is he going to use my father's necklace on me? But wouldn't it kill me like he just explained to the room? My ears are ringing as I face the room, my eyes finding Dimitri. He's watching me with a look of terror etched into his features. My breathing speeds up as he focuses on me, and Cyrus holds my father's necklace above my collarbone.

"No!" Dimitri lunges from behind Felix, his eyes wide in desperation as he moves for me. Felix is fast, however. He quickly grabs Dimitri's arm, ripping it back with a loud crack that sounds off the walls. Dimitri's scream is cut short as Felix presses his foot into his leg, forcing Dimitri's legs out from under him. I watch in horror as Felix uses Dimitri's falling momentum, pressing his palm against his head to smash him into the floor.

"Dimitri!" My instincts kick in to go to him, but Cyrus's arm is around my throat, wrenching me to his body. His grip is like steel as he presses the necklace against my skin. To my shock, the sharp stab of a needle from the necklace penetrates my flesh, latching on just as a surge of energy rushes through me, filling every cell and vein until my body feels like it's on fire.

My legs give way from the intensity, and I collapse, my breathing heavy as I try to pull it under control. To my shock, my nails break through the layer of marble with a loud screech, causing murmurs to erupt. I look up, and Felix is holding Dimitri by his hair, his face bloodied from the impact as he watches me in regret.

He knew.

As I breathe, I notice the room seems vivid. My body feels constricted and somehow much stronger than before.

"The humans have gained knowledge. We have stopped the spread, but now the hunter's camp is our main concern. They are using these camps, our power, and our people. And while they are doing little to affect this kingdom, they are hurting our kind. And I will not stand for it," Cyrus says.

I cry out as Cyrus pushes his foot into my back, pinning me to the ground. "We must wipe them out. If we continue to allow them on this path, they will infiltrate the kingdom, and we will have a real problem on our hands."

Cyrus glares down at me as he speaks, his gaze filled with hatred. He looks away, gesturing to the guards.

"Take her."

Chapter Sixteen

ANNALISE

I don't know who I am. Cyrus's words from the meeting and my knowledge of my life don't add up. How could I withstand the power of that trinket? How did my father come into possession of one so valuable, and why would he give it to me knowing I did not know how to use it? I immediately think of Dimitri's reaction when the necklace was revealed.

Of course.

Dimitri knows, somehow. My father probably expected Dimitri to tell me the truth about it someday. I flinch as the door to the empty chamber opens to reveal the king. I've never been in this room. Instead of the lavish decor and pristine walls of the palace, the room has stone walls and only a window on the far wall. I try to stand, my hands chained in front of me as Cyrus steps into the room, his expression unreadable as he studies me.

"Your Majesty," I bow the best I can, hoping he isn't here to beat me within an inch of my life.

Instead of approaching me as I expected, he takes a seat at the small table, still gauging me. I want to ask him about my past. I want to ask him if Dimitri is okay, but I know both questions will bring me punishment.

"I know nothing, Your Majesty, I swear—" Cyrus holds his hand up, silencing me.

He studies me intensely once again before filling the silence. "I didn't understand it at first. I thought it was strange that you came from a village with such a heavy hand in the war, yet you were so naïve to it all. I figured you were lying initially, but it turns out you truly knew nothing. And the one that knew everything was right under my nose the entire time."

My eyes widen. He's talking about Dimitri. He smiles at my reaction, angling his head to study me.

"You spoke so highly of him. You craved his very existence without knowing what you are and what he is. And he willingly kept it from you. Even in the end, when telling you the truth could have saved you, he chose wrong. He failed to do the one job your father entrusted him," he says. A light knock sounds at the door, and Cyrus keeps his gaze trained on me as he responds.

"Enter."

Tears spring into my eyes as Dimitri enters the room with Felix in tow. His eyes are downcast, his face bloody from the beating he received. Felix's expression is blank as he roughly shoves Dimitri into the room, forcing him to lose his balance as he falls to his knees. I take a step forward without thinking, stopping in my tracks as Cyrus's glare pins me to the spot.

"All this time, you have loved and defended him. And he's been lying to you your entire life," Cyrus says in disgust. His glare shifts to Dimitri, and out of disbelief, I also look at Dimitri.

"That isn't true," I whisper.

The sound of my voice pulls Dimitri's attention, his eyes settling on me.

"Tell her." Felix's voice is like a whip, striking fear into both of us.

"I'm begging you, don't make me do this." Dimitri's sobs echo in the room. I've never seen him so broken. Felix bends to his level, whispering something in his ear—something that makes Dimitri tremble, his eyes widening as he focuses on me.

Cyrus decides to step in, standing from his seat to cross the room with my father's necklace in his hand. "The man that raised you was very clever. But not clever enough. He never expected you to set foot in my kingdom. I sensed the power this little trinket radiated from the moment you stepped into my kingdom. I couldn't understand why he would give such a powerful item to you and not use it himself. Especially when he hid from you the world that it came from."

Cyrus looks at me, amusement in his gaze. "The world that *you* come from, Annalise."

Cyrus's gaze now falls on Dimitri. "Ask him."

My mind is swirling with questions as I look at Dimitri once again. But now, he won't look at me.

"I'm so sorry, Anna," he whispers.

Cyrus has lost his patience. His amusement dissipates within seconds, and he kneels, ripping Dimitri from Felix's grip. His hand is around his throat as he glares at him.

"Tell her. Tell her of the past you've helped conceal. Tell her, or I will end her journey right here."

Silence stretches over the room as Dimitri has an inner battle with himself. Whatever it is he has to tell is something he wants to take to his grave. Dimitri chuckles softly, looking at Cyrus. His face feigns false bravery as he looks at the king.

"Kill me," he says. His threat does little to sway Cyrus. Cyrus smiles in response, throwing Dimitri across the room. My legs feel like lead, but I can't move as I watch him struggle to sit up.

"Kill you, you say?" Cyrus repeats. Cyrus walks in my direction, and Dimitri is up, trying to prevent it. But Felix is ready for him, grappling him easily to hold him flush against his chest. Dimitri screams and struggles as Cyrus approaches. I am frozen in fear. I can't move; I can't breathe.

Cyrus stands over me, evil apparent in his gaze. He doesn't speak, holding his hand out to me. My gaze focuses on his palm as fear washes over me, but I have no choice. I place my hand in his, and he gently leads me to stand in front of him, facing Dimitri. Our eyes meet, defeat passing between us. We are both prisoners to our masters. We are trapped and have no future. We are completely at their mercy.

I tense when Cyrus pulls my hair from the tight bun. My hair falls around my shoulders in waves, and he pushes it to one side, his lips hovering over my throat. A whimper escapes me as his grip tightens.

"Who would protect her?" he says mockingly. Dimitri snarls, trying to break free of Felix's grasp as Cyrus's hand slowly moves to the front of my dress, dipping beneath the fabric. His hand grips my breast, pulling me flush against him as he squeezes, chuckling at Dimitri's struggle.

"Weren't you just ready to die? Leaving her all alone with me? With no protection?" he taunts. Cyrus's free hand snakes around my throat.

"Your Majesty," I whimper. He ignores me, pressing a kiss along my throat. My breath quickens, my brain trying to comprehend my situation. Cyrus's hand grips the fabric of my dress, pulling enough that a tear ripples through the room. Cool air blows against my chest, my breast inches from being exposed.

"No—"

"Shh, Anna. You weren't this vocal the night I returned from battle," he chuckles against my throat.

Dimitri has a burst of adrenaline-fueled strength from Cyrus's words, rage in his eyes as he attacks. Felix tackles him to the ground, wrapping his forearm around his throat as he holds him steady to watch the king taunt both of us.

"Bastard!" Dimitri screams in rage, but Cyrus is prepared. He steps around me, kneeling to where Dimitri lies on the ground.

"I'm not the one in this room that is a bastard." Cyrus looks at me, roughly gripping Dimitri's hair as he speaks. "Who is her father?"

Dimitri still won't answer, and Cyrus's patience has run out. He stands, coming to me with purpose. I cry out as he snatches me around the arm, throwing me into the wall. I don't have time to recover as he rips away the top of my dress, exposing me to everyone in the room.

"Don't touch her!" Dimitri's nails are scraping the floor as he tries to claw his way to me, screaming my name. Cyrus ignores him, his hands already slipping under my skirt. My eyes widen, and I press my hands against his chest as he finds my folds. My body immediately reacts, coming alive at his touch. Cyrus smiles wickedly, his eyes sharpening into serpent-like slits as he looks down on me, leaning in to suckle my throat.

He pulls a gasp from my lips.

I flinch as Cyrus rips me from the wall, throwing me to the floor between him and Dimitri. His gaze narrows as he studies Felix.

"Break his leg." The action comes seconds after the king's command, the loud snap of Dimitri's leg filling the room, followed by his screams. I hold my hands over my breasts, kneeling with tears in my eyes. I don't know what to do.

"This will end if you answer the king." Felix's voice is low, sending a chill through Dimitri and me. Dimitri's gaze meets mine, tears filling them as he drops his head.

"I'm not what you think I am. I am a half-breed." Dimitri keeps his eyes down, sobbing.

"People like me were brought into the world so that hunters could withstand the power of the beasts without it killing them. They discovered full-blood beast's power was too strong and corroded their bodies within a few years under the constant strain, eventually killing them. This was before your parent's time. By the time your parents were born, hunters realized that if they tried for and had children while the power of the trinkets was active in their system, their children could withstand stronger and stronger power with each generation." My eyes widen as Dimitri spills the secrets of the hunter's world. Secrets that he kept from me my entire life. His pained sob fills the room as he fights himself to speak the truth.

"Paul and Alexandria were the perfect examples that this was possible. They were the strongest of the hunters because of selective breeding. But they never had children. The war was moving too fast, and their ideals differed from the others. Paul may have raised you, but he wasn't your father. Your father was another hunter who was just as strong as Paul and Alexandria. He also had the respect and ideals that everyone around him felt were the correct path in this war. He knew that he and Alexandria would have a child that could withstand the power of the beast king, so he... forced himself on her and had you." Dimitri finally raises his gaze as he finishes, looking at me.

I shake my head, my vision blurring as tears fall. "No, you're lying. Why would he-how did I—"

I flinch as Cyrus grips me from behind, pushing my hair away from my shoulder as he looks at Dimitri.

"Answer her, half-breed. Why would a stranger raise her as his own?" he asks.

To my horror, Cyrus's hand slips over mine, gripping my breasts. I flinch, pulling away from Cyrus, but he grips me harder against his chest, his lips at my ear as he whispers to me.

"Don't be like that, Anna. While we're revealing secrets, why don't you tell the half-breed how you moaned on my cock all hours of the night?"

My eyes widen. I don't know what he's talking about. But lying is out of character for Cyrus.

"I never—"

"Yes, you did. I believe you had been drinking with the servants earlier that night," he chuckles. Horror washes over me as he shifts his fingers under my dress.

"How about I prove it to you?" He pushes his finger inside of me, and to my horror, my body is already wet for him, allowing him to slide in easily.

"Let go of her, you sick fuck! Why are you doing this? I told her everything!" Dimitri sobs. His nails are cracked and bloodied from his desperation, and I squeeze my eyes shut, looking away.

Cyrus adds another finger, stretching me further. My body comes alive, my nipples beading under his touch as he slowly thrusts his fingers. I bite my lip to fight the moan threatening to escape me. Suddenly, Cyrus releases me, pulling his fingers from my body. A gasp leaves my lips, and I focus my eyes on the floor, trying not to let everyone know the frustration I feel from Cyrus removing his fingers.

He chuckles, stepping around me to address Dimitri. "If you ever so much as look in her direction again, I will execute you. I do not care that you've found favor with Felix's cock."

To prove his point, Cyrus's gaze shifts to Felix. "Break his arm."

Felix instantly follows his instruction, Dimitri's screams once again filling the air.

"Now get him out of my palace," Cyrus commands. Felix roughly hauls Dimitri up, and he continues to scream and fight even though both his arm and leg are dangling uselessly.

"No, Anna! No!" he screams.

Felix chuckles behind him, a wicked smile on his lips. "Save her, Dimitri. Once we leave, she is at the mercy of the king."

I hold my hand out to Dimitri, pleading with my gaze.

"Please, stop." My voice is no more than a whisper. I watch Dimitri fight and struggle, the sight fueling my fire. I fear Cyrus more than anything, but I love Dimitri more. I rely on my instincts, rising from my knees as I sprint to him in the doorway. My hands are outstretched as desperation fuels me. They can't take him away. He can't leave me, not like this. We were meant to be together, no matter what the past held.

"Dimitri-Ah!" I cry out as Cyrus roughly grips me around the waist, pulling me back with ease. He uses his leg to kick the door closed, tossing me to the floor all in one motion. I cry out, colliding with the floor just as Cyrus turns to face me.

He scoffs lightly, kneeling to my height.

"Annalise. I am not done with you yet."

Chapter Seventeen

ANNALISE

He's gone.

I no longer hear his screams or struggles. Once again, Dimitri has been ripped away from me, as if our lives hold no meaning. The door remains closed as I continue to stare at it. And although it has only been a few seconds, it feels like hours. I shift my gaze to Cyrus, my anger bubbling to the surface. Amusement finds its way onto his face as he quirks a brow at me, laughing.

"Oh, don't look at me like that. You'll break my heart." He continues laughing as he steps away from the door. My tears fall freely as I glare at him, letting my emotions show. I have nothing to lose now.

"Why? Why would you do this? Do you find happiness in our misery that much?" I snap.

"Where did this confidence come from, slave? Did you forget your place?" he quips back.

I know I should be frightened, but I let my anger fuel me.

"I won't let you win. I will fulfill what I was created for. I will spend every second of my life trying to kill you—" Cyrus is across the room in an instant, his hand over my mouth as he pushes me into the wall. I cry out under his arm, my eyes we come face to face. His grip tightens, and I try to pry his hand away from my mouth. He's too strong, and my hands are nothing to him.

"Your entire race has spent their every waking moment trying to kill me, Annalise." His eyes darken as he squeezes me harder, studying me. "If you think you can kill me when you only found out what you are minutes ago, then you aren't as intelligent as I thought you were."

His hold tightens to an unbearable grip until I am screaming under his palm. Cyrus is unfazed by my struggles, his gaze narrowing as he shifts closer to me. His gaze continues to move over my face with interest, dipping lower to the tears of my dress. His nose gently runs over my throat, his lips lightly playing at the sensitive flesh.

"When I returned from battle, and you were in my chambers drunk off your ass, I figured I'd send you back with the servants and have you flogged the next day," he says. His free hand roams between my legs, finding my sensitive bud. He slowly rubs in a circle, causing my body to react to his knowing touch. I try to move his hands from between my legs, but he releases my mouth to grip my arms above my head as he holds me steady with his body. I try to pull my arms out of his grasp, but my strength is pathetic compared to his.

"The longer I watched you, the more desire took hold of my thoughts and reason. The blush staining your cheeks, the way you lick your lips when you're nervous, the sweet scent of your blood..." He trails off, nuzzling my throat. I gasp as he kisses me once before latching onto the soft flesh. My body follows his every command. He dips a finger inside of me, my quivering sex already wet with my juices, thanks to him.

"I knew that if I didn't take you that night, I would regret it," Cyrus murmurs as he adds another finger, stretching me further. I shudder in pleasure as a warm wave washes over me, building to something more intense.

The promise of greater pleasure.

He finally pulls his fingers out and lets go of my hands. I tense when both of his hands grip my ass, pulling me flush against him as my legs wrap around his waist. I feel his cock positioned at my entrance and expect him to shove into me roughly, but he doesn't.

"Look at me, Annalise." His voice is gentle, and I obey him. I slowly open my eyes, meeting the dark depths of his gaze. His eyes remain lined to mine as he slowly pushes past my entrance. My eyes widen, my mouth opening with each inch until he fills me entirely with himself. A moan escapes my lips from the pleasurable sensation that comes from the shaft of his cock. I expect pain, but there is none—only pleasure.

"Feel my cock, Annalise. Take all the pleasure only I can give you; Only I will ever give you." He slowly pulls out, only to sheath himself back inside, his pelvis flush against mine. I cry out as he thrusts the same way he did with the women before me, adding to the heat I feel deep in my belly. My inner walls quiver, dripping with arousal as he fucks me. My body isn't my own anymore. It belongs to Cyrus, to do with as he pleases. Pleasure is all I feel. It's all I know. My nipples rub against the material of his shirt, sending bolts of pleasure to my pussy. I feel his hands gripping my ass, pulling me closer to him as he thrusts, holding me between him and the wall.

Cyrus knows my body better than I do and spends every second letting that fact be known. My back arches, my eyes widening in shock as my inner walls begin to contract around him.

"Wait, wait-Ngh!" My body tenses, my hands flying around his neck as I cling to him. He continues his thrusts, drawing out my body's climax with powerful strokes. Cyrus's lips find their way back to my throat, pulling the skin between his teeth. He then pulls away, closing his lips over mine, swallowing my moans.

I finally come down from my high, sagging against Cyrus as he continues to hold me up. As I catch my breath, tears form, slipping onto his shoulder. Cyrus's cock is still fully erect inside of me. He still hasn't found his release, meaning he isn't done with me.

"Why are you crying when I am giving you nothing but pleasure?" Cyrus steps away from the wall, kneeling with himself still lodged inside of me so that I am on my back and he is over me. He gently cups my breast, his thumb rubbing my nipple as he speaks.

"You should be happy. You have earned the favor of the king. No slave has ever earned anything but lashings and death from me," he says over me.

"Why me? Why, when you said you would never touch me?" I sob.

Cyrus looks down at me with a strange expression, a frown on his lips. He tilts his head, finally coming up with an answer. "I want you. That is all."

His deep blue gaze roams over my face, lingering in interest. I try to look away, but he grabs my face, holding my gaze steady to his.

"Look at me," he says. I feel swallowed up by the intensity of his gaze. It's a gaze I don't understand. I tense when I feel him pushing against my entrance. My hands fly to his chest.

"Wait-Ah!" I cry out as he thrusts inside of me, my body immediately accommodating itself to him. The dull ache that was dying down has reignited almost instantly, my body reacting to his stimulations. A smile pulls at his lips as he stares down at me.

"Wait?" His thrusts grow more violent, forcing cries from my lips. My tear-filled eyes meet his, and a smile forms on his lips. Excitement radiates from him as he takes in my distress. He's much rougher this time, jarring my body violently with each thrust until I can no longer hold back the cries he forces from my lips. I tense when I feel his shaft grow larger inside of me until warm spurts of liquid bathe my insides, pushing me over the edge. My orgasm hits me once again, and I cry out, spreading my legs wider for him just as he shudders above me, grinding against my pussy.

My soft moans wash over the empty room, the same room Dimitri and I were fighting for each other in only earlier.

Our labored breathing fills the air, a light sheen of sweat forming on my skin as Cyrus looks down at me. I try to pull away from him, but he remains lodged inside of me, a smile forming on his lips as he lightly pulses his hips, forcing his seed out of the sides of my pussy, spilling to the floor beneath us.

"How sickened do you think your father would be to see his precious 'hope' squirming on the cock of the king?" he chuckles.

He pulls out of me, my body feeling cold from the loss of heat as he stands, tucking himself away.

"How disappointed the entire hunter clan would be to see their greatest hope reduced to this." Cyrus's gaze narrows as he studies me. I slowly sit up, crossing my arms over my chest as he glares down at me. "Now you know that in any shape or form, the past and the future you had is irrelevant. You will never become the woman your king expected you to be. You will never save the people who are counting on you. You will never become the woman that half-breed will love. You will never leave this kingdom."

His words cut deeper each time he speaks, and he knows it. A smile creeps onto his face as he takes in my reaction.

"Do you know why, slave?" he asks.

I slowly shake my head, wanting nothing more than to look away, but I can't.

"No, Your Majesty." My breath feels like it's been knocked out of me as Cyrus's dark gaze swallows me up.

"Because I want you, Annalise. And I will have you as many times as I must to sate my desire."

Chapter Eighteen

ANNALISE

The textured towel I use to scrub every inch of my body forces blood to the surface of my skin, but I don't care. I ignore the pain, the cold water soothing the burn. I lift the bucket, dumping the chilled water over my body. It's all I can do to refrain from screaming. Anytime I close my eyes, I can feel him. His hands roam over my body, making me do as he wants. My eyes fly open, and I release the scream I've been holding back, throwing the bucket to the wall.

His words hammer against my skull, torturing me.

"You will never become the woman your king expected you to be. You will never save the people who are counting on you. You will never become the woman that half-breed will love. You will never leave this kingdom."

He's right. Even if I somehow got the power from the necklace, my father never taught me combat. The one time I tried to fight Cyrus, he easily dodged me and sliced through my back with his blade. He's clearly been in several battles with hunters, none of them doing any damage.

I'm pulled out of my thoughts when the door to the slave's bathhouse is pushed open, revealing an angry servant I've come to loathe. Brigida stands in the doorway, her gaze narrowing as she looks at me. She doesn't speak, storming across the room to pull me up. "What are you still doing in here? The king is ready for his day, and you are not! You useless slave!"

I cry out in pain as she strikes me across the face, throwing me to the ground. She's using the king being ready as an excuse, but Brigida has hated me from the moment servants were put to death over me. My naked body smacks the floor just as Brigida's feet come barreling towards my body, kicking my open belly. Sharp pain explodes in my ribs, but she continues to kick me with no care for how weak I am under her.

It feels like a lot of time has passed in the time since the king returned. Not only did the king do something unspeakable to me upon his return, but he also revealed many secrets while simultaneously torturing me. It's left my mind in such shambles that it feels like it's been longer than four days.

But the ball is tomorrow.

Cyrus and Felix spar in the center of the courtyard, the loud clash of their blades sending shivers up my spine. Servants and slaves surround the beasts as they spar, but Dimitri is nowhere in sight. The last I saw of him, he was being dragged from the room, his limbs broken from his desire to fight. My mind aches to know if he's okay, but with Cyrus and Felix's possessiveness, it's better to pretend I don't care.

Cyrus dodges Felix's blade, using his momentum to flip the beast, but Felix is up in an instant, retaliating. Their movement is so fast that it's hard for my human eyes to keep up with them. Although I feel shame about the past that I came from, I understand why the hunters were so extreme in their methods to battle the beasts. There would be no battle otherwise. If the way Cyrus and Felix spar stretches to their armies, it's no wonder they easily lay waste to our own.

I approach Cyrus and Felix with linens in my hands as they step away from the sparring area in light conversation. The weight of Cyrus's gaze is heavy as I approach until he pulls one from me, wiping away his sweat.

Felix eyes me with a vicious smirk.

"She's alive," he takes in the bruising under my eye, his smile widening as he finishes his sentence, "Barely."

Cyrus also looks at me, a frown forming on his lips as he takes in my face. He reaches for me, grabbing my cheek to angle my head so that he can better inspect me.

"I didn't put this here." He says it low, as if speaking more to himself than Felix. I pull my face out of his grasp, but he doesn't react like I expect him to. He only eyes me for a moment longer before going back to conversing with Felix. As they continue their conversation, they make their way to the table that has been set up for their leisure. There's an assortment of fruits and wines and a water pitcher sitting atop the polished marble table.

I remain behind Cyrus, filling his glass as they continue their conversation.

"As expected, the last battle put a hole in their defenses. I'm sure we'll easily be able to smoke the king out," Felix says. Felix tilts his head, looking at me. "I'm sure it would be much easier to use the king's bastard to draw him out of hiding. Or at least make him make a mistake."

I want to throw the crystal pitcher at his head, but I am not foolish enough to invite such trouble into my life. So I do nothing but clutch it tighter to my chest.

Cyrus absentmindedly waves him off, taking a sip of his water. "The king will not reveal himself for a bastard he lost track of years ago. Our best course of action is to continue with the current battle plan. He's been weakened significantly, meaning he will become desperate soon. There is no need to indulge this any longer."

Felix nods in understanding, rising as he speaks. "I should get going. I am meeting with Rowan today about the materials used for the weapons. I think with his help, we'll be able to single out the location of the camps."

Cyrus stands with him, nodding. "Very good. Let me know what you find."

Felix bows, stealing one last glance in my direction before exiting the palace. I don't understand the dynamic between the two, but Felix seems content to follow his king's orders without so much as a complaint.

"Leave us." Cyrus's voice pulls me out of my thoughts, but he isn't speaking to me. The surrounding servants bow, leaving me alone with the king. Cyrus motions for me to come around the table, his face still holding the same irritation I saw earlier as he studies the bruise.

"What happened to your face?" he asks, reaching for my cheek.

I step back from his touch, avoiding his gaze. "I was beaten for making you wait, Your Majesty."

Silence stretches over us.

"Who did this?" His tone catches my attention, causing me to look up against my better judgment. My breathing hitches in my throat when I notice his eyes sharpening in front of me.

"A servant, Your Majesty. I do not know her name. Beatings are normal for slaves to receive." I try my best to diffuse the situation. I may dislike Brigida, but the last thing I want is to watch Cyrus kill another servant in front of me with his bare hands. He narrows his gaze and, to my relief, doesn't push the issue.

"They are not to lay their hands on you, Annalise," Cyrus says as his irritation continues to grow.

"Your Majesty, slaves do not—"

"You are not just a slave anymore," he says. His eyes hold an intensity that I cannot match, forcing my lips to remain sealed. Silence stretches over us as a chilled breeze drifts over the courtyard. I involuntarily shiver from the cold. Winter has set in, and the snow should fall any day now. But being a slave, we do not get warm clothes. Several slaves die from sickness or freezing to death around this time.

"Did the man that raised you never tell you about the human king, at least?" Cyrus asks.

"No, your Majesty." Anger rises within me at the audacity he has to bring up my father when he shattered the memories I had of the man who raised me in such a wicked way.

"Do you think your people will ever succeed in this war?" he asks, an amused grin forming on his lips as he toys with me.

My grip tightens on the pitcher, but I respond. "No, Your Majesty."

"Why not? They are harboring weapons that have caused worry. They are breeding their children to be strong enough to withstand a full-blooded beast's power. Do you not wish for them to win this war? Do you not hope that they will give you the freedom you crave?" he says with a smirk on his lips.

"I've seen personally what you can do to an army and hunters in the same battle. I have no doubt you will come out of this war victorious," I say.

Cyrus finds my response amusing because he tosses his head back, laughing. "They have learned over the years. I will hand them that. They use the battles as an excuse to pick us off individually. But only the strong. They use the cover of battle to capture a beast and use their power to create the atrocious trinkets you people love to use," he says.

I don't understand exactly what Cyrus is trying to say, but I don't think I'm allowed to pry. Cyrus stands abruptly, shocking me out of my thoughts. He stands tall over me, looking down at me before speaking his following sentence.

"You are a brilliant one as well, Anna. But I will keep watching you. And I will never let you reach your potential," he smiles.

He steps around me without turning back.

"Come. Your shivering is irritating me."

Cyrus has decided he wants a private bath tonight. The bathroom is smaller than the large room he usually bathes in, with no servants in sight. It's still nicer than anything I've ever seen.

Cyrus sits silently in the clawfoot tub, one leg dangling over the edge of the golden side. His head is tilted back, his eyes closed as he breathes deeply. The room is warm and steaming from the heat of the water. I study him silently from my corner of the room. He's an evil creature to tell me how pathetic and weak I am constantly, yet he still came for my body with no qualms. It doesn't add up, his infatuation with me. I only wish for it to end. And soon.

As if sensing my gaze, he opens his eyes immediately, locking onto mine. A surprised gasp leaves my lips, earning a grin from the king. He closes his eyes, angling his head towards me.

"Join me."

I take a deep breath.

"Your Majesty-"

"Now, Anna."

I slowly bring my fingers up, pulling at the strings of my dress to loosen it. Cyrus opens his eyes upon hearing the sound of my clothing, his gaze focusing on me. My dress slowly falls from around my shoulders, and Cyrus is instantly in front of me. He opens his mouth to speak when he suddenly pauses, his eyes roaming over my skin. His gaze narrows as he roughly yanks my arm up to reveal the skin that I rubbed raw.

"What the fuck is this?"

I try to pull my arm from his grasp, but he tightens it, his anger growing by the second.

"Let go," I whisper, trying to free myself from his grasp. He finally releases me, forcing me to stumble back.

"Answer me."

Cyrus's naked body drips with steaming water as he awaits my answer.

"I wasn't paying attention, and I—"

"You're a terrible fucking liar," he snaps. "Did you do this to yourself on purpose? Did you try to rub it from your bone? Do you think it will erase what has happened between us, Annalise?"

Cyrus steps so close to me that I don't have the time to react as he pushes me against the wall, forcing his body flush with mine. My skin immediately heats up from the feel of his body being so close. The imprint of his erection pushes against my naked belly. He uses his hands to pin my arms by my head against the wall.

"I own you, Annalise. I have given your life meaning by showing you favor. Do not insult me by doing something so grotesque to your flesh," he growls.

His eyes narrow slightly as he takes in my pained expression, and he steps back from me, inspecting my body. His hands trace over my bruised rib, causing me to cry out in pain. Cyrus notices, his eyes narrowing on the bruised flesh that has turned a ghastly purple and green.

"Who. Did. This." Even though the room is steaming, I shiver at his tone. It takes a great deal of strength for me to find my voice and respond.

"A servant, your Majesty."

Cyrus places his palm flat against my injured ribs, his eyes lifting to meet mine. Our eyes remain locked, and I feel warmth emitting from his palm. It's soft at first, but it grows until it spreads all over my body, including my arms. He continues to glare at me, not reacting to my terror-filled breathing. His eyes roam over my face and down my body, causing my heart rate to increase. I know he hears it because he smiles as his eyes focus on mine. He finally lets me go, stepping away.

Cyrus doesn't say another word as he moves towards his clothes, sitting on the chair near the door.

"Wash yourself and come to my chambers." He doesn't wait for a response as he leaves the room. I immediately inspect my body upon his exit, shock coming over me. My ribs are no longer in pain. Even my arms that once held hideous scabbing from this morning are now healed and smooth. I look back to the door that he just left through.

I don't understand the beast king, not in the least.

Chapter Nineteen

ANNALISE

The ball has arrived. The palace is alive and bustling with slaves and servants alike, all trying to get the palace ready for the King's Ball, a celebration of the victory of a momentous battle, a giant discovery, and a turning point to end this war.

"Take this straight to the king. Do you hear me?" The cook glares at me with the same set of eyes all beasts have as he shoves the tray of food into my hands. I quickly nod my head, reassuring him I will get the job done. The servants have come to acknowledge the king tolerates me more than others as of late, sending me with anything that needs to be done for the king. But I know today will be a busy day for him. According to the gossip around the palace, this is the first ball in five years.

The last ball was held in honor of Cyrus's coronation.

The gossip also says the palace balls were the highlight of the season. Only the most elite of the beast society were invited to attend. Even the servants gossip about how much of an honor it is to be considered to serve at such an event. I also know that slaves aren't allowed within the area unless it's for "entertainment" purposes. I shudder to think what the king has planned to entertain the brutes of his society, especially on this night of celebration.

The guards standing outside the king's chambers push the doors open upon my approach. I step into the king's chambers, fighting the chill threatening to consume me. I hate this room. I hate that bed. I hate each corner and flat surface. Every inch is a reminder of the things he's done to me. I push the door closed, looking around the room for the king.

I find him standing near the window. The shutters are open, and there's a bone-chilling wind sweeping into the room, but he doesn't seem to notice it or care. He isn't wearing a shirt, and his hair isn't pulled away from his face. It flows freely, billowing in the wind. The longer I stare, the more I realize he's holding the necklace my father gave to me. He's staring at it with an intense expression.

I place the tray on the table in his room, stepping back.

"Good morning, Your Majesty. Breakfast is ready for you," I say.

I begin setting up the spread, trying my best to ignore the sound of his footsteps as he approaches.

"The cook sends his regards. He hopes you appreciate the special breakfast he created in honor of the ball and your victory," I say, reciting what the cook told me.

Cyrus chuckles behind me, looking at the spread on the table. He gestures to it, taking a seat across from where he usually sits.

"Are you hungry?" he asks.

I blink in confusion. I don't know what game he's playing, but I don't like it.

His smile widens.

"You didn't leave my chambers until the crack of dawn. I know you haven't eaten yet, Anna," he gestures to the food, "Eat."

I bow my head.

"I wouldn't dare sit at your table and eat your food, Your Majesty—" I gasp when he's in front of me, his dark blue depths boring into my soul. He has a strange expression on his face as he takes me in, lifting his hand to lightly caress my cheek.

"Sit. Eat."

I immediately obey the command, fear controlling my will. I reach for the toast, bringing it to my lips. Once I nibble on it and Cyrus is satisfied with my obedience, he turns his back to me.

"Five years. Five years since I held a ball in honor of something." He holds up the necklace, looking at it, releasing a bitter chuckle. "Five years since...," he trails off, turning to look at me.

"Have your people ever told you the story of the king before me?" he asks.

I stop my nibbling, looking up at Cyrus. I slowly shake my head.

"My father wanted nothing to do with the war... or the beasts. All he ever told me was that the war was a waste of time," I say.

Cyrus chuckles softly.

"It sounds like the man that raised you was wise. Even if he was foolish enough to challenge me," he says carelessly.

His words catch my attention, and I'm asking before I can think of the consequences.

"Did he suffer?" I ask.

Cyrus looks at me, his eyes softening before quickly covering it up. He looks back at the necklace, malice dripping from his every pore as he speaks. "Not nearly as much as mine."

He places the necklace on the table between us, standing to move across the room before I can respond. His back is to me as he opens a gilded chest, his voice carrying across the room.

"Strip." His voice comes out cold, and my eyes widen. I immediately sink to the floor on my knees, bowing before him.

"Please, Your Majesty, I didn't mean to offend." My voice trembles as I speak. I can't imagine him taking me right now with so many servants and slaves roaming the castle halls. I also can't imagine the torture that awaits me should anyone find out about my nights with the king.

I hear him coming to where I kneel until he stands directly over me. "Anna. Strip."

I slowly rise, my trembling fingers reaching for the strings holding my dress to my body.

"Look at me," he murmurs. I obey his command, my eyes meeting his. He's holding expensive fabric in his hands, his eyes twinkling in amusement as he takes in my fear. Once I'm naked, he drops the fabric in front of me.

"Change."

I reach for the fabric, shock consuming me when I realize what it is. It's a dress. A beautiful gown. One that a noble would wear. I look at Cyrus in confusion, but he doesn't seem to have any hidden agenda as he watches me. I quickly move to put the dress on, but I can't stop myself from taking in the fabric. It's so soft and smooth against my skin, unlike anything I've ever worn in my life. I tense when I hear Cyrus behind me, but he doesn't touch me intimately. He works on the intricate strings of the dress, pulling it tight so that it hugs my frame flatteringly.

Once he finishes, he steps back from me, his eyes roaming over me in appreciation.

"This dress was the most sought after by the nobles to wear to tonight's ball," Cyrus says as he places his hand in mine, leading me to the large mirror hanging on the wall. I stand in front of it in awe. The dress is beautiful. It's blood red with gold trim. The front of the dress dips, leaving little room for the imagination. The sleeves are embroidered in gold as well, the small puff of the sleeve giving it a full look. It hugs my frame perfectly. I've never worn anything so elegant.

Cyrus stands behind me in the mirror, reaching for my hair. He pulls the pin, holding it in a high bun, letting it fall to my upper back in wild waves. He places his hands over my arms, the heat of his body seeping into my own.

"I knew you'd be stunning," he purrs.

I know he hears my heartbeat because he smiles. I muster up all the courage I can, forcing myself to speak.

"I don't understand. Why are you doing this?" I ask.

He looks at me in the mirror, his smile widening. It makes me uncomfortable.

"Do I need a reason to gift the woman that has kept me satisfied for the past few nights?" he asks.

I drop my gaze, my cheeks burning in embarrassment. I'm a glorified whore, nothing more. I slowly step away from him.

"Your Majesty, I should be getting back to work. There is a lot to prepare with the ball—"

"Did you forget your first priority, Anna? Serving me. The ball can wait," he snaps. I bow my head, not wanting to anger him further.

"My apologies, Your—" I'm cut off as his lips come crashing to mine. His hands roam over my body with familiarity, caressing the spots he knows draw out my moans.

He pushes me against the wall, pinning me there with the weight of his body. Even through the thick material of my dress, his erection strains against his pants, his hands already at the hem of the dress as he hoists it up above my waist. His hands wrap underneath my thighs, spreading me for him as he anchors me against the wall, quickly sheathing himself inside of me. I cry out from the sudden intrusion, the pain already ebbing as he finds his pleasure. A dull ache forms as he stretches me to fit him, each stroke taking me closer to the edge.

Cyrus's hands grip my thighs tighter as he uses his strength to pull me in closer to his body, his strokes reaching impossibly deep. I can no longer contain my cries, and he knows it. His thrusts turn violent. He fucks me roughly against the wall of his chamber, not giving me time to recover or breathe. My inner walls contract, squeezing him tight. My hands fly to his back as I toss my head back, letting my cries fill the room. I can't stop myself as my hips involuntarily grind against him, drawing out my climax.

My orgasm finally fades, and I slump against Cyrus, my head lying against his shoulder. He chuckles softly and carries me towards the bed, his cock still resting inside of me.

"Anna, look at me," he murmurs.

I look at him, and the fear I've always felt comes bubbling back to the surface.

"Your Father may have wanted to keep you from this war, but you have just become a very important part of it." He slowly pulls out of me before pushing back in, deliberately drawing pleasure from me. He pushes my hair away from my shoulder, placing a kiss on my exposed collarbone.

"The dress, the food, my bed. It can all be yours. Your days as a slave can end. But you must first do something for me. Your *king,*" he murmurs.

My body grows cold as Cyrus speaks over me.

"I want you to infiltrate the hunters' camp." He pushes the stray hair out of my face. "And I want you to tell me where they are keeping my father hidden."

My eyes widen, and I shake my head. "N-no. I can't- I could never—"

Cyrus's amusement drops drastically, and his eyes visibly darken.

"No?" he chuckles, his hand snaking around my throat.

"What makes you think you have a choice in the matter, slave?"

Chapter Twenty

CYRUS

I haven't held a ball since my coronation five years ago. It is not a pleasant memory. It was a coronation forced on me upon the disappearance of my father in battle. The council said it was time to let him go and lead the people. But I refuse to believe he is dead, especially now since Annalise arrived in my palace with a trinket carrying his blood.

A bitter chuckle escapes me at the thought of Anna. I never thought lusting after a human would carry me this far from grace, but it has. If anyone found out about my little trysts with her, it would cause a scandal. There is nothing left for me to do but embrace it at this point until I grow tired of her. But it doesn't feel like I am growing tired of her. Even now, as I wait to enter the ball, I want her to be with me as well.

I've come to realize that I enjoy looking at her. She is a striking woman. There's no denying that. And knowing that underneath the servant's clothing lies a body I've claimed as my own over and over brings me a feeling I can't control. But she cannot attend the ball. It is for beasts only. No exceptions. There's already been talk since I have her at my side constantly, but with no hard evidence, all they can do is speculate, especially since I am the one personally bringing humanity to its knees.

"Your Majesty." I turn to see Marzia walking towards me. She's dressed in a beautiful gown laced with gold. The colors coincide with mine as they should. Her hair is pulled into an intricate updo, while jewelry adorns her throat and arms. She's beautiful. But as I stare at her, all I find myself doing is comparing her to Annalise. I frown as the thought manifests itself.

Annalise is a body. Nothing more.

Marzia notices my sudden shift in mood and falters in her steps. I quickly wipe my face of any emotions, offering her a smile. I dislike her. That's no secret. But with the ball just beyond the doors and the rumors of our engagement swirling, I must at least pretend.

"Marzia. You look ravishing," I say as I take hold of her hand, placing a soft kiss on it.

"I see the dress I sent looks as beautiful as I knew it would on you," I add.

She smiles, dipping her head at my compliments. Initially, the dress I let Anna wear was for Marzia. But the longer I had it in my possession, the longer I felt Anna would be better suited for it. And I was right. An erection threatens me at the thought of Annalise in that dress. Her dark hair splayed around her shoulders, the red that beautifully contrasted against her skin, matching that incessant blush on her cheeks. The way her eyes glaze over as pleasure courses its way through her system. And the way her body squeezes mine...

The doors open to the ball, pulling me out of my thoughts. Marzia drapes her arm through mine, smiling as the nobles of society erupt in applause upon our introduction. Marzia knows that marrying me would bring her misery. But she also knows it would bring her the crown, something she is all too eager to have. She would do anything to call herself queen, and that's what I hate most about her.

As the night drags on, I constantly drift away from the festivities. I wanted no part in throwing a ball, but my council insisted on having one to reassure the people how well the recent battle went. Not only did we put a damaging blow to the human forces, but we found the fort that the hunters used to create their weapons. I am confident my father is hidden there somewhere. Once we retrieve him and kill the human king, this "war" will be over.

I look up as Felix approaches, bowing to me and Marzia.

"Are you enjoying yourself, General?" I ask.

"Yes, Your Majesty," Felix says knowingly.

"That makes one of us," I mumble, pulling my arm away from Marzia. I gesture for the open floor, walking away before looking back at her.

"Enjoy the night, darling," I call to her. I don't miss the look of shock and irritation on her face as she watches me leave, but she knows how I am and what I enjoy doing. Being around her isn't one of them.

"I see you left the human in hiding," Felix says with a smug grin.

He's the only one I would dare trust with my secret. He is still of noble birth but cares little about what society thinks. He has the luxury of being a general and the successor of many battles. Not just against humans. No one blinks at his endeavors any longer.

"And you decided to leave your whore," I counter.

Felix's smile widens, and he takes a sip of his drink. "Yes, I felt it wouldn't be best to bring him to such an extravagant event. But if you decide to hold a more private event, he will definitely be in attendance."

I eye him curiously. "So you still haven't killed him? Even after he tried to attack me?" I ask.

Felix shrugs.

"You and I both know he couldn't do any damage. Besides, he's too broken right now to go anywhere," he smiles.

I shake my head, looking back over the crowd.

"And what of yours? Now that you've gone down this road, you know the pleasure of a human." He's teasing me. I used to scold him for his behavior of messing with anyone from a slave to a beast. And now look at me. I'm no better.

"I plan on using her to infiltrate the hunters' camp," I say.

Felix's amusement disappears instantly, and he faces me.

"Your Majesty... Are you sure that is wise?" he asks.

Not it's my turn to shrug.

"Whether or not it is wise is not my concern. I know the hunters are a dangerous group. I do not want to risk my men when I can simply send her in and break them down from the inside," I say.

Felix scoffs.

"What makes you think she will obey? She could go into the camp and stay. She could help them against us," he says.

I shake my head.

"She's becoming too much of a distraction. If she betrays me, it will be her death. I only said I do not wish to risk casualties on my side. But if she fails, I will have no choice. I will lead the attack myself and kill them all, starting with her," I say.

Felix is silent as he mulls over my words, and finally, he speaks. "What if we sent someone with her?"

I eye him in confusion.

"Surely you do not mean—"

"Yes. I do," he says with a twisted grin.

"No. Absolutely not. They will encourage each other to try such a betrayal. And who knows what else?" I say quickly, trying to mask my irritation.

Felix chuckles next to me.

"You're jealous of a half-breed?" he asks. I have to fight the sudden urge to wrap my hands around his throat.

"Felix," I warn.

My anger radiates, and I know Felix senses it. He bows his head slightly.

"My apologies. I did not mean to anger you. I know he will not betray me, Cyrus. Nor will he let her betray you. I only fear you're putting too much trust in her, and I don't want to see what happens when she breaks it. As for your other concerns, I am confident that Dimitri will not touch her in that way. He'll never touch another woman for the rest of his life," he says.

I think about his words, going over the plan in my head when the doors to the ballroom open. Felix looks up before me, immediately paling from what he sees. I follow his gaze, my eyes falling on the group of slaves that have been brought in just as Marzia speaks out over the room.

"The entertainment has arrived!"

My gaze narrows when I see the one woman I've been wishing to see the entire night. I release a bitter laugh at the irony as I take in Annalise. She's dressed in that filthy nightgown, her hair wild and her eyes wide with fear. She's clearly been ripped from her bed just for this occasion.

My gaze whips Marzia, who is watching me with a beaming expression just as the crowd circles the slaves. They point and laugh and whisper, taking in the filthy state of the humans. Humans who believe they should be a part of our society. Usually, the display wouldn't bother me in the least. But I know that with this event and this group, none of these slaves are going to make it out alive.

Annalise

The last time I stood before the king like this was the night he held a private party and whipped some of us for entertainment. And now, as I look around the gloriously decorated room, I know that this is the same situation. The beasts surrounding us watch us in resentment, hating that we even exist.

"Entertainment."

That's what she called us. We are definitely going to die. I look around the room at the unfamiliar faces, pausing when I see Cyrus. He looks as regal as he did the first day I saw him in his palace. His clothes fit perfectly, his hair tied up and away from his face. He's a distance away, standing next to Felix. His expression looks calm, but I can tell by the whites of his knuckles as he grips his glass he's furious.

He makes his way toward the future queen, a small smirk on his lips. I'm terrified. Only hours ago did Cyrus threaten me with consequences if I didn't do as he said. Does this mean he decided to end my life?

I stumble as the chains around my arms are pulled, forcing all of us to the center of the room. There are bars sitting, waiting for us to be bound to. I look around at the slaves' faces. Some are sobbing, while others are too shocked to react. I take note Marzia has a strange grin on her face as we approach, though Cyrus does not look happy as he approaches her.

"What is this?" I know that tone. He's furious. His voice emerges cold.

Marzia steps closer to him, adjusting his shirt.

"A little entertainment for the nobles, of course. Your skills are legendary throughout the kingdom. I'm sure they would love to see a demonstration on the pests that caused this war," she smiles.

Cyrus's eyes slightly narrow, but Marzia turns away from him.

She looks at us, smiling, and immediately points to me. "How about this one?"

The guards step around me, pulling me towards the iron bar, and that's when my panic sets in.

"No, No! No, please!" I scream and struggle, causing the room to erupt in a fit of laughter and excitement. My heart is pounding in my chest as they lock my arms around the steel bar, forcing me to my knees. I pull frantically against the chains, looking at Cyrus as I plead, but he's watching me with a strange expression.

"Please don't do this! I beg of you-Ah!" I'm cut off as Marzia slaps across the face, blood filling my mouth from the force.

"I see you still have yet to learn any manners," she snaps, turning away from me. I keep my eyes down, spitting the blood onto the floor as it fills my mouth quickly. I hear her footsteps going to where Cyrus stands, but I don't look up for fear of being slapped again.

"It will be good to have this one out of the palace. She lacks basic manners and has yet to learn after all this time. Oh! Now that I think about it, this is the slave you favored as of late, isn't it?" Her voice lowers, but I can still hear her since she and Cyrus are standing so close. "My apologies, your majesty, I know how attached you've become to the human. If you would like, we can—"

"Strip her." My blood runs cold as Cyrus's voice easily carries over the room. I hear footsteps before my dress is ripped from my skin. Cool air hits my back, causing me to shiver.

"Pay very close attention because this is all I will demonstrate tonight." Cyrus's voice rings out over the murmurs of the beasts, commanding attention. Excitement rises in the chatter as they anticipate what is to come.

"Five lashes." The room falls silent upon his words. "We shall see how many bones I can break, how much skin I can take, and how deep I can cut after five lashes."

The room erupts into a fit of cheers, and I drop my head, letting my tears fall. I am helpless. Cyrus offers me no words of comfort or any warning of when he's going to start. I immediately feel the white-hot sting of the whip, followed by the crack that ripples over the ballroom.

"Ahhhhh!"

Chapter Twenty-One

CYRUS

I yank Marzia by her arm into the nearest room, looking around at the servants who are frantically following us.

"Leave us. Or you will die this night. I can promise you that," I hiss.

I turn away from the door, slamming it before approaching Marzia. She's looking at me with a smug expression, her eyes not holding enough fear for me. I strike her across the face.

"You miserable bitch," I hiss. I don't give her the time to react before I have her around the throat and smashed into the nearest wall. She cries out in shock, her eyes meeting mine. They're wide.

"What the fuck did you hope to accomplish by challenging me in front of the entire kingdom!" I shout.

She flinches but finds her voice anyway.

"Did I hit a nerve, Your Majesty? Or are you just angry you had to do away with your favorite slave?" She says it to provoke me but does not know just how correct she is. I let out a bitter laugh, releasing her.

"Is that what this is about? Favoring a slave?" I ask.

Her eyes grow defiant.

"You favor her more than you should, Cyrus. You humiliated me in front of her! Rumors are spreading about how you rarely punish her and how she is still alive after all this time! You've never kept a slave alive for so long!" she shouts.

My gaze narrows.

"I have humiliated you in front of slaves, servants, and nobles alike. Yet you never tried something so foolish with any of them," I growl.

"You cannot keep treating me as if I am nothing. Eventually, you will have to acknowledge the union between us, and I will not stand for you lusting after a slave!" Marzia counters. I inhale deeply, looking at the ceiling as I try to reign in my anger. Marzia has grown greedy and defiant. Her desire for the crown outweighs her fear of me, especially now that she's seen my favor toward Annalise.

"Did your father put you up to this? Did he send you here and tell you to eliminate any distractions in front of me?" I ask.

Marzia is silent. I release a sigh, stepping past her.

"I told you I had not decided yet to pursue the engagement. And you felt you should give in to rumor because your name, as possible queen, would be tainted? You have overstepped," I say.

Her face noticeably pales at my sudden shift in mood. "Your Majesty, I didn't mean to offend, I—"

"Didn't you? You knew I favored her. Yet you chose her to be beaten and thrown out like the rest. Are you sure you didn't mean to offend me?" I ask.

Marzia still doesn't speak, earning my anger.

"Answer me!" I shout.

She drops to her knees, trembling as she presses her face into the floor.

"I swear, I only meant to keep my name as your betrothed. Please forgive me," she whispers shakily.

Her apology does nothing to sate my anger. I stand over her, kneeling where she is on the floor. I place my hand under her chin to lift her gaze to mine.

"Let me give you a sample of the power you wish you had and shall never receive. Your father will be demoted. You will lose all your servants and your title. And Marzia, if you ever cross me again, no matter the reason, you will die as well. I am doing fine ruling this country without a woman jealous of a slave by my side. I have no qualms about killing you for your stupidity."

Annalise

My body is on fire. The pain is unbearable. The sheets are soft, like silk, helping by cooling the wounds and not causing irritation. My eyes slowly open as an unfamiliar room comes into view. It's elaborate in its decor, but I don't recognize it as a room in the palace.

"And so she returns." My gaze shifts in the voice's direction, my heart sputtering in my chest at the beast leaning against the wall. It's Felix. He's dressed in simple clothing, his dark hair pushed away from his face as he smiles at me. A smile that does little to hide his intimidation, even though he holds no weapons.

"The king asked that I take care of you while he's dealing with pressing matters in the palace. It was quite the task, sneaking you out of the cart of dead slaves. But you cannot be in the castle while the king purges it. Or else you would have been killed as well," he smirks.

I bite back my instinctual reaction, keeping my face void of emotion as he studies me.

"I've done all I can for your back to keep you from dying, but Cyrus will have to fix it to its original form. I'm afraid he excels in the art of healing, whereas I am just mediocre. In the meantime, I will have breakfast brought to you." Felix continues to wear that smirk as he leaves the room, closing the door behind him.

I attempt to sit up but can't because of the pain in my back. The events that caused this pain play in my mind repeatedly. I have to bite back the wave of nausea from the memory of Cyrus whipping my back to ribbons: the blood, the flesh, the pain.

The door opens and my eyes widen as Dimitri steps in. He looks much better than he did the last time I saw him, other than the haunted look in his eyes. I fear that will never go away.

"Dimitri?" I flinch from the pain of sitting up. He's carrying a tray of food that he places on the nightstand, refusing to look at me.

"Dimitri?" I try again. He doesn't respond as he makes his way to the door. Tears well into my eyes as he walks away from me. Felix has done it. He has broken him. Just as Dimitri reaches the door, the beast of my nightmares enters the room. My blood runs cold at the sight of him. His hair is pulled up and away from his face, his dark eyes focused on Dimitri in irritation as he steps out of the room, only pausing to bow to the king.

Cyrus steps past Dimitri, closing the door as he enters the room. He doesn't speak, stepping around me and pulling a chair close to the bed.

"How much does it hurt?" he asks.

I narrow my gaze. He almost sounds genuinely concerned. But I'm not foolish enough to fall for his false sincerity.

"A lot," I whisper.

His frown deepens as he reaches for me, and I immediately flinch away from him.

"Anna, let me see. I'm only trying to fix it," he says as if he's speaking to a child.

"Why? Why are you trying to fix this, Your Majesty? Is this not what you wanted?" I say bitterly.

He notices my shift in mood and smiles. "I have caused a lot of pain for you, Annalise. But don't I fix it every time? This time is no different."

I don't protest as he reaches for the bandages wrapped around my body. I hiss in pain as he pulls them from the blood-crusted wounds. He traces his fingers over the deep gashes, releasing a disappointed sigh.

"This will leave scarring," he murmurs to himself more than me.

Cyrus places his palm against my back, the familiar warmth coating the wounds until I feel them tingling.

"I couldn't hold back as much as I wanted to because of the audience. I cannot show a slave favor by any means," he says softly.

I stare at my hands in confusion. I don't know what's come over the king today. He almost sounds regretful.

"You are the king, are you not?" I ask, testing my theory.

He chuckles softly. He doesn't seem angry or irritated in the least. He's strangely calm.

"Being the king does not mean I can change rules that build the society I rule over. That would only lead to corruption and disorder. The people's needs come before my own. And the people need to know I have only their interest at heart. Your people started this war. Your people took the former king before his time was up. And your people kidnapped the beasts' prince to exert their power," he says.

His palm leaves my back, and just like he said, there's no more pain. He healed me. I feel him running his palm over my now scarred flesh.

"You and I are similar now," he murmurs. I turn in the bed, looking at him. The scars that cross over his face and neck disappear into his clothing. I've seen him naked enough times to know how far and wide those scars go. He tilts his head slightly, taking in my features.

"One thing I've come to admire about you is your beauty. I'm sorry I was the one to place something like this on your back permanently. That was never something I wanted to do. Not unless it was my seal." His gaze swallows me whole as he speaks.

The rest of the room falls away, and I feel like I'm suffocating under his glare. I don't know where his sudden mood came from, but it's unnerving. I drop my eyes, not knowing how or if I even should respond. He was in this same mood the day of the ball when he let me wear the dress before he told me of his plan for me.

"You saved me from death... why?" I whisper. I look up at him, and his features hold nothing to give away his feelings.

He leans into me, placing his hand on my cheek. "I told you I want you, Annalise. I am not done with you yet."

I shake my head.

"But you could easily find another slave, Your Majesty—"

"Hear my words, Annalise. I will never touch another slave that isn't you. You have piqued me to break the rules of my people. I will admit that. But I will never do it again."

My heart beats faster against my chest, and I try my best to keep it down.

"Speak, Annalise. You look as though you have something to say." His gaze is intense, and I can no longer handle it as he watches me expectantly. I immediately look away, trying to get up from the bed as I speak.

"I will speak with the Overseer of the estate to figure out my duties," I say.

Cyrus chuckles, shaking his head.

"You are at Felix's estate now, and he keeps a strict and selective staff that isn't you. Your only job currently is to heal. Once we feel you are better, you will begin your mission."

My eyes widen.

"My mission?" I ask.

"We already discussed this. I will stay here in the coming weeks to assist with your recuperation, and then you will bring my father, or I will infiltrate the camp myself and kill every single hunter there. Man, woman, or child. It's your decision on whether you want that blood on your hands," Cyrus says as he walks to the door.

"Rest, Annalise. I already miss the feeling of being inside of you."

Chapter Twenty-Two

DIMITRI

"It must burn you up inside. Seeing the beast you hate the most have the body of the woman you loved. Over and over and *over* again." I tense as Felix approaches me with a smile on his face. I look away from him, back to where Anna is seated with the king of the beasts across from her as she nibbles on her breakfast. Felix knows how much I hate this. And he's reveling in my suffering.

He looks past me to where they are seated.

"He has her body, and soon he'll have her mind," he says.

She's beautiful in this light, as she's always been. I know exactly why she caught the eye of the king. She's more beautiful than any of the beasts surrounding him with her bright amber eyes and dark hair.

I purse my lips before forming a response. "It must burn you up inside. Knowing she'll always have a part of me, you never will."

Felix chuckles, stepping closer to me. I flinch away from his touch, a gasp of fear leaving my lips. His hand caresses my cheek lightly before he grabs my chin, forcing my gaze to meet his own. I don't fight the shudder that crawls up my spine at his cold gaze.

"And what part is that half-breed?" His dark eyes roam over my body, lingering on the parts he knows awaken my senses. He's challenging me to say more. To make him angry. But I've had enough. I can't take any more of his games. I step back before he tries anything, bowing my head.

"No part. You have everything," I murmur.

I feel Felix's eyes on me, and it terrifies me, so I keep my head down, hoping that he will take my submission and move on.

"The king is sending her into the hunter's camp. He wants her to retrieve his father. The former king," he says.

I look up in shock at his revelation.

"What—"

I immediately stop when I notice the look on his face. Blood drains from mine as an uncontrollable tremble washes over me. I clench my fists to calm myself down, but it does nothing. My heart is already beating fast, and I know he hears it. He can smell my fear.

"You are going to accompany her," he says.

"No. Please don't send me back there." I whisper. Memories of the cruelty from my childhood surface as Felix glares at me, immediately destroying any rebuttal I thought to have formed. My words evaporate from ever leaving my lips. I hate myself. I hate how much I fear him yet crave his touch at the same time.

I hate him.

"You are going to make sure she does nothing foolish to betray the king's trust. And you are going to find out the location of the human king. Do you understand?" he growls.

I slowly nod my head, tears already forming in my eyes. He steps closer to me, forcing my breathing to quicken.

"You will not run away. You will not betray me. And you will not touch her. If you do, I will find you, and you will never leave my chambers for the rest of your miserable life. Do you understand, half-breed?"

I'm shaking as he towers over me, his dark eyes boring into my soul, controlling me with only a look. In the past, I would have stood up to him. I would have run away regardless. I would have touched her and convinced her to leave. But every day is a living hell here. And I fear what would happen to me if I ever betrayed him. Betrayal is the last thing on my mind. I cannot do it. I will not.

"Yes, I understand," I whisper.

Felix grabs my chin with his hand, forcing my gaze to meet his. He smiles cruelly at me, revealing his teeth.

"Very good."

Annalise

"I've missed your presence in the palace," Cyrus's voice pulls me out of my deep thoughts—something I hate to be sucked into more and more these days.

It's been five days since Cyrus dropped me at Felix's estate. At least the estate is beautiful. It overlooks the river that cuts through the kingdom and leads into the forest. It's strange waking up and not fearing for your life or having to ready the king's meal quickly. The servants here are too fearful to pay me any heed. They keep their heads down, mouths shut, and hands to themselves.

"Are you enjoying your time away from the palace?" he asks.

I eye the king curiously, unaware of how I should answer. Rumor has spread throughout the kingdom of the Marzia's fall from grace. Cyrus had her father demoted, her slaves and servants all executed, and he refuses to grant her an audience. Even the servants believe her to be beneath them. I don't understand why Cyrus would make her punishment so cruel.

"I have begun preparations for your task. It will be a seven-day trip to reach the hunters' camp. I will have to train you before you depart and teach you how to use the power in the trinkets. It is the only way you will be able to protect yourself if you are discovered," he says in response to my continued silence.

I let out a shaky laugh. "Your Majesty, surely you don't believe I can actually pull this off?"

He smiles, making me nervous.

"I think you will do whatever you must to earn some semblance of freedom."

My eyes widen as he continues.

"I have an estate in the mountains. If all goes well with this mission, you will live there for the rest of your days. You will have an entire staff to care for you in the months I am away. You will never serve another beast again," he says proudly.

"You're making me a mistress?" I ask in disbelief.

His eyes watch me carefully. He's reading me. He knows my reactions.

"I am making you comfortable. Which is more than any slave can say." His voice grows dangerously low as he speaks. But what he is sending me to do is a big deal. So I straighten my back, hoping to feign bravery as I try to negotiate.

"If I am bringing back your father and betraying my race, I want my freedom... And Dimitri's."

Cyrus doesn't give me a chance to react. He is out of his seat in an instant, his hand around my throat as he smashes me into the wall. I cry out in fear, gasping for air that Cyrus won't allow.

"You dare to dictate to me, slave? I am your king. You do as I say. Not the other way around!"

He releases me, stepping away from my body as I crumple to the ground in a heap. I rub my neck in pain, trying my best to keep my composure, but I can't. Tears spill down my cheeks, hard and fast.

"How dare you mention that half-breed's name to me? I never want to hear his name come from your lips again. Do you hear me?" he growls.

I rub my neck, trying to stop the pain, but nod my head as he continues. "Freedom isn't something you can have, Annalise. *Ever!* Your life will never be as it once was. You will find no semblance of that life. Everything you are should be devoted to me!"

"I-I'm sorry, Your Majesty. I didn't mean to offend," I whisper.

He lets out a humorless chuckle, and I hear him moving toward me. He towers over me, looking down in irritation before reaching for his pants. My eyes widen and I try to move away but to no avail. His engorged cock springs free of its restraints as he stares down at me.

"Open your mouth."

I feel my heart thundering in my chest as I stare at the very thing that brings me unwanted pleasure. The bulbous head is aimed at my lips.

"I said, open. Your. Mouth."

I close my eyes, letting the tears fall before opening them and rising to my knees. I open my mouth, taking him in like I've seen the women in his chambers do before me. The skin is soft against my tongue. I can feel the heat radiating from his shaft as he pushes himself deeper into my mouth. He lets out a pleasure-filled breath, pushing my hair out of my face.

"Look at me."

I slowly raise my eyes to look up at him, and his eyes dilate before me. He thrusts harder into my throat, catching me off guard. The force causes me to cough, and I try to pull away, but he grabs onto my face, keeping me still. He fucks my mouth as if he's fucking me, his thumb running lightly over my cheek, testing the texture of my skin under his own. My eyes are watering from the lack of air, and just when I think he is going to suffocate me, I feel his hard length grow in my mouth, the veins seeming to move against my tongue as he finds his release.

I attempt to pull away, but he holds me close, letting himself pour into my mouth.

"Swallow. Do not even think about getting my clothes dirty," he says over me. I swallow the thick liquid, the foreign taste causing me to shudder as it slides down my throat. Cyrus finally pulls out of my mouth, and I find relief in breathing freely again. He lifts my chin to meet his gaze, his eyes filled with death. He wipes his thumb over my bottom lip, looking at me with such intensity that I want nothing more than to shrink away.

"You will be the only woman to have the heart and body of the king, Annalise. Freedom is not an option for you. It never has been. Not from the moment I had you," he says.

Tears well up in my eyes from his words.

"I suggest you make peace with this future. If you betray me, I will find you. And make the half-breed suffer in your place. Then I will drag you back to the mountainside and lock you away to fuck whenever I feel like it. So you can take my offer, or I will force it upon you. It is your choice." He pushes my face away, standing at his full height.

"Get up. We have a full day planned to prepare you for this mission. And I do not plan on wasting a second of it."

Chapter Twenty-Three

ANNALISE

"Argh!"

I cry out in pain as my body collides with the ground. The thick blanket of snow effortlessly seeps into my clothing, giving me some cushion but adding to my discomfort. We've been training every day before I depart for the hunter's camp, and every day, Cyrus has lost his patience with my lack of skill.

"You're hopeless," he says, throwing his sword down in the snow.

He looks past me towards the estate before focusing his gaze on me.

"It's a good thing your parents are dead. They'd be disappointed to see what a failure you've become."

I drop my head in embarrassment, holding back my tears. He will not make me cry, not like this. I slowly rise from the snow, fighting the chill that has been seeping into my clothing all day. I reach for the blade that was knocked out of my hand, flinching in pain when I try to pick it up. A whimper escapes my lips from the pain radiating up my wrist. I hear Cyrus approaching me in the snow before he's standing over me, reaching for my hand.

He gently rubs his thumb over the swollen bone poking from my wrist, releasing an irritated sigh.

"It's broken," he murmurs.

My eyes widen.

"How do you know?" I ask in disbelief.

It hurts, but it doesn't look like any broken bone I've ever seen.

"I've memorized your body. I know when something is out of place," he says. My hand remains in his, and after a few seconds, the warmth I've become familiar with over the past few days appears.

"I told you to absorb the blow. Tensing like this will get you killed."

I know he is speaking to me, but his explanation as to why I need to do things a specific way slips right through my ears.

"I cannot do this, your Majesty," I whisper. "Even if you aren't giving me a choice, I've never done combat a day in my life. There's no way I can hold my own against people who have done it their entire lives."

Cyrus doesn't seem to be inclined to listen to my excuses, though. He only heals my wrist before looking up at the setting sun. A small bit of happiness flows over me. He always leaves at nightfall. He must return to the castle to do his duty.

"Come. Your shivering is irritating me," he says, whipping away from me.

We make our way back to the estate in silence. Cyrus's mind seems to be elsewhere. As we approach, Felix is waiting for us with a grin on his lips. I take note Dimitri is standing silently next to him. That constant look of misery is plastered on his face. I don't dare make a move or acknowledge that he's there. I just lower my gaze as the king approaches another superior.

"Your Majesty, I trust training has gone well with this one?" I don't miss the amusement in Felix's voice as Cyrus walks past him into the estate.

"No. She's terribly useless," he says in irritation. "Have my belongings arrived?"

Cyrus's words catch my attention, and I immediately look up at the two of them speaking.

"Yes, Your Majesty. My staff has already placed everything in your room. You will stay in the west wing, of course, and I have cleared the halls. It is an honor to have you as a guest in my home." Felix's gaze meets mine as he speaks. He's enjoying crushing my spirits by using a few words. Cyrus rolls his eyes, shoving him.

"Stop it. I wish to speak to you about something important," he says before turning away.

He pauses, looking between Dimitri and me. "See her to my chambers."

Cyrus's eyes linger on Dimitri before he turns away with Felix in tow. I watch them both as they disappear up the marble hall, leaving us alone together.

"Follow me," Dimitri says as he walks knowingly through the large estate. The halls are magnificent. I've barely seen any of it since my arrival. I only ever see my room and the fields Cyrus trains me in. But as we walk through the halls and make our way to the west wing, I am in complete awe. My interest shifts to Dimitri, who is walking silently ahead of me. He hasn't so much as acknowledged my presence. I let out a bitter laugh.

"So, this is how it will be between us? You will act as if I never existed?" I ask. There are no servants around—only the darkened halls. Dimitri doesn't offer a response.

"They have both taken us away from each other. I know that. I would never put you in a position to be at the end of the king's anger. But I wish you would at least smile at me like you once did. I wish you wouldn't treat me so coldly," I say.

Dimitri's steps falter, but he continues the silent walk to our destination. We climb a flight of stairs and reach the double doors that Dimitri pushes open. There are two servants waiting for us outside of the king's doors. They bow to Dimitri as we approach.

"The king has instructed we draw a bath for her." One of the servants keeps her eyes down as she speaks to Dimitri, revealing his status on this estate.

Dimitri nods his head before turning to look at me. His eyes are cold and empty.

"The king has requested you stay in the west wing with him while he is here at the estate." His eyes soften as he speaks his next sentence. "You cannot leave this wing without the king accompanying you... please."

His voice slightly trembles, and my eyes widen. I nod my head slowly before he turns away from us, leaving me with the two servants.

The bath is warm. Steaming really. It feels amazing against my skin, especially since I was in the cold snow all day. The servants scrub my skin clean and continue to fill the tub with scented oils that cling to me. I'm sitting in the warm water as one servant massages soap into my hair when the doors to the room open. The king silently enters the warm chamber, and the servants immediately step back, bowing to their superior as he enters.

His eyes fall on me in the tub as he pulls his shirt off.

"Leave us." His voice echoes off the walls, sending a chill down my spine. The servants immediately scurry out of the room, leaving me alone with the king, and I begin to stand when he stops me.

"We are no longer in the palace. You can drop the formalities," he says.

He continues his path toward me until he is standing directly in front of me. A small smirk appears on his lips as he takes me in.

"Nobility suits you," he says before walking around the tub. He pulls up the seat behind me, and I tense when I feel his fingers in my hair, continuing the servants' work.

"Your majesty—"

"Shh," he hushes me while continuing the task he has set himself on. A wave of sleep washes over me from the feeling of his fingers gently working through my hair. It feels nice.

"I should have known training you would be this hopeless," he murmurs, more to himself than to me. I feel my cheeks burning from his words.

"Your father really taught you nothing about combat?" he asks.

I shake my head in response.

"It's as I said before. he wanted me to have as little to do with this war as possible," I say softly.

Cyrus chuckles, pouring the vase of water over my head to wash out the soap.

"What were you planning on doing with your life if not becoming part of the war?"

I bring my knees to my chest, my gaze focusing on the rippling water in front of me.

"I was going to get married. I was going to start a family. I was going to travel across the sea and get away from all of this," I whisper.

I expect to be pushed under the water at any second, but surprisingly he doesn't.

"Get married..." Cyrus repeats my words, placing his seat next to me. His dark blue eyes focus on me harder than I would like, but I say nothing as he deciphers whatever it is he wants to get out of this strange conversation.

A small smile appears on his lips.

"You were marrying out of love?" he asks.

I slowly nod my head.

"To the half-breed." I don't know if he's asking or telling me, but I nod my head regardless.

"And you were going to bear his children?" he continues.

I slowly nod my head again. My response brings Cyrus amusement because he chuckles softly, shaking his head.

"I don't understand the ways of humanity. You would start a family and marry in the middle of a war? You had no guarantee of keeping your child safe if you were to have one," he says.

His smile widens at my expression. I feel myself growing smaller as he glares down at me, naked and vulnerable in the tub before him.

"You would have been a formidable opponent had you been allowed to reach your full potential," he says.

His eyes shift, and I feel a chill sweep through the room.

"We will have to remedy your lack of combat skill."

Cyrus makes his way to the door.

"Finish washing up. I will be waiting."

Once I finish cleaning myself, I wrap the robe left for me around my shoulders making my way into the king's chamber. I breathe in a shaky breath, looking around the king's temporary quarters to calm my nerves. The room is much larger and nicer than the one I've been staying in, but that is to be expected from the king.

I'm terrified to know what Cyrus has planned for me this night. I've slept with him more times than I care to count at this point, but I've always had the comfort of knowing we were in the palace, and he wouldn't take it too far. But now he is staying in a place where he is free of those restraints, which is terrifying.

I notice him standing near the fireplace. My breathing hitches in my throat at the sight of him. His hair has been released from its usual updo, so it flows freely down his back. The fireplace casts an ominous glow over his intimidating form. I can also see the scarring that wraps around his chest and neck disappearing into his pants. He's a terrifying creature to behold. And I'm alone with him, away from anyone that could possibly help.

He finally notices my presence and looks away from the flames. "Aren't you a lovely sight to see?"

His dark eyes meet mine, and he gestures for me to approach. A slight shiver ripples up my spine. His attention is completely focused on me. I silently cross the room, clinging to the robe that keeps my body hidden from his gaze. He smiles as I approach, his hand gently grazing my lower back as he pulls me in closer to him. Heat radiates from his body. His eyes roam over my face, taking in every last detail.

"Nobility really would suit you, Annalise. It is too bad you were born into such scandal and weakness," he says as he pulls me towards the bed. He takes a seat on the edge, pulling me between his legs. His eyes focus on my body as he gently undoes the tie holding the robe together. He holds the tie in one hand while using the other to push the fabric from my shoulders, and I notice his eyes dilate at the sight of my exposed flesh.

"Did you enjoy your bath?" he asks.

I slowly nod my head, clearing my throat before speaking.

"Yes," I whisper.

He scoffs lightly, looking past me to the fireplace. "Good. I'm glad you could enjoy one thing tonight."

He gestures to the bed. "Lie back."

He continues to watch me as I make my way onto the bed. I lay on my back, focusing on the ceiling as Cyrus crawls over me. He studies me intensely, pushing my hair away from my shoulder as he gently takes hold of both of my hands. He still has the tie from the robe, quickly wrapping it around my arms. He then ties the other end to the bedpost, anchoring me to the center of the bed. My eyes are wide as I study him, pulling against the bonds.

"Your Majesty?" Panic is evident in my voice, but Cyrus doesn't acknowledge it.

"You are not a fighter, Annalise. Honestly, I do not understand why your father gave you such a powerful trinket with no knowledge of combat or how the thing even worked. If your intentions are discovered in the hunter's camp, you will be completely at their mercy. So, I shall give you something more powerful than a mere trinket. Something that I hope your breeding has equipped you to handle."

I gasp as Cyrus gently nuzzles my throat, placing a soft kiss over my pulse.

"I shall give you me."

I tense as a deep growl emits from Cyrus's throat, his legs pushing mine apart as his free hand grips my jaw, holding me steady.

"You are going to bear my seal, and with it, you shall bring me the world."

Pain surges through me as Cyrus's teeth sink into my throat, directly into my artery. My eyes widen as my screech fills the chambers. I try to move, but I can't, my arms held over me by the ties. I pull and wrench, the pain excruciating as the tie slowly burns at my skin. A cold mist seeps into the same area where Cyrus continues to bite, causing my vision to blur. My screams slowly break down into choking as I gasp for air, my throat closing up. I can't breathe, my vision blurs, and to my horror, a cloud of black smoke surrounds me. I can still feel the weight of Cyrus on top of me, but it does nothing to ease the pain. I feel like I'm dying. I am looking death in the face as it surrounds us, plunging the room into darkness.

Chapter Twenty-Four

CYRUS

What were once screams have now become moans. Moans that I can't get enough of. I can feel the warmth of her pussy gripping me as she reaches her climax, her back arching in pleasure as she involuntarily brings herself closer to me. I don't hold back, continuing to fuck her through her release just as I find mine. The warmth grows hotter as I fill her with my seed, and I can't help but look at her face as I do.

Her lips are parted, her cheeks stained red from arousal. The fire from the fireplace casts a warm glow that makes her eyes light up, and her hair is slick to her face from the sweat. She's fucking gorgeous. And she's completely out of it from my seal settling in her veins. Her veins still burn black from me, giving her my seal. My gaze shifts to her ribcage, where the seal has already formed. As I stare at it, I feel more possessive of her than I ever have before. I slowly pull out of her, and she shudders as tiny ripples of pleasure move within her.

I can't help but smile.

If anyone found out that she now has my seal, there would be hell to pay. And she would lose her life. When I first mentioned the seal, I did so absentmindedly. I never meant to actually give it to her. A seal is sacred among beasts. It's also where the hunters coined the idea of trinkets. It's a way for her to use me and my power. I gave her a piece of the beast that runs through my veins, and now it settles in her body to lie dormant until she calls upon it.

The more I trained her, and the more she failed to pick up any form of training, I realized I was sending her to her death. If she's caught, that's it. She has no hope. And I refuse to send her into the enemy's camp without my protection. At least now she can use my strength to escape should things go wrong. But only if things go wrong.

"Your Majesty?"

I'm pulled out of my thoughts by her timid voice, and that's when I realize I've been staring at her. I pull away from her, sitting up in the bed. She immediately sits up as well, pulling the cover to her chest. I frown at the action, reaching for the blanket. Her loud gasp fills the room as I pull it away.

"Don't hide from me," I say.

The longer I stare at her, the more I think back to our conversation. She was so ready and willing to become a mother for that half-breed. Each time I think of it, my obsession grows—my possessiveness. I need to be a part of every desire she has. She's weakening my usual resolve regarding humans, and I don't like it.

And I will no longer fight it.

"Do you still want a family?" The question leaves my lips before I can stop it. She tries and fails miserably to hide her surprise. Her head drops before she speaks.

"No, your Majesty—"

"Cyrus." Once again, the words are out of my mouth before I can stop them. I told her to drop the formalities, yet she still refuses to say my name. I move closer to her in bed, angling my face under hers to see her amber gaze.

"Say my name," I urge.

She parts her lips, and I can tell she's struggling with saying it. I lean in closer to her, where I can smell the natural scent she gives off. My cock grows hard, just inhaling her scent. And I find myself full of need just to hear it.

"Say it," I whisper.

She takes in a shuddering breath and finally does as I ask.

"Cyrus," she whispers my name, the sound heavenly coming from her lips. And suddenly, her whisper isn't enough. I want to hear her screaming my name until it is all she can cling to for stability. I press my lips against hers, pushing her back into the bed, ravaging her beyond oblivion.

Annalise

"You are to go into the hunter's camp and find my father's location. Once you locate him, free him. That is all you have to do." Cyrus speaks to me as he ties the front of my cloak around my shoulders. I look over his shoulder at the horse waiting for me. He's actually doing it. He thinks he can send me to the hunter's camp to free his father.

He's either crazy confident that I won't disobey him or has some other plan up his sleeve. I look up at him as he stands over me, taking in his features. Only last night, he was so intense. Everything from the way he would look at me to the way he commanded me to voice my desire and his name. I feel my cheeks burning as I think of it all. The pleasure. The possessiveness he exuded. I fear it will grow into something dangerous. Something that involves him being a part of my life in that way permanently.

"My seal will protect you should anything unfortunate happen with the humans." His hand hovers over the area beneath the fabric of my clothing, and I feel the warmth of his seal on my skin. "All you must do is summon my strength, and it shall be yours. Use it wisely, Anna. You can only use it once. Then you cannot stay where the hunters can take you. They will use you as they use the beasts in their camps for my strength."

My eyes widen as I listen to his words.

"Your strength?" I ask in confusion. He nods his head.

"Where do you think the hunters got their weapons from? They're fighting fire with fire. Learning our ways and trying to use them against us. The seal is like the trinkets they use," he says.

"Will you be able to find me with this seal? If I get lost?" I ask. Cyrus's eyes visibly darken as he sees right through my lie. And I feel the world grow immensely more frigid as he steps closer to me. He grabs ahold of my chin, pinning my gaze.

"Don't run, Annalise."

I feel my legs growing weak just being under his dark gaze when Felix comes to my rescue.

"Your Majesty!" he calls out to Cyrus as he approaches. Cyrus holds my gaze as Felix approaches but finally releases me. I take a deep breath, trying to relax my nerves, but to no avail. Cyrus eyes Felix, and I take note of Dimitri alongside him, dressed in warm clothing and pulling his horse along with him. My eyes widen as I put what I'm seeing together. I look at Cyrus, but he ignores me.

"Is the half-breed ready?" Cyrus asks.

Felix turns to Dimitri possessively, running his finger alongside Dimitri's face.

"Yes. He's ready. He knows what will happen should he fail," he says with a wicked smile.

My stomach drops and I can't tear my gaze away from Cyrus. He walks to Dimitri, standing over him with a look of disgust on his features.

"Protect her, half-breed. Ensure that this mission runs smoothly." Cyrus snatches Dimitri by the throat, pulling him in close to him as he growls his last sentence. "And do not entertain the idea of touching her," he growls before throwing Dimitri to the ground.

Cyrus turns away from Dimitri and Felix, grabbing my horse by the reins and placing his hand along the small of my back to lead us to the gate.

"You know your mission. The half-breed is going with you to protect you and ensure that you do not fail," he says. Cyrus helps me onto my horse, eyeing me with a strange look as he glares up at me.

"Do not tell anyone that you hold my seal. You will not live if you do."

Dimitri is already mounted on his horse, making his way past me. I look back at Cyrus with fear in my eyes. I take note that the corners of his mouth twitch slightly before he speaks again.

"Come back to me, Annalise."

Dimitri rides silently in front of me as the sun slowly sets. The winds are picking up, meaning more snow is coming in tonight. I can already feel my face burning from the icy winds. Dimitri slows his horse, looking back at me, and for the first time, he speaks.

"We'll make camp in the nearby caves."

We travel a few hours into the night before finding a decent cave to make camp. It's away from the main road, and Dimitri made sure to move us deep within the cave so no one would see the fire. I watch Dimitri as he pets his horse in the corner. He's been avoiding me all day. I let out a deep breath after the long bout of silence, staring into the fire.

"Do you remember when we were children, and my father would take us with him to set the traps in the winter?" I look over to Dimitri, who still has his back to me. I don't know if he's listening. Maybe he hates me for sleeping with the king. I don't blame him. I hate myself. I look back into the flames, enjoying the warmth they give off.

I smile as I speak.

"And you got caught in the rabbit trap trying to steal the berries?" I laugh.

He still doesn't respond to me.

"I miss those days. When life was simple. And we were innocent," I murmur. Dimitri finally moves away from the horses, taking a seat across from me. He looks into the flames as well, and I can't help but focus on the sadness in those crystal eyes. The despair that is reflected at me is enough to break anyone's heart.

"I'm sorry, Dimitri. For whatever I did to make you loathe me so much. I've had no choice in anything," I say.

For the first time, his eyes light up in shock, and he focuses on me. "Anna, you've known me your whole life. How could I ever loathe you?"

My eyes widen, and tears spring up. The sound of his voice is music to my ears. I move towards him, a smile on my face when he flinches away from me. I immediately notice the fear in his eyes as I do. I then remember Cyrus's threat before we left, and I sit back down, moving further away from him.

"I'm sorry," I say.

Silence envelops us once again, the crackle of the fire echoing off the walls.

"... You baited me into messing with the trap."

I look up, and Dimitri is smiling at me. It's a sad smile. One that doesn't reach his eyes. And I find myself mirroring that smile.

"Yes, I did," I laugh softly.

I pull my knees to my chest, looking back into the fire when Dimitri speaks up.

"Is he kind to you? The king," he asks.

I'm hesitant to answer. But I see a glimpse of the old Dimitri. The one that was always concerned for my well-being. I let out a bitter laugh.

"Do you think he is capable of kindness?" I ask.

"I wish there was something I could do, Anna. I'm so sorry I got us into this mess. I knew we couldn't leave that night, but I didn't know how to tell you—"

"Don't do that, Dimitri. We never had a chance. The war was moving faster than we knew was possible. It was only a matter of time before they caught us," I say, hoping to ease his guilt.

Dimitri looks at me, concern on his face.

"Does he hurt you? You know, when he..."

My cheeks burn bright red. I know exactly what he is asking.

"Sometimes. Sometimes, he is gentle. Other times, he is rough."

I think about last night. After I spoke his name, he wasn't rough at all, but he wasn't gentle either. I don't know how to describe the way he was last night. It was like he was trying to possess me. To own every piece of my body and coax me into needing nothing beyond him. I look at Dimitri, shoving my thoughts down.

"Why have you ignored me?" I ask.

His eyes darken at my question, but he finds it in himself to answer.

"Felix is a very jealous beast. He knows of the past we shared. If I so much as look at you, there will be consequences."

My heart aches at the shakiness in Dimitri's voice.

"You fear him?" I ask.

Now it's Dimitri's turn to laugh.

"Pathetic, isn't it?" he says.

"No. These are monsters. We are ants compared to them. There is no shame in fearing something that is stronger than you," I say.

Now Dimitri looks at me, letting his emotions shine through.

"What about finding pleasure in his touch?" he asks.

I see desperation in his eyes as he looks at me.

"Wha—"

"I hate him. I *loathe* him. But when he touches my body... when he forces himself on me... I find pleasure... is there shame in that?"

His voice breaks as he speaks, and I shake my head.

"Dimitri—"

"I couldn't be the man you wanted then," he drops his head into his hands, "And I am less than a man now."

"I find pleasure in the king's touch, Dimitri," I say.

He looks up at me in shock, and I offer him a sad smile reflecting the same brokenness that he gives.

"I am terrified of the king. He beats me. He speaks to me with no regard for my emotions. He makes me watch and do unspeakable things, and yet when he touches me in the right places, I find pleasure. I hate him, yet I crave the release that only he can give." Tears fall down my cheeks as I speak the words to the man I was supposed to marry. The man I was supposed to start a family with. The man I once loved.

"I cannot tell you there is no shame because I feel shame as well, Dimitri," I say.

I think of his question earlier and decide to ask.

"Felix hurts you, doesn't he?"

Dimitri drops his head, nodding. I think of all the times I saw him and Felix interact. And when Felix easily broke his arm and leg without hesitation at the war meeting. I can't imagine the horror Dimitri has lived through. I look over at the horses, an idea forming.

"Let's run away," I say.

Dimitri's head whips up as he looks at me in disbelief.

"What?" he asks sharply.

"They won't find us if we travel east instead of taking the ocean. We can move towards the war and go straight past the battlefield. Maybe find the king of the humans and start our own lives away from this all. Just you and me—"

"Stop! Just... stop." Dimitri's face is a mixture of anger and sadness. "You and I can never live together, Annalise, don't you get it? I can never touch you, hold you, or even kiss you! I cannot protect you from them! He has broken me. He has crushed any semblance of my old self into nothing but this pathetic shell you see in front of you!"

I slowly reach for him. "Dimitri—"

"No! We cannot run. *You* cannot run. You cannot betray the king, Annalise. Do you not understand what would happen if you betrayed the king? Everyone would feel his wrath. Everyone! They are not called beasts for no reason."

He immediately stands from his seat, moving away from me.

"But Dimitri—"

"Stop! He is my king. He is your king! And I will not betray my master. Not for you. There is nothing between us. There never will be," he says quickly.

Dimitri gets a look of panic on his face before looking at me in anger.

"I will not help you. And if you try to leave him, I will stop you, Annalise. So, never mention such a reckless thing again. Ever!"

He doesn't look back as he makes his way to the supplies, pulling out a blanket. I don't know what to make or think of his outburst or our conversation. But I can see Dimitri is feeling such anguish and turmoil. It's eating him up inside. I wipe the tears from my cheeks, rolling away from the flames as I let the crushing despair of this reality lull me to sleep.

Chapter Twenty-Five

CYRUS

The day is lovely. Light snow falls around Felix's estate, blanketing the area beautifully. I find myself wishing Annalise were here to enjoy the snow. In the palace, she could never do such a thing. But keeping her at Felix's estate gives her much more freedom and leniency. And I've seen her open up more in her time here, something that I enjoy watching when she doesn't realize that I am.

Felix gestures for his servant to set up the serving tray, and she silently begins her duty. It's silent at the estate without our favored slaves around. And it's torture waiting to see if they will fail the mission or not.

"If you are worried about the half-breed touching her, he will not. He wouldn't dare do such a thing. I have beaten that desire out of him," Felix says next to me, gauging my silence.

I laugh softly, shaking my head.

"I believe you. It's her I am skeptical about. Her face when she left… it was strange."

I never speak my mind to anyone but Felix. We've been friends our entire lives, and he's the only person who can be honest with me, treating me as an equal.

"Strange? How so?"

The servant bows slightly before leaving us, and I reach for the warm cup, bringing it to my lips.

"She seemed vengeful," I say.

Felix chuckles next to me.

"Vengeful, you say? After you took her away from her fiancé, took her virginity, beat her within an inch of her life, and forced her into the enemy camp, vengeance should be the least of your worries," he chuckles.

I bite my tongue. He's right.

"Why do you care so much? If she can't fulfill her mission, her usefulness has run out," he says after I don't respond.

I look at Felix in irritation. He's right again. He's constantly pushing me. He loves to see people squirm. It almost makes me feel bad for the half-breed. Almost.

"And what of you? Do you plan on welcoming *him* back into your bed?" I ask.

Felix chuckles, looking out over the estate.

"Yes. Dimitri is always welcome to my estate. And my bed. So long as I know where his loyalty lies. And right now, it is to me and the beast empire," he says.

I shake my head at his confidence.

"How are you so sure he is loyal to you?" I ask.

Felix leans back in his seat before looking at me. His dark eyes have lost all amusement.

"Because I own him, Cyrus. I own his mind. I own his body. I own every part of him. Men are much harder to break than women. They have these ideas in their heads. These years of strength and endurance that have made them into hard, strong beings. But once you break them, there is no fixing them back. It goes against everything they've been taught to believe about themselves. Dimitri is broken. Beyond broken, if there is a term. And he will never be able to function unless I give him purpose. That is how I know I have his loyalty."

I look at him. Really look. He's always reveled in violence and battle. Even when we were children, he would torture the other kids, doing everything in his power to make them afraid of him and respect him at the same time.

"You are one sadistic beast, Felix."

Felix shrugs, leaning back in his chair. "Maybe. But I embrace that. Unlike you, my king, who tries to tame it for the sake of your people. You and I both know you are worse than me. That is why you're so adamant about getting your father back. You need someone to control you."

I don't respond to his prodding, but he is right. My father is a different beast than I am. His way of ruling was firm but understanding. He believed in a world that led humanity—not enslaved them. I believe in a world where humanity is annihilated. His leniency with humanity is what got me captured in the first place and these scars placed on me. He treated them as lesser beings, regardless of living alongside each other. And lesser beings will always feel entitled to power.

"Have you thought about what you're going to do if your father isn't alive, Cyrus?"

Felix's words pull me out of my thoughts, and I look at him.

"If he isn't alive, we will proceed with the slaughter. I have no room for any of them in my kingdom. But I know he is alive. They wouldn't kill him. He was my predecessor. He holds power that rivals my own. And the necklace Annalise brought into my kingdom had his blood in it. They're using him to make weapons."

"So you sent her in to aid in the possible destruction of her people?" he asks.

I shake my head.

"I sent her in to protect him. If I showed up with my army, they would kill him or use him to control me. She can slip in, confirm he is alive, and get out. And if he isn't, she will still tell me. She is the only human I trust enough to get the job done," I say.

Felix chuckles, flipping my question on me.

"Trust? And why would you trust her?" he asks.

"Because I know her, Felix. I have spent every day since she stepped into my kingdom training her to be obedient. To know my likes and dislikes. To follow me without hesitation," I say.

I can feel Felix watching me, and I hate it.

"You're indulging in humans now? Whatever happened to them being vermin? Every last one of them?" he says, quoting me in the past.

"She is the only exception. I do not indulge in anyone but her. She is the lowest I will ever go. And I will never glance in that direction again," I ground out.

Felix looks over my shoulder, gesturing for one servant to come to us. As she approaches, he pulls her down on his lap and begins placing kisses on her throat. His eyes meet mine, and he smiles wickedly.

"You must learn not to indulge too much in lower beings, Cyrus. They easily disappoint."

Annalise

The trip to the hunter's camp has been hell. Ever since Dimitri's outburst, he refuses to speak to me. Not even a glance. He keeps ahead of me on the trail and only speaks to me when telling me the plan to stop for the night. I don't fault him, though. Dimitri was a proud man once. And Felix has twisted him enough to turn him into a man that fears everything. Especially betrayal. The man that Dimitri was is gone forever, just like he said. It makes me wonder what type of person I have become as a result of Cyrus's reign.

I only spoke of running away out of pity for Dimitri. I wasn't thinking when the words left my lips. I just wanted him to no longer feel pain at the hands of Felix. But now that I think about it, could I really have run?

"Don't run, Annalise."

Cyrus's words are burned into my brain. Dimitri fears what Cyrus would do if I ran away. It's something I hadn't thought about. Just thinking of being caught by him after running gives me a chill I do not wish to acknowledge. I am just as much a prisoner as Dimitri. I hate to admit it to myself, but the idea of running has me terrified. I fear Cyrus has broken me as much as Felix has broken Dimitri.

We have both been manipulated into their obedient puppets.

I look up when Dimitri slows his horse, coming to a stop next to me. His deep blue eyes are determined as he gestures to the surrounding area.

"The camp should be just over this—Ah!"

Dimitri's body is ripped from his horse, colliding with the ground. I cry out in shock and fear, my horse rising from being startled as well. I jump down from my horse, running to where Dimitri is groaning in pain.

"Dimitri!" I scream.

There's an arrow sticking out of his shoulder. I reach him, placing my hand on his chest to still him, when I feel a blade touching my back.

"Do not move unless you want your head removed from your shoulders."

My hands are shaking as the hunters drag us blindfolded through their camp.

"Dimitri?" I call out for him but get nothing in response. A hard shove causes me to stumble forward, losing my balance, and I fall to the ground. I'm instantly yanked up by my arm and pushed again.

"Keep it moving," someone hisses behind me. The desire to use Cyrus's seal and escape is all but clawing at me, but I fight it. My survival instinct is kicking in as our fellow humans treat us like prisoners.

We finally reach our destination, and my blindfold is pulled off. I blink, trying to figure out the situation. I see humans—five of them. But what I don't see is Dimitri.

"Where is he? Where's Dimitri?" I shout in a panic.

A woman clad in armor steps forward, pointing her blade at my chin.

"You do not speak here unless you are given permission, girl," she hisses.

I narrow my gaze at the woman. She is covered in dirt as well, and I take note that the glowing necklace around her throat looks similar to the one my father gave me.

"Elisa." The man in the center of the room speaks her name with authority, and she steps back, digging the tip of her blade into the dirt as she stares at me. The man who spoke looks at me as if he's trying to figure me out. He has brown eyes that are as cold as the beasts.

"Dimitri. That is the name of the man you were traveling with?" he asks.

I slowly nod my head. The man sits back in his seat, motioning to the guards. I hear them running away before the brown-eyed man looks back at me as if he's studying me. Being under Cyrus's constant gaze makes it easy to look this man in the eyes. Their gazes don't compare. He laughs lightly before the doors are opened. I turn around to see Dimitri being dragged in. They drop him roughly on the ground, causing him to groan in pain.

"Dimitri!"

I try to move to him, but a blade blocks my path. I look back at the man in charge.

"Why are you doing this?" My voice is shaking, but I don't care. The man stands from his seat, making his way toward me.

"What is your name?" he asks.

I look between him and Dimitri. Dimitri has a strange expression on his face. He finally looks at me and slowly nods his head.

"Annalise," I say.

The man doesn't show any sign that he is aware of my identity. He stops walking, standing over me before kneeling to be at eye level with me.

"Annalise, my name is Liam. I am the commanding officer here at the hunter's main base."

His eyes roam over my face as if he's trying to figure me out without me speaking. He finally moves back, standing to his full height.

"I apologize for the surprising greeting, but we are a little concerned about your traveling partner." Liam's eyes roam over to Dimitri, filled with disgust. "Why is it you are traveling with a half-breed?"

Liam pulls his blade from its resting place, making his way toward Dimitri. My heart leaps in my chest, and I try to move toward them, but a guard easily holds me down. I look at Dimitri in panic, but he's watching me with a calm expression. The guards surrounding Dimitri force him to lean forward on his knees so that his neck is perfectly visible for Liam to cut off his head.

I let out a scream.

"No! Stop! Please!"

Dimitri narrows his gaze at me, slightly shaking his head, but I don't care.

"Here in the hunter's base, the half-breeds are no better than the full-bloods. We do not even let them out of their cages. So, tell me why you are so attached to this one?" Liam asks.

I feel the heat growing on my side the more panicked I become, and I suddenly realize what's doing this. The seal. Cyrus's strength. I feel my whole body growing warm as I call on his strength. I don't care if it will ruin the plan. I don't care if I have to kill any of these people. They will not take him from me.

"She's my fiancée." Dimitri's voice pulls me out of my thoughts, and everyone looks at him. Liam takes the hilt of his sword, smashing it into Dimitri's face.

"You don't speak here, half-breed," Liam emphasizes his disgust by spitting.

"He grew up with me in my village. A beast recently destroyed it, and we had nowhere else to go. We thought this place was a good idea," I whisper.

The lie pours easily off my tongue, but I use the desperate look that Dimitri's eyes hold for strength.

"I'm sorry, we didn't know—I didn't know. We will leave and be on our way—"

I'm interrupted by the doors opening just as another hunter enters. His eyes are wide as he looks at us. Liam is the first to speak into the silence.

"Why have you interrupted our interrogation?"

The guard quickly recovers, looking out over the room.

"The king, sir. He has arrived."

Chapter Twenty-Six

ANNALISE

I cry out in pain as I collide with the ground, turning just in time to see the female hunter, Elisa, close the door behind us. The loud click of the lock adds to my panic as I scramble to Dimitri, checking him for serious injuries.

"Are you okay?" I ask.

He gently pushes my hands away, nodding.

"I've had worse than this, Anna," he smiles sadly.

I drop my hands, feeling sorrow at his words. My gaze roams over the room, taking it in. It's been modified so that no one can get out. Man or beast. I look at Dimitri, letting my fear show through.

"What are we supposed to do now?" I whisper.

Dimitri doesn't miss a beat.

"Now, we find a way to get you out of here. The hunters are too hostile. They're on edge from the recent battles, and I don't think it's safe for you."

My eyes widen from his words.

"Go back? Without his father?" I ask.

"We have no choice, Anna."

I take a deep breath before rising on my knees and lifting my shirt. Dimitri's eyes widen.

"What are you—"

He immediately stops as his eyes take in the seal that Cyrus gave me.

"He gave you his seal?" Dimitri's face has grown pale as he looks at the seal. He slowly shakes his head as horror washes over his features.

"Anna..." he trails off.

"Cyrus said if we encountered any troubles, I could use this to get us out—"

"No! Annalise, no."

I look at Dimitri in confusion.

"But—"

"No! Just... we'll figure a way out of this. But that is not the way," he snaps.

My eyes widen at his sudden change in mood, but I listen.

"Okay," I whisper softly. Dimitri's entire demeanor has changed. He seems anxious.

"When did he give that to you?" he asks.

"The night before we left, why are you—"

"It doesn't matter. Annalise, listen to what I am saying to you now. You cannot get hurt here. You are the priority now, okay? If something happens to you, everyone is doomed. Please, I won't be able to help you. The hunters are going to lock me up and use me to make their trinkets. And when they do, I need you to be smart, Anna. The first opportunity you get, run," Dimitri says with sheer panic in his voice.

"Dimitri, why are you being like this?" I ask.

He opens his mouth to respond when the door opens and more guards enter. They ignore me, snatching Dimitri up by his arms.

"Hey! Stop!" I shout.

I move to run after them when one turns, shoving me away roughly.

"Anna, remember what I said!" Dimitri calls to me. He looks more terrified for my well-being than his own as they drag him away.

I shake my head in disbelief at how things have turned out in this camp.

I have been invited to dinner with the king. I don't know why I've been given this special opportunity. Most of the hunters in this place never see the king. And yet, I have been invited. I make my way through the dining hall, and I take note that the hunter who holds disdain for me, Elisa, is here as well.

"Annalise!"

I look up at the sound of my name to see Liam. He has a smile on his face as he comes towards me.

"You will sit at my side tonight," he says.

I look around the room at all the unfamiliar faces in fear of what this means.

"I really appreciate the honor, Liam, but I don't quite understand what's going on. If Dimitri and I have offended you in any way, we'll be happy to continue our journey and find another place to go," I say, hoping this entire predicament will end.

Liam laughs at my words.

"And you say the half-breed was a part of your village as well?" he asks.

"Dimitri's Father was the blacksmith. We grew up together. I never suspected he was a... half-breed," I say.

Liam nods his head in understanding.

"Yes, they can easily hide within our ranks if not properly branded. I don't know how he got out to live an entire life away from us, but he won't be able to wreak havoc any longer," he says.

Liam's words shock me as I look at him.

"You're keeping him as a prisoner?" I ask.

Liam's face holds an indifferent gaze as he studies me.

"Of course. A half-breed is dangerous. We cannot have him roaming about the world as one of us," he says matter-of-factly.

I shake my head in confusion.

"Dimitri is not dangerous! He was raised human," I say desperately.

Liam finally cracks a smile and laughs, shaking his head. "It doesn't matter. By blood, he is a savage beast. He was only created for one purpose, and now he gets to fulfill that purpose."

"You mean using him as a weapon?" I ask in disbelief.

"What other purposes would there be for him?" he counters.

I shake my head in disbelief.

"Dimitri came here with me. Not as a prisoner," I say.

"It doesn't matter. The half-breed only exists because of us. He is our property and our responsibility," Liam says.

"You can't possibly think that I would be okay with this?" I say, feeling hysterical as he studies me.

"Of course not. But you don't have a choice in the matter. Your home was destroyed, you have nowhere else to go, and I doubt you'll leave here without your fiancé," Liam says.

I want to scream in frustration. This makes things much more complicated. Not only are the hunters hostile towards the person who was sent to help me, but they also don't seem too trusting of me either. I can't leave Dimitri here. And if we take too long, Cyrus will enter this camp with all the horrors of hell.

"So you plan on keeping me here against my will?" I ask.

Liam shakes his head just as the doors open.

"I plan on doing whatever my king tells me. He seemed very interested in meeting you when he heard of the nature of your arrival," he says matter-of-factly.

My eyes widen and I look towards the doors to see the king of the humans stepping in. He's a brute of a man. His dark hair is wild and pushed out of his face, his eyes narrowed and slightly crazed. I recall Dimitri telling me the story of my true parentage, and I can't help but feel shame in my gut as I think of the truth behind my existence. This man is no king. He's a coward. I feel nothing for him as he enters the room.

"Now, will you sit, or will I have to tie you to the table?" I tense when I hear Liam's voice behind me but move to take my seat next to him. That's what this is all about. He's monitoring me. Making sure I comply.

The king enters with his head held high, taking his seat at the head of the table. The stark difference between the way he commands the room and the way Cyrus commands the room is noticeable—two completely different kings, both ruthless in their own rights.

Liam speaks up for everyone. "It is an honor to have you join us tonight, Your Majesty."

The king gestures for everyone to sit, and I don't miss the look in his eyes as he focuses on me. My stomach dips. I wasn't expecting to see the king, and now that he's here, I'm hoping he doesn't see my mother's features in my face. The longer he stares, the more discomfort I feel. Finally, a smirk breaks his expression.

"So this is the girl. The one that showed up with a half-breed?" he asks.

The hunters all look at me with unreadable expressions.

"Yes. This is Annalise. She said her village was destroyed by the beast king," Liam answers for me.

The king's eyes light up at the mention of the king of the beasts. He narrows his gaze at me.

"You came into contact with the king and lived?" he asks, genuinely interested.

The doors open before I can respond pulling everyone's attention. My blood runs cold as I take them in. There are half-breeds, chained and broken, as they hold the food and drinks for tonight. Most of them have brands that show on their necks and shoulders. Among them is Dimitri. And there's a fresh brand on his face.

His face.

I move to jump up from my seat, but Liam grabs my arm roughly. He watches me with a warning gaze, but I don't care. I let my anger fuel me.

"What the hell have you done?!" I shout as I look at Dimitri.

He looks up in shock at my outburst, his eyes warning me to calm down.

"You fucking branded him?" I screech, looking at Liam.

"Annalise—"

"No, this is cruel!" I shout. The king across the table chuckles at my outburst, leaning back in his seat.

"Cruel?" He laughs even harder.

"Have you seen the aftermath of the battlefield? Have you witnessed the horrors of the slaves in the kingdom? Beasts are monsters, the whole lot of them. These half-breeds exist so that we can win this war. But you wouldn't know anything of that, would you, girl? Living your sheltered life in the forest, and you think you can come into my war zone and tell me what's cruel?"

I muster all the rage I feel and spit at him.

"You're a coward!" I shout.

"Anna!" Now, it's Dimitri who is looking at me with a panicked expression. He shakes his head at me, but it's too late. The king is already out of his seat. His eyes are focused on Dimitri. He glares at Dimitri with an interest that I don't like. His gaze leaves Dimitri, focusing on me, and he finally smiles. He pulls out a blade, holding it to Dimitri's face. I move forward in a panic, but Liam grabs me, holding me back.

"All this fuss. For a half-breed?" the king asks, looking at me.

He places the blade against Dimitri's flesh, pushing it into his skin. Blood wells to the surface, and I feel myself growing warm again. I know it's Cyrus's seal. I have to use it. I have to. This is the best chance I have. Dimitri is here, and I can just grab him and go.

I look around the room.

But there are also hunters present. I can't beat them all. Like Cyrus said, I have no skill.

"Please... don't," I whisper.

The King glares at me for what feels like an eternity and finally rips the blade away from Dimitri's skin. He makes sure to slice a piece of his cheek, leaving a trail of blood.

"I know you've never had a hardship in your life, girl. You come into my camp after experiencing one interaction with the king and try to tell me what's what?" He chuckles in irritation, and I have to bite back the scream threatening to leave my lips. He has no idea the hell I've been through. He has no idea the many encounters I've had with the king of the beasts.

"I can kill that halfbreed anytime I want. Because he is disposable. He is nothing but a weapon created for the greater good of humanity. And I am the king. In this camp, we do not treat them as our equals because they are not. I had you come here because I want you to see the true nature of these monsters," he says.

The king gestures for the guards at the doors, and they nod their heads, quickly exiting the room. The king finally walks away from Dimitri, and I feel myself relaxing only a bit.

"When they told me the half-breed was your... fiancé, I couldn't believe it. I didn't believe it. How could someone love one of *them*? And I realized it was because you have never seen the true nature of these monsters," the king says, looking past me.

The doors open, and in comes the two guards with a full-blooded beast. His eyes are dark and empty. His hair is also dark and falls into his face as he keeps his gaze down. He's chained. Branded. And there are cuts and bruises all over his body. As I look at his face, I can't help but notice the resemblance he shares with Cyrus. I look over at Dimitri, who is watching me with a terrified expression, confirming my fears. The former king is here. And he is very much alive. Our plans have just become more complicated.

The human king walks over to the beast, blade still in hand.

"You wouldn't be so in love with them if you knew their true nature," he calls to me.

Cyrus's father looks up, his face twisted in confusion. His eyes land on me, and I feel my body tense. His gaze is intense and filled with darkness. He glares at me, a myriad of emotions washing over his face until he finally scoffs.

"Behold. The true nature of the beasts!"

The king takes his blade, plunging it into the restrained beast king's back. He drags it across his shoulders, causing the king to let out an inhuman screech. His body seizes up as the pupil of his eyes visibly sharpens like a serpent. My ears are ringing in pain from the sound he's emitting, his teeth elongating into sharp fangs. A growl rips through the chamber, and I feel an unfiltered fear crawl over me as he jerks at his restraints, his body shifting to a strange form. The hunters on either side of him have trinkets attached to their wrists that are lighting up with the sound he makes. The human king isn't done, though. He plunges the blade into him again and again.

"Stop! Stop it!" I scream.

There's a rough pull on my arm, and Liam shoves me into my seat. "Shut your mouth!"

I look around the room at all the hunter's faces. They are watching with smiles. Joy. All the half-breeds have visibly paled, including Dimitri. They look unable to stand. I look back at Cyrus's Father, a newfound fear stroking my spine. I have been thrust in between two cruel worlds, forced to choose the lesser of the two. But I know that if Cyrus learns about the torture his father is going through, he will never let humanity see the light of day.

Tears well up in my eyes as I realize the true weight of my situation and why Cyrus even sent me here. Not only to free his father but to test my loyalty. He knows what this means to me. His words to me before I departed are ringing in my ears.

"*Don't run, Annalise.*"

Chapter Twenty-Seven

ANNALISE

The snow falls even harder these days. I had almost forgotten how bitter winter could be, but I've had much more to worry about than the cold as of late. I trudge through the snow, making my way to the dungeons that the hunters keep the beasts locked in. For all their hatred of the beasts, the hunters don't seem to care when I visit them. Of course, I get lectures and looks of disgust upon my return, but they seem inclined to stay away and leave me be.

Liam's words play in my head over and over.

"I plan on doing whatever my king tells me."

It makes me wonder if the human king has something to do with the freedom I've experienced in this place. The human king is a tyrant as much as Cyrus is. Both of them are evil in their own ways. I feel the human king is playing with power he doesn't understand and can't control. He has unknowingly revealed to Cyrus that his father lives. Cyrus will come for this camp eventually, with or without the release of his father. If I've learned anything from being by his side, it's that he is not a patient beast.

The guards don't look in my direction as I step into the building, going in search of Dimitri. They keep half-breeds on the first floor in cells that remind me of my time in Cyrus's palace before I started spending my nights in his chambers. The full-blooded beasts are kept below ground in cells that are the bare minimum of what anyone should have to live in. They deprive them of sunlight and food and are constantly bleeding them out to use their blood for weapons. Only a handful of weapons have been created using Cyrus's Father's blood. No one can seem to withstand the strength, dying within the week.

Cyrus gave me until the second full moon to carry out his plan. And the more days that pass, the more stress I feel. If I find a way to release his father, I will subject humanity to a life of enslavement. If I don't release his father, I will subject the world to a life of war until the beasts wipe us all out. The only way we are even holding our own in this war is because we are using the beast's own power against them, and Cyrus has figured that out. It's only a matter of time before he uses that knowledge against us.

I pull open the heavy door to Dimitri's cell. He's lying in the bed, staring at the ceiling as I approach. My eyes travel to the brand on his face. It's healed quicker than it would if he were human. My stomach churns in discomfort as I imagine what that must have felt like.

He looks in my direction, sitting up in the moldy cot before moving to the bars of his cell. His once bright blue eyes are dull and tired. His hair is wild, and his body sports bruises and cuts all over. They've started bleeding him as well. It's a gruesome process, where they open multiple wounds on the bodies, letting the blood run out for collection. They aren't shallow wounds, either. They are life-threatening wounds. The only reason any of them survive is that they are beasts and half-breeds. They heal quickly.

I offer him a soft smile, pulling the loaf of bread I saved for him. I take a seat in front of the cell, passing the bread through the bars. He eyes me before moving from the bed to the floor, gently taking the bread from me.

"How did you get this?" he asks.

I shrug.

"The hunters give little attention to what I do," I say softly.

He laughs softly before taking a bite of the bread. I remain silent as I watch him devour it. He's starving in here. It makes me loathe the hunters even more.

"Have you figured out a way to escape yet?" he asks.

I shake my head.

"Dimitri, we've been over this. I'm not leaving here without you," I say.

He stops his chewing, eyeing me carefully. Finally, he releases an irritated sigh.

"I'm not the priority here. You are," he says sternly.

"I don't care. I won't leave you. Not again. There's no telling what the king will do to you if I escape. He might kill you out of spite," I say firmly.

Dimitri laughs again, looking at the ground.

"Would that be so bad?"

I know Dimitri has suffered since Cyrus entered our village. I know he's suffered more than I have. And I know I'm selfish in wanting him to stay alive. I'm selfish to want him to escape with me back into the arms of the beast that causes his life such pain. But he's the only thing I have left of my world before it changed so drastically.

I drop my head, unable to face him. I'm no better than Cyrus.

"Dimitri..." It takes all my strength to look him in the eyes. He's watching me with the same expression he always does. Concern. He always carries such deep concern for me, no matter his situation. "Yes. That would be bad."

His eyes widen slightly and tears well up in them before spilling over. He takes in a shuddering breath before nodding his head. He has such a broken smile on his lips.

"I won't abandon you, Dimitri," I say. "I can use Cyrus's seal and get us out."

Dimitri once again tenses at the mention of the seal. "Anna, the seal isn't what you think it is."

"Why don't you just tell me the truth about it, then?" I ask.

Cyrus only said I needed to call on it, and it would give me his strength. But Dimitri knows something about it he won't tell me.

Dimitri shakes his head, eyeing me.

"It's just dangerous, Anna. You shouldn't use it unless you have been pushed into a corner. It should be your last resort."

I draw my knees to my chest, not bothering to push the issue. Dimitri's fear of the beasts far outweighs his feelings for me. If Cyrus doesn't want me to know the true extent of the seal, Dimitri won't be the one to reveal it.

"Then... what do you propose?" I ask.

Dimitri releases a breath, looking at me. "Are you really prepared to betray your own race, Annalise? Really?"

I remain silent, unsure of how to answer. I've been thinking the same thing for days now.

"Are you?" I ask, turning his question on him.

Dimitri chuckles bitterly. He glares at the ground for a moment, and I see something flash behind his gaze that I've never seen before. Something that doesn't fit the nature of the man I grew up with. He finally looks at me, the depths of his eyes holding emptiness, and I feel my blood run cold as he speaks.

"I'm not human, remember?"

I slowly make my way back to the entrance of the building, Dimitri's words making my chest ache. The hunters have forced Dimitri to see himself as something other than human. I have to find a way for us to get out of here soon. I don't know how much more of this torture his mental state can handle.

I'm almost to the door when I pause, looking towards the heavy door that separates the half-breeds from the beast's holding cells below. My gaze shifts to the exit doors. The hunters only have men stationed outside the compound, but none stand watch within. My stomach churns to think of the despicable things they are keeping from one another to not have men stationed inside.

Cyrus did say all I had to do was release his father. The longer I stare at the doors that separate the beasts, the heavier I feel compelled to follow Cyrus's orders. Dimitri's words to me about betraying my race are like a distant memory, my feet moving before I can talk myself out of it.

I make my way down the steps, the spiral staircase leading into the dark abyss below. The closer I get to the bottom floor, the cooler it feels. The chill adds to my fears as well, making it difficult for me to keep from shivering. I don't know what I'm going to see, but I know it can't be good.

The warm glow of torches greets me as I reach the bottom floor. The floor is covered in stale-smelling water; the walls have dried blood and scrapes on them, and moans of discomfort sound behind some doors. I slowly pass each of the cells, pausing in front of a random one as my curiosity gets the best of me. I bite back a wave of nausea as I take in the sight. A female beast lies in the center of the cell. Her clothes are tattered and torn, and she's extremely emaciated. She looks like she's barely clinging to life. Gashes adorn her arms and legs, her blood pouring down the drain in the center of her cell.

I quickly step away from the cell, continuing my walk down the dark hall. There's a door at the end of the hall, not on either side but directly in the center. It's bigger, heavier, and marked on the front.

This must be Cyrus's father's cell.

I push open the door to reveal the conditions they have the former king of the beasts in. He doesn't look up at my entrance, but there's a small smirk on his lips. He's leaning against the wall, his arm split open like someone took a blade and ran it completely through. I can see the separation of his flesh, his blood pouring out like a chalice. He's staring at his wound, a bored expression on his face.

"You're either here because my son sent you, or you got very lucky and somehow escaped from him." He finally lifts his gaze to look at me. The emotions I get when Cyrus looks at me come back in this beast's presence. I don't know how to respond, or if I even can, so I don't.

"Judging from the lack of shock to see me, I'm assuming my son sent you," he says.

He shifts in his cell, dropping his arm to focus on me. "Come closer."

I don't know what it is about the sound of his voice, but I feel compelled to obey his command. So, against my better judgment, I move closer to the cell. His eyes roam over me.

"You carry him with you." His words are matter of fact. The corner of his mouth twitches as he fights a smile.

"I never expected my son to be the one to favor a human," he says.

He shifts again, his dark gaze leveling as he studies me.

"Humans put those scars on his body. They captured him, dipped barbed chains in an elixir, and wrapped him in it. They kept him suspended for hours, damaging his skin permanently. Now I see the mistake I made putting so much trust in such an entitled race," he says.

Silence washes over us, and he continues to study me. I'm not sure if it's out of curiosity or irritation.

"I see why he favors you. My son has always liked the finer things in life. You're exquisite. Elegant. Docile. Very fitting for my son. Probably the type of woman I should have betrothed him to. Did he ever follow through with the engagement to Sorrel's daughter?" he asks.

I slowly shake my head, assuming he's speaking of Marzia.

"Last I heard, he stripped her of her title," I whisper.

The former king smiles, resting his head against the stone.

"Still bullheaded as ever, I see," he murmurs to himself.

His gaze shifts to me, and confusion finds its way onto his features.

"So, what exactly did my son send a human girl here to do?" he asks.

He raises a brow at me, and I realize I still haven't answered him. I blink, trying to find my voice as I lower my gaze. All of my training in the palace kicks in as I speak.

"I was to confirm you were here and release you, Your Majesty." My voice does little to hide my true emotions, and I know he notices.

"You can't release me. Not from here. And not in this state. I'm weaker than I've ever been. And they have reinforced these bars with the same elixir used to harm my son. Leave this place. Return to my son and tell him I am alive and well. Tell him I sent you back. Tell him at the most crucial times of war, it is best not to make haste," he says.

"But—"

I stop mid-sentence when the door to the underground cells opens. I whip around, facing the door of the king's cell. Someone has come down here. My heart jumps in my chest.

Shit. This is it. I've been caught.

They're going to drag me out of here and kill Dimitri, and it's all my fault.

"Calm down," the former king orders.

His voice is soft and oddly calm. I keep my gaze on the door, glad that I closed it on my way in.

"It's the commanding officer of the hunters. He's found a toy down here among the beasts he so loathes," he says. I look at the former king in horror, but he has his head leaned back against the wall, his eyes closed. The sound of another cell door opening echoes off the walls, followed by the sound of it shutting and a lock latching in place.

"Make yourself comfortable. He will be here a while," he adds. So far, the former king hasn't shown me any hostility, which is strange compared to his son. He doesn't regard me as incompetent and doesn't treat me with disgust. I can't get a proper read on his emotions. He's a closed book.

He finally opens his eyes, looking at me. "Tell me about yourself. I'm curious why my son has grown so softhearted towards one of you."

His eyes visibly darken, a frown appearing on his lips as his eyes travel to the door. Then I hear it—the scream of a woman. A chill finds its way up my spine. I know that scream. It's the same scream I had when Cyrus began using me to sate his desire. So I sit in front of the cell of the former king and answer his questions.

Anything to block out the screams of another helpless woman in these dark halls.

Chapter Twenty-Eight

ANNALISE

The world is corrupt. Humans and beasts alike. They deserve each other.

The fire in the center of the camp blazes bright, casting a warm glow over all sitting by it. Only humans can sit near the fire. The beasts are chained to nearby trees for the pleasure of humans. They're to serve as a reminder that humanity is just as capable of enslaving them.

I chuckle bitterly to myself as I look over the corruption happening in this camp. My eyes fall on Liam. His eyes aren't focused on the celebrations happening around him. They're focused on the poor beast that he forces himself on daily. She's among the strongest of the beasts, which is why they keep her in the basement. But tonight, she is a part of the celebration. A beacon of how far the beasts have fallen.

I wonder who she was in the beast empire. Was she a commanding officer? Did Cyrus know her? She looks broken. Her eyes are dull and lifeless, her dark brown hair matted. Her clothes remind me of the clothing we were forced to wear as slaves in Cyrus's palace. She's even shivering from the cold, which is out of character for a beast. Winter has set in. It's enough to kill a human if they're in the cold for too long. I couldn't imagine the torture she feels, especially since she is drained twice as much as the half-breeds.

The hunters cut open the prisoners, draining them of their blood. They then use the blood to forge weapons and trinkets. I understand why Cyrus was so angry when he realized the necklace I carried belonged to his father. He'll be even angrier if he sees the conditions his father has been in for the past five years. They bleed his father the worst among the prisoners. He must have at least five wounds open at a time. The max for the rest is two.

In the weeks I've been here, I've found several weaknesses for the hunters. I know how many beasts they need to continue to create weapons at a steady pace. I've seen their battle plans. I know how they use the trinkets and how they assign them by rank. I know what paths they use to ambush the beasts, and I know they plan to capture Felix next.

The only thing I haven't been able to get is the location of the human king's stronghold. With all the information I've gained and the command from Cyrus's father, all I have to do now is escape. But I can't bring myself to do it without Dimitri. I know they will kill him if I leave. The human king always makes sure I see them torture him. He resents me for loving one of "them." And he's hell-bent on proving that there's nothing I can do about his treatment.

"You look glum for someone free of the beast's reign." Liam comes towards me with a mug in his hands. I gently take it from him, not bothering to drink its contents.

"We are not free. You have created a delusion you happily live in," I say.

Cyrus's words are burned into my brain.

"*Freedom is not an option for you. It never has been. Not from the moment I had you.*"

"You seem so sure of that," Liam laughs.

My eyes travel to Dimitri, who is once again being used as a slave to serve the hunters. My anger once again builds as I see the way they treat him. I chuckle bitterly, looking at Liam. "I am confident that this is all a waste of time. You can't possibly think this will last."

He narrows his gaze at me.

"If you hate humanity so much, why stay here? Why not go be a part of the beast's society where you'll be beaten and raped to death," he hisses bitterly at me.

I glare at him, fighting myself tooth and nail to control my anger. The hunters love to insult me about the "sheltered" life they believe I had. They have no idea what I have endured to be here, what I will endure when I leave. I keep my eyes locked on Liam's as I pour the drink he handed me out into the snow. I slowly release my grasp on it as well, letting the cup join its contents.

"Fuck off," I growl, looking back into the fire.

Liam is silent for a moment before his laugh finally permeates the air. He slowly places his cup down on the log next to me before he snatches my arm quickly, bringing me in close to him. I pull against him, trying to free myself, but he pulls me in close, whispering in my ear.

"Don't you dare make a scene, or I will cut off the head of the half-breed right here in this fucking camp," he growls.

He knows exactly how to get me to do what he wants. Against my better judgment, I let him drag me away from the fire, away from any witnesses. When he feels he's pulled me far enough, he smashes me into the nearest tree. The force of my back colliding with the tree forces a cry from my lips, and I feel him pressing into me.

"You know, I'm about sick and tired of your fucking attitude. You know nothing of the war. You know nothing of how the beasts are," he hisses.

He presses even closer to me, and terror wracks my body when I feel the hard press of his erection against my thigh.

"You let that half-breed fuck you whenever he likes, tainting you over and over while you frolic in your fuckwit village away from the real world, and you think you're better than us? Do you think you can high road us because of what you've only seen on the human side? You're no better than the beasts we fuck to breed those monsters you love," he hisses.

I try to push him off of me, but it only makes him angrier. I feel the heat on my side again as the seal tempts me to use it. But I can't. I won't. I recall Dimitri's panicked expression when he found out about it. He pleaded with me not to use it. So I fight the urge, closing my eyes and calming my breathing.

"Let go of me," I growl.

"Maybe you need to be knocked down a peg," Liam hisses as his hands grip my clothes. I let out a panicked cry, struggling. I close my eyes, ready to use the seal Cyrus gave me.

"Liam."

We both tense, whipping our gaze in the voice's direction. It's the beast Liam forces himself on. She's watching us with a steady expression, the sadness in her gaze gone.

"You are needed back at the base," she says.

Liam studies her before looking down at me, gripping a handful of my hair—his free hand slips under the collar of my clothing, crossing over my bare chest. Tears of anger burn my eyes as he gropes my breast, keeping his eyes locked on mine. I refuse to let the tears fall. I've survived worse than this against the king of the beasts. I'll be damned if I let a human make me cry.

He roughly pinches my nipple before shoving me back roughly into the snow.

"Women. You're all the same. You think you can look down on us from whatever pedestal in life and judge us, but at the end of the day, you all squeal the same," he chuckles.

He turns away from me, making his way back to the camp in the snow. I don't miss the sound of his cackle carrying on the night air. My fingers are shaking in anger from the cold of the snow seeping into my clothing. The beast that interrupted us makes her way towards me in the snow, bending to my height. She studies me intensely, holding her hand out to me.

I eye her, gently placing my hand in hers as she helps me up.

"They are growing hostile towards your presence. Whatever your purpose is here, fulfill it and go. You don't have long before their king disposes of you."

My eyes widen as she speaks to me, but before I can respond, Liam is screaming at her.

"Calista!"

She doesn't flinch as she continues to study me and finally stands to her full height, walking away.

I don't know how long I stay in the cold, but I finally gather my wits and make my way back to the camp. My mind is a whirlwind of emotion. I'm tired. Exhausted, actually. But as I trudge through the snow, a new plan forms in my head. I never had the option of betraying Cyrus. He's been instilling that in me from the moment I awoke in Felix's estate.

"I think you will do whatever you must to earn some semblance of freedom."

He was right in some ways. The only person I care about is Dimitri. I bet that's why he sent him with me, to remind me of what is really at stake. I doubt they knew of the hunters' hostility towards half-breeds, but despite that, this works in Cyrus's favor. I would never abandon Dimitri like this. The treatment he has received is despicable, and it makes the hunters my enemy. I no longer care about humanity. I don't feel a connection to them. All I feel is my connection with Dimitri. The love we share is too deep to abandon him for hunters who would treat him this way. Either way, Cyrus wins.

I make my way to the fire, slowing when I see that the number of people in attendance has trickled down. Calista said the hunters needed Liam back at the base, so something important must be going on for them to abandon the celebration so suddenly.

Most of the beasts have been left outdoors, and I say a silent prayer of gratitude when I see Dimitri is one of them. I look around as I make my way toward him. My plan suddenly seems ridiculous as I take in the state of his body. He's battered and bruised and has a fresh wound on his arm from being bled all day. I don't know if he can make it past the barrier in this state.

"Dimitri."

I call to him softly, just in case there are hunters lurking nearby. His gaze shifts to me in confusion.

"Anna, what are you—"

"Shh, we're getting you out of here tonight," I whisper.

Dimitri eyes me like I'm crazy, his gaze narrowing.

"Anna, I don't have the strength that I did when we arrived here. How do you expect to get me out of these chains?" he asks, holding up his hands.

I don't respond immediately, and his eyes widen.

"No. I told you not to use that unless—"

"I don't have a choice! If I don't do this tonight, I don't know when I'll ever have an opportunity to free you again. You can't stay here, and you can't help me like this," I say desperately.

Dimitri studies me intensely, but I continue to speak. "I can't do this without you. I need you. I need you to live. I'll be okay. But I know if you remain here, you won't be."

Silence passes between us before Dimitri finally releases a breath, and I know I have him. I eye the chains around his wrists, my gaze focused when Dimitri snatches my wrists.

"A seal is something passed between beasts. I've never heard of a human having one and using it safely. If you feel any kind of pain, promise me you'll stop, and we'll find another way. This is about more than just you, Anna," he says.

I slowly nod, focusing my gaze back on the chains. I inhale a deep breath, my heart beating slightly faster as my nerves take hold of me. I feel the heat from the seal on my side spread through me, settling in my veins. Dimitri's eyes widen slightly in front of me, and when I look at my arms, I can see my veins turning black as Cyrus's power courses through me. I flinch as the heat becomes too much. It adds weight to my body that I can't handle, and as I grip Dimitri's chains, I collapse.

"Anna!" Dimitri falls next to me, his hands running over my shoulder in comfort.

"Annalise, stop. Stop!" he shouts. I blink rapidly, trying to steady my breathing as the world around me dulls. It takes me a minute or two, but I finally focus on Dimitri. His expression is worried as he studies me.

"Did it work?" I whisper.

Dimitri makes a face, dropping his head in relief. "No. You collapsed."

Frustration bubbles through me, and I slowly try to sit up, but Dimitri holds me firmly.

"No, dammit! Are you trying to get yourself killed? I told you it was dangerous. There's a reason halfbreeds exist. And even if you were bred for it, Cyrus's power is too strong. There has never been a beast like him. He's rare."

I lean against Dimitri, tears of frustration burning my eyes. If I can't use Cyrus's seal without collapsing, we're actually trapped here.

"What do we do now?" I whisper.

Dimitri's gaze shifts past me as someone approaches. I whip my gaze around, and to my shock, it's Calista. She watches us intensely with her dark gaze, coming to stand over me. Her gaze runs over me, lingering before she looks at Dimitri.

"I knew there was something strange about you two. I just didn't quite expect you to be so... close with the king." She chuckles, stepping past me to Dimitri. I watch her in shock. She is nothing like she was only hours ago. The brokenness in her eyes is gone, and she's fully alert as she studies Dimitri's chains. She must be a warrior in the beast empire.

"Not sure how you did it, but these are loose enough for me to pull apart," she murmurs.

She's quiet as she places her hands over the chains, her lips pursing in a line as she uses all of her strength to pull the chains apart. By the time she's finished, Dimitri can barely slip his hands from the chains.

I watch her in confusion.

"Thank you... why would you help us?" I ask.

She watches me with an unreadable expression, her gaze shifting to Dimitri. Dimitri's expression is one of desperation as he looks at her, a silent conversation passing between them.

"Head to the south gate. There shouldn't be any hunters standing watch. They're all going over war plans now that they have captured a large scale of beasts. It won't be long before they launch an attack that will affect the civilians. Now is the only time you can escape. And you tell Felix if he gets captured, I'll fuck him up myself," she says.

I open my mouth, but Calista shoots me a glare.

"No questions. Go. It won't be long before they notice he's gone."

Dimitri pulls me away, but I continue to study this beast. She's not only risked her life for two strangers, but one is a human. She doesn't seem to show any regret as she watches us disappear down the hill, turning away to return to the hunters. Dimitri stumbles slightly as we make our way to the south gate. At this rate, I don't know if he can make it back to Cyrus. I see the south gate in the distance, and just as Calista said, there are no hunters. I slow my steps, and Dimitri notices, looking at me.

"What are you doing? We're almost there?" he says hastily.

"I'm not going," I say.

Dimitri's gaze narrows.

"You can't possibly think I'm going to leave you," he says.

"You have to. Only I can stay. I have access that you don't. Tell Cyrus all the information I've given you. And make sure he tracks me not to the hunter's camp but to the king's stronghold," I say.

Dimitri gently grabs my shoulders, his expression filling with concern.

"Do you hear yourself? This isn't like you to be so hasty. What's going on?" he asks.

I hate how gentle his tone is. It pulls more tears from my eyes. Dimitri's grip tightens, pulling me in for an embrace. I rest my head on his chest, taking in his warmth and feeling his heartbeat just like I used to.

"Anna. We'll both go tonight, okay? We'll both escape—"

"No!" I pull away from him, hastily wiping my tears.

"I can't. Once the human king returns to the stronghold, he'll take Cyrus's father with him. I have to go with him. If I go, Cyrus can track my scent, or at the very least, I can leave a trail for him to follow," I say desperately.

Dimitri's expression shifts from confusion to shock.

"Annalise. You can't—"

"I can! I can't release him because he's too weak. You saw how he was tortured. The king will take Cyrus's father to his stronghold, and Cyrus won't be able to find him. If they begin to lose this war and kill Cyrus's father in retaliation, there will be no more humans. Me included. Cyrus will wipe them out. I have to do something!" I shout.

Dimitri stares at me with a strange expression.

"Anna, this doesn't fall on you. You know that, right? This was just a plan Cyrus put together at the last minute, and if it didn't work out, you were to report back to him in one piece. What are you trying to prove by doing this?" he asks.

"That I'm loyal!" My voice is shaking, my tears coming hard and fast. "I don't want to go back to him, Dimitri. And I can't run away. I don't want him to hurt me for failing. I don't want to live a life of suffering, wondering how different things would be if I had just stayed. I have to prove to him I am loyal and I am not like all the other humans he loathes. This is the only way I can take control of my life. I have to, or I'll die another slave in that palace."

Dimitri's eyes grow sadder the more I speak. He drops his head, his shoulders shaking, before he looks back up at me.

"Annalise, you are the most valuable thing in both the human and the beast empire. *You*. What's important now is that you make your way back to Cyrus," he says. The desperation in his voice is thick as he looks at me, pleading.

I blink in confusion.

"Why do you keep saying that?" I ask.

Dimitri is having an inner battle. He slowly shakes his head before dropping his eyes. He can't look at me.

"Cyrus didn't just give you his seal. I noticed it a few days ago. You're carrying the king's heir."

I don't have time to think about his words or even respond.

"Hey!"

We both tense as a hunter sprints toward us. He's a guard, and he's armed, his body taking on a glow as he presses the trinket into himself. Dimitri grabs me, pulling me in close.

"It's too dangerous for you to leave now. I'll make sure they think I betrayed you. Cyrus won't be far behind."

Dimitri shoves me hard into the snow, not looking back as he takes off in the direction of the south gate.

Cyrus

As much as I hate to admit it, I miss her.

I look up at the night sky. The moon is almost full. I told Anna she had until the second full moon to fulfill her task. It would seem that she has failed me. I release a disappointed sigh. I thought she would come back to me on her own. I really did. Irritation surges through me for getting so attached to her.

My gaze shifts from the moon when I see Felix, along with a few beasts approaching. We left Felix's estate for battle weeks ago, slowly but surely making our way to the hunter's camp.

My gaze narrows as I take in Felix's grim expression.

"How many are missing?" I ask.

"Twenty-three."

I nod, containing my anger. I can't lose my temper now. I am the king and ruler of the beast empire. Now is the time, more than ever, to be cool, calm, and collected.

"Any casualties?" I ask.

Felix nods again. He faces the beasts behind him, gesturing for them to bring something. My eyes widen when I take in the unique-looking blade that Felix brings to me. It radiates heavily with my father's essence. They've gotten better at fusing their weapons. I grab hold of it in my hand, testing the deadliness of it. It easily slices through my palm, sending tendrils of pain up my arm all the way to my spine. Against my will, my body locks up, and I feel paralyzed for an instant. I stagger, leaning against the desk to steady myself.

"Your Majesty!" Felix is next to me in an instant, and I wave him off. I toss the blade to the ground, glaring at it in anger. My gaze shifts to Felix, gesturing for him to follow me into the tent.

Silence washes over us until I finally decide to speak.

"Do you think living in harmony is attainable?" I ask. I keep my gaze on my blade resting on the wall. It's still crusted in the blood of hunters. I have no desire to clean it. I love the reminder of their heads rolling around me.

"I don't think I am qualified to offer an opinion on state affairs, Your Majesty—"

"Felix," I interrupt in irritation.

He releases a breath.

"No. And I do not wish to live in harmony with them," he says.

"My father believed they could live alongside us. But they rebelled. And he still believed that diplomacy could be attained up until he was captured. Is it my duty to uphold my father's last wish?" I ask.

Felix is silent before stepping forward. "Cyrus—"

"Your Majesty!" We both look towards the tent entrance as a guard comes rushing in. He looks between us, dropping his gaze.

"Well? What is it?" I ask.

He raises his gaze. "There's a wounded half-breed, sir. He wandered into our camp, saying he needs to see you."

My gaze narrows, and Felix stands before I can respond.

"Bring him in."

The guard immediately bows, making his way to bring the half-breed. I take note Felix is tense next to me. But what I don't get is why the half-breed would be returning without Annalise.

The guards come into the tent with the half-breed, and panic floods through my chest as I take him in. He's bloody. Not just injured bloody but battle bloody. His arms are gashed, he's full of arrow holes, and his face is barely recognizable from the swelling. My eyes widen as I take in the large brand on the side of his face. They fucking branded him.

He's broken, bloody, and battered.

And Annalise isn't with him.

Chapter Twenty-Nine

ANNALISE

The night is cold. They always are. Especially when I choose to sit away from the warmth of the fire that the hunters all gather around. I refuse to sit with them. I refuse to be associated with them. I am disgusted by the very existence of them. I think back to Dimitri and his desperate attempt at fleeing this hell. They tried their best, hunting him down with weapons created to destroy beasts. I hope that their return without his body means he got away.

I drop my head, thinking of his words before he left me.

"*You're carrying the king's heir.*"

I knew it was only a matter of time. Cyrus is an insatiable beast. I don't know the specifics of how our bodies are compatible, but I had hoped during our time together that maybe it just wasn't possible. As far as I knew, no one had ever produced a half-breed. That is until Dimitri's origin was revealed to me. Now, I only wonder if he did it on purpose. I wonder if he knew about it before sending me to the camp. Did he send me here to die with his child? Was he setting us up so that he wouldn't have to kill me himself? I hastily wipe my tears, trying to rid myself of the thought.

Dimitri said he noticed it a few days ago, meaning Cyrus couldn't have detected it before I left. I must not have been pregnant at the time. Even if he is evil, he was talking about hiding me away before I left. Cyrus has never been one to hide his emotions. If he wanted me dead, he would have killed me himself. I feel a multitude of emotions at the revelation of carrying Cyrus's child.

How could he do something like this? What does this mean for my future? Will he kill me to rid himself of the mistake? Will he make me keep the child and take it away from me?

I tense at the sound of cheers coming from the campfire. When I turn back to look at the commotion, I feel my stomach churning at the sight. They are bleeding more beasts and beating one in particular for sport. Calista's aid in Dimitri's escape has earned her punishment; no beast should have to endure. She's now bled just as much as the king, and when she is weak enough, she is beaten down. They think she and Dimitri planned this.

We've been traveling in a caravan for days to the king's stronghold. And just as I'd overheard, Cyrus's father is being transported as well. I'd expect no less of the king. He's a coward. Cyrus's father is the perfect leverage to protect himself should the king of the beasts come looking for him. And now that they have captured so many more beasts, they know it won't be long before Cyrus hunts them down.

It makes keeping who I am and my condition even more crucial.

I look back towards the river, focusing on the running water. The moon casts a bright glow over the land, illuminating us all in its light. I was supposed to have returned to Cyrus by now.

I chuckle to myself as I take in the river. This is how it all started—a river.

I can't help but wonder if it was me that led him to my village that day. If I had never run into him by the river, would he have found us? Would my life end up the way it has? Would Dimitri have been free of his suffering? I see clearly now why my father stole me away from this world. He knew it was corrupt. He wanted me to have no part of it. And I silently thank him for loving me like his own, even though I represented the world that did nothing but take from him.

"Tears for the half-breed who betrayed you?" I don't bother looking up when I hear Liam's voice. His footsteps are so sure. So uninhibited by fear of any kind. He chuckles at my silence.

"You only have yourself to blame for this. Now, you've been abandoned. You'll be just another refugee within the king's walls, praying for the ones you look down on to bring you victory," he chuckles.

I still don't respond.

"There's no way a half-breed could outrun our elite. He's dead. You should thank us. We did the job you couldn't do," he says.

I whip my gaze to meet his head-on. I don't feel fear—only disgust.

"Dimitri was good. You tortured him out of your own pathetic need to feel superior. He would have fought by your side. He would have been loyal to his dying breath. But you never gave him that chance," I hiss.

Liam narrows his gaze at me, a dark smile crawling onto his face. "He will fight by our side. And he will die for us. We got plenty of weapons out of him. He's fulfilled the role he was created for."

"You're all sick," I snap.

Liam seems to be happy with my outburst.

"Not sick enough to fall in love with one," he chuckles.

"Yeah, only to fuck her in secret when she can't even fight back, right?" I growl. Liam's amusement disappears from my words, his gaze narrowing as he strikes me across the face. His hit is hard, but it is nothing like Cyrus's. I cry out, holding my face as I look at him.

"She deserves everything that I give to her," Liam snaps. He continues to glare at me before turning away, finally leaving me alone with my thoughts.

I watch his retreating form, anger pooling inside of me. I want nothing more than to watch him suffer. I immediately stand, the need to get further away from the noise the hunters create outweighing my disdain for the temperature. I continue my walk along the river until I find myself among the cages of the beasts that have been added to the caravan along with Cyrus's father. A deep chuckle fills the air, and I turn in the sound's direction, coming face to face with Cyrus's father.

He studies me, smiling.

"And suddenly, my cage isn't so cold," he taunts. "What brings you here this time? Are you seeking help to escape? Or do you just find yourself wandering to the strongest presence?"

I don't give him a response, and he leans back, closing his eyes.

"You caused quite a stir the other night, helping the half-breed escape," he says.

I don't fight my shock.

"How did you—"

"Being stored below ground doesn't dull my senses. There is a reason I was king before my son. And Calista hasn't been left alone since that night. She's always been bullheaded. I'm sure she had something to do with it," he says.

His eyes open, and he focuses on me.

"Why haven't you left this place yet, as I told you? What's keeping you here?"

"I..." I trail off, not knowing how to respond. It doesn't exactly seem like the proper argument to give to the former king that I stayed to prove my loyalty to his son. He chuckles at my silence.

"Your naivete is both sad and endearing. You don't have the slightest clue of how dire your situation is, do you?" he asks.

I slowly shake my head.

"My son has given you the greatest gift you could ever receive from the king. He's given you a pardon. A living, breathing, pardon." His voice is terrifyingly serious as he glares at me. "You are the most valuable thing in both the human and the beast empire. *You.* You carry the seal and his heir. Can I not make things any clearer for you?"

He takes in my silence and finally speaks.

"Whatever plan you have in your head will not fall that way. My son is impulsive. He is driven by emotion, not reason. He will come for you sooner than you think. And it will forever change your life. I suggest you distance yourself from the hunters. If they find out about your condition, you will be in danger. You will be nothing more than an easy target carrying a weapon. And they will use your child as soon as it's born to create more weapons."

His eyes drift over to the campsite, and I see the lack of warmth or compassion for them that lies in his eyes.

"My son will come for you, and he will bring the fires of hell with him."

Cyrus

I glare at the half-breed's battered form, trying to find the right words, but I can't. My mind immediately snaps as one prominent emotion comes to the forefront. I'm on him before anyone can stop me. My hands close around his shirt, pressing him hard against the beam that holds my tent up.

"Where. Is. She." The words pour from my lips like ice. I know at the back of my mind I'm not being rational. He's here bloodied and barely clinging to consciousness. But the rage that consumes me is more than I can account for. All I want is to know where she is and why she isn't with him.

"Cyrus!" Felix's hands are on me, yanking me away from the half-breed, who drops in a heap on the ground. Felix continues to hold me back, but the outer edges of the room are darkening as I take in the half-breed.

"How dare you return here without her!" I shout.

"She told me to leave! She told me to come back so that I could give you all the information!" he barely gets out.

A growl rips through the tent, and I realize it's me. "You left her there, *alone*?"

"Cyrus." My gaze shifts to Felix, who is watching me with a strange expression. But I take a deep breath before whipping away from the both of them. I look at the soldier who brought the half-breed to us.

"Get a medic."

She's pregnant.

Annalise is pregnant with my heir. My flesh and blood. My child. She's carrying it as we speak. I don't know what emotion to feel at the news. The irrational part of me is excited about it.

Procreation was always a duty to me. I knew I would have to produce an heir with Marzia someday. But Annalise is the one carrying that heir.

The rational part of me doesn't know what to do about it. My muscles are tense in anticipation. My mind is filled with anger. Annalise. The human, the slave, is carrying my child. But as I sit in the middle of the war meeting, gazing at the map of the camp that's been laid out before us, I cannot focus on anything else other than getting her back.

I stand from my seat, and the room falls silent.

"Everyone out."

Each of my military personnel leaves the room in a hurry. All except Felix. He slowly stands from his seat, eyeing me curiously. He already knows the directions of my thoughts but doesn't share them with me.

"You've been strangely quiet," I say.

He smiles softly, looking towards the entrance to the tent.

"It's a war meeting, Your Majesty."

The information that was given to us by the half-breed was more than anything I expected. Not only did Anna send an accurate layout of the camp, but the news that my father is alive, how they're creating weapons, and their upcoming battle plan.

In light of this, Annalise stayed to follow through with my plan. She couldn't release my father because he is too weak, but she will follow him into the stronghold and wants me to track her there. I gave her complete freedom. She could have run away, and I wouldn't have been able to find her. But she didn't. She stayed, and now she puts herself uselessly at risk to prove her loyalty to me.

Felix was right about one thing: Once you break them, there is no putting them back together. I own every part of her now. I move past Felix, pulling open the tent. There's a guard on the other side.

"Bring me my horse," I say.

Felix approaches with a shocked expression on his face.

"Where are you going?" he asks. I ignore his question, quickly relaying my plans.

"Gather my army. Send an elite force into the hunter's camp and wipe it out. Use the plans during the war meeting. Starve them out, then kill them all. I want no prisoners." I say as I move hastily around the tent, grabbing my sword and supplies.

"Cyrus, don't tell me you're going after her," Felix says. I don't bother looking at Felix as I leave the tent. I hear him following close behind me as the sounds of the war camp fill the air.

"Cyrus! Don't act irrationally. She will be freed when we—"

"No. The longer I wait to get her, the more danger she will be in. I don't know how long it will take for us to destroy the king's stronghold and kill him. It could be months, and that is time I do not have."

"What do you plan on doing once you retrieve her? The child she is carrying will be a half-breed, Cyrus. You have no future with her. You are the king, and she is a sla—"

"I don't care. She is what's important right now, Felix. You saw what the hunters did to their own creation. You heard how they are. I'm sure it's only a matter of time before they realize Annalise will not be an ally to them. I cannot wait that long!"

Felix roughly grabs my shoulder, whipping me around to face him. "Cyrus. You're being irrational!"

I shove him away from me, a snarl escaping me. He immediately backs away with wide eyes, dropping his head.

"...I didn't mean to overstep," he says.

I reign in my anger, stepping closer to him.

"I will reward Annalise for her role in this war, Felix. The half-breed will be rewarded as well."

His eyes raise at my words. I find myself using my father's resolve as I speak my next sentence.

"Half-breeds are as much a victim in this war as the beasts. Half-breeds will be granted the same rights as beasts. They are more my people than the humans," I say.

I see the guard coming near us with my horse's reins in his hands.

"Annalise is now carrying a half-breed. And that half-breed is my child who I will not abandon," I say.

I greet my horse with a simple pat on his nape before hoisting myself atop his back.

"Have my army ready in the morning. Follow my trail to the king's stronghold. We will toast our victory in the remains of his palace," I say.

Felix chuckles bitterly before holding his hand out to me. I smile, clasping his hand in mine.

"You weren't supposed to indulge this much, Your Majesty," he says, eyeing me. I laugh at his words, thinking back to our conversation that day.

"She didn't disappoint."

Chapter Thirty

ANNALISE

Cyrus's father was right. The plan I had in my head didn't at all fall how I thought it would. The king's stronghold was an extremely long trip. The trip has taken two weeks, to be exact. And in that time, I got to know more about the hunters and their despicable ways. It isn't a wonder how Cyrus never found the stronghold. The king's stronghold sits within the mountains, far from Cyrus's kingdom. Not only that, but it sits beyond a river that cuts through the mountainside. I fear Cyrus may be on his own when finding it now. I'm sure the river has washed away any trace of my scent.

Physically, the stature of the king's stronghold is magnificent. It makes me wonder how long it took to build this place. The stones are thick enough to withstand any blow from the outside. The columns have also been built with watchtowers for the soldiers to see anyone coming for miles. The stronghold is also big enough for all the refugees or close subjects of the king. The only people that live within its confines are the hunters, their families, and the nobles of humanity. Other than that, the rest of us live on the outskirts of the stronghold. Our only protection is the sentries that patrol the border.

I have also lost track of Cyrus's father. I was not given the same freedoms I had in the camp. They are much stricter here. Once we arrived at the stronghold, I was told to see the man overseeing the new arrivals. Since my arrival was so last minute, I've been placed on the very outskirts of the stronghold. I can see the edge of the castle from the small hut that's been built for me. The only time I see the inside of the stronghold is when I bring in supplies, like water or wood. I've also had time to reflect on the life I will lead now. If Cyrus never shows, then this is it for me, and Liam was right. I will live off their land, praying that by some miracle, the hunters will win the war for us. But I don't know how I'll explain the child I will give birth to in the meantime. It's been terrifying nights alone that I stay awake wondering what kind of monster is brewing inside of me.

What will Cyrus do when he sees me? When he finds out?

His father seems to think of it as some kind of pardon, but Cyrus hated Dimitri for being a half-breed. And Cyrus isn't very fond of me as well. He only tolerates me because, for the moment, he lusts for me. I've been in his chambers enough to know how quickly his lust for women changes.

I look up as the guard opens the stronghold gates for me. Today, I am bringing in more wood. The trip to the stronghold takes an hour from my hut, but it's worth it to get a look inside. I mainly try to see where they could be keeping Cyrus's father. But as I walk through the hallowed halls, I can only assume they keep him somewhere below ground as they did in the hunter's camp. And I am not allowed access to certain parts of the stronghold.

I'm placing the wood in the bin near the fireplace in one bedroom when I hear a light knock on the door. I almost drop my head and bow out of habit, but I have to remind myself I am in the humans' castle. Here, I am equal. Sort of.

I turn to see Liam standing in the doorway. He has a wicked grin on his lips as he takes me in.

"Enjoying the freedom provided to you by the hunters you so loathe?" he asks smugly.

I don't bother with a response. I grab the rest of the wood that needs to go to other rooms and make my way to the door. Liam grabs my arm roughly, causing the wood to fall to the ground.

"Hey!" I snap.

"The King has invited you for dinner. I have come to escort you to his dining hall," he says.

I narrow my gaze, pushing against his chest. I don't trust any invitations, nor was I informed of this when entering the palace.

"You can tell the king I declined his invitation," I hiss.

Liam places his hand on my chest before shoving me with a strength that he shouldn't possess. My body flies across the room, crashing into the wall. I cry out as pain wracks itself up my back, my eyes widening when I take in his towering figure.

His eyes darken, and I can see the trinket that is attached to his arm begin to glow. He's using the beast's power to intimidate me.

"I'm afraid it wasn't a request."

The condition of the king's stronghold is sickening. The walls are magnificent. Not even a scratch would dare to adorn these walls—only the blood of beasts. I'm led through the halls of the stronghold, the sounds of the higher class laughing and jeering beyond the doors as we approach.

The halls of this place are big enough to house the people who want to hide from the beasts. Even the village that is safe within the walls could house more people. But the king wants to keep order. The refugees don't belong within the walls—only the elite. The ones bred for this war. The ones who fought for their place.

Liam steps ahead of me, pushing open the double doors to reveal the room full of hunters, nobles, and the king himself. I look around at the plates full of food and glasses filled with wine. Some furs lie across the ground, and a large hearth in the corner gives five times more warmth than my tiny pile of wood ever could.

There are also half-breeds and beasts alike in the room, chained up for entertainment or being forced to serve the wretched likes of the king. The human empire is no different than the beast empire. The difference lies in the beasts having an established society that doesn't so blatantly fuck over the unfortunate. Whereas the human king doesn't seem interested in winning the war. He seems more interested in enjoying the riches of the life he's claimed for himself while trampling over anyone who gets in his way, including my mother.

I take note that at the head of the room, chained up by his neck and arms, is Cyrus's father. There are spikes on the edges of his chains, stabbing into his flesh, and I bite back the wave of dizziness that bombards me at the sight of blood trickling out of each puncture wound. He seems to sense my presence as he always does and raises his head to look at me.

His expression shifts to that of a warning. Though what it is he is warning me of, I don't know.

"Annalise! The girl who met the beasts' king and lived! The woman that fell in love with a half-breed and was abandoned. Welcome to my kingdom!" the king calls to me. I continue walking, keeping up with Liam as he leads me to my seat. The king watches me with interest, but I keep my eyes down, not wanting to show the disgust I feel. I don't know why he suddenly wanted me to join this strange atmosphere, but I'm sure I'll soon find out.

Once I'm seated, he begins speaking to me.

"Tell me, Annalise. Have you enjoyed your time in my kingdom?"

I look up from the plate of food a beast places in front of me. I take note her arms have long scars from being bled constantly. I wonder how much of the elixir they use to weaken these beasts daily.

"Yes," I say.

The king nods his head, gesturing to the men who are all seated at the table. I drown out his words as he introduces them. I find myself looking at Cyrus's father. He has an indifferent look on his face as he studies the room. He keeps glancing at me. Not out of fear but something else. He seems to know what is going to happen and is trying his best to prepare me for it.

"What say you, Annalise?"

I'm pulled out of my thoughts when the king addresses me. I clear my throat.

"I apologize. I am all out of sorts at the moment," I say.

The king's features grow irritated, but he repeats himself.

"Recently, we've had several successful raids on the beasts' military camps and have captured more each time we attack. I think it may very well be time to go for the beasts' kingdom. We can take them from the source and cripple their king," he says.

I blink in confusion.

"Why do you think I would be insightful about this plan?" I ask.

He laughs as if the answer is obvious.

"Your very own village was taken by the king. You've seen his army in action, and you've seen ours," he says.

I don't fight the chuckle that leaves my lips.

"Did you forget that the beast hierarchy is based on strength? The king could kill twenty of the beasts you captured. Why do you think you are ready for such an ambitious feat?" I ask incredulously.

The king smiles, gesturing for the guards surrounding us. The doors suddenly open, and they wheel in a strange-looking contraption. My eyes widen as I take in what it is.

It's a harpoon. And it's attached to a spring-loaded weapon.

"A weapon?" I ask.

The king laughs. "Not just any weapon. A weapon designed for the king himself."

The guards grab the weapon, aiming it at the former king, who is chained and unable to defend himself.

"What are you doing?" I ask aloud.

Cyrus's father's eyes meet mine, and I finally realize what it is he's been trying to communicate.

Don't react.

It's the same for the other beasts that are in the room. None of them move to protect their king.

"Demonstrating, of course," he laughs. "We've finally discovered a combination strong enough to pierce even the most powerful beasts down to their heart. It takes weeks and over six of the most powerful beasts to synthesize this weapon. And now, we have finally created it."

My eyes widen, and I watch in horror as the guard pulls back the lever of the weapon. He's going to use the weapon on Cyrus's father. I don't think as fear rushes up my spine. I make my move to stop the man from shooting when someone roughly grabs me around the waist. The beasts in the room don't move as they watch their predecessor. The emptiness in their gazes is now filled with a hopelessness I'm all too familiar with.

"No, Stop!" I screech.

My pleas fall on deaf ears. I watch in horror as the thick weapon flies through the air at a speed I've never seen. My body is thrown as my offender roughly pushes me to the ground. At the same time, the weapon pierces the former king.

I open my mouth, letting my scream of horror erupt through the chamber. The former king's eyes meet mine, and I don't see anger. I don't see regret. I see comfort for me. He offers me a soft smile, even though there is a large spear through his chest. His eyes stay connected to mine, and I know he is dying. I can see the light in his eyes dim. I think back to his words to me.

"My son will come for you, and he will bring the fires of hell with him."

My son will come for you. *You.* Not him. He knew he wouldn't make it out. He knew he would die here. And he tried his best to prepare me for it. His struggling breaths fill the air, his desperation to hold on to life audible. As his eyes meet mine, I feel a deep sense of sorrow. He offers me a small grin, the last thing he will be able to give anyone in this world before his head hangs. I watch in complete horror as the life leaves his body.

Applause erupts throughout the room.

"You've done it!"

"It works!"

"And now, we can end their own king with this!"

The men congratulate the king, but I just stare. I stare as my last hope of salvation is tied up, lifeless, at the front of the room. Cyrus will never forgive us. I failed. I failed him. I failed his father. I failed Dimitri.

I failed.

The king looks at me with a wide smile. "What do you think? It should be more powerful and faster than their king, correct?"

I stand up, feeling the sudden onslaught of heat consume me.

"I think... you've just condemned the human race to death," I say. I turn away from him, not bothering to look back as I make my way to the door. I have to get out of here; I have to escape before Cyrus reaches and kills us all. I flinch when Liam grips me around the waist, pulling me back.

"No, let me go! I want to leave!" I screech as he drags me back into the room.

The king looks taken aback just as Liam brings his hand toward my face. He strikes me, but he can't silence me as I continue to struggle.

"You're a coward. You've doomed us all! We're all going to die!" I cry.

The heat continues to warm up my body and I suddenly recognize the feeling. It's Cyrus's seal. It's coming alive with my anger. It easily consumes me, and I can't think of anything other than destroying Liam. I grip his hands around my waist, squeezing until I feel the bone crush beneath my grip. His cries fill the air, forcing everyone to look in our direction. I then bring my elbow down, striking him in the chest. He releases me immediately, stumbling back as he struggles for breath. I'm confident with that blow that I crushed his lungs. His eyes look at me in shock as he struggles to breathe, and blood comes rushing violently past his lips. But I can't move as my legs grow weak under me from the force of the seal.

I can no longer hold myself up, collapsing in the middle of the hall.

Chapter Thirty-One

ANNALISE

I jolt awake.

I try to move my arms, but they're tied to a chair. My gaze whips around the room, but I don't recognize it. I must still be in the stronghold. My body is on fire, my limbs numb with pain. It must be the effects of the seal still resonating in my bloodstream.

"You're awake."

I flinch, my gaze whipping to the corner of the room. The human king stands, eyeing me with a guarded expression. His hand rests on the hilt of his sword, ready to strike at any moment if he needs to.

"Who are you?" he asks.

I blink in confusion.

"What?" I ask.

"Don't play dull girl," he hisses.

His grip on the blade tightens as he takes a threatening step toward me. He's clearly suspicious of something, but I don't know what.

"I don't know what you're talking about," I rush out. He now pulls the sword from his scabbard, aiming it at me. My heart thunders in my chest as I take in the possibility of death.

"Liam's dead. You killed him without a trinket. You arrived from a village, clinging to that half-breed. Are you a spy?" he asks. I narrow my gaze at him, letting my bitter resentment come to the forefront. This seems to be the only route I can take to get him off the scent of me being a spy.

"Do you not recognize me? Do you not see my mother's face?" I snap. His grip doesn't slacken at my words, but his gaze narrows as he steps closer to me, pressing his blade against my throat. I hold back my fear as he pushes the tip of his blade, drawing blood.

"Paul raised me. He only told me the truth because our village was destroyed. He's the only reason we all got away. I know what you did to my mother," I try harder, and this time, the king hears me. His grip slackens, his gaze wide as he takes me in. His sword slowly lowers, horror finding its way onto his features.

"How did I not see it?" he whispers.

He watches me as if I am a ghost. Maybe to him, I am.

"So that's it then? You've come to kill me?" he asks.

I shake my head, my gaze drifting to his sword as he looks toward the ceiling, battling his inner demons.

"Your mother was a necessity in the war. Just as you were. Paul didn't understand that. He didn't understand what was needed for the greater good. He took our greatest hope from us. Even in death, he taunts us with your existence," he says, laughing humorlessly.

"I'm not here to kill anyone," I whisper, pulling his attention.

The king raises his brow. "And yet you did."

He's referring to Liam.

"He deserved it. He's sick and kept harassing me. I tried to let him slide, but he just wouldn't stop," I say, hoping he'll accept my lie, chalking it all up to vengeance.

He chuckles, pulling my attention. "Had Paul left you here, Liam would've been your match for the next generation. I can see now my decision to create you wasn't the wrong one."

I bite the inside of my cheek to keep from responding, but the king is still considering what to do with me.

"It's time you took up your place among the hunters. Paul's ideals have tainted you, no doubt. But we will fix you. You will be of great use to me in this war," he says.

He looks up, a wicked smile on his lips. "I still win, Paul."

Terror wracks its way up my spine as he speaks of my future. I cannot remain here. I cannot stay within these walls, especially now that I am carrying Cyrus's child. It won't be long before I begin to show, and Cyrus's father's fears come to life.

"I will send an escort with you to take you to your hut and gather your belongings. You will move into the stronghold and begin training immediately."

Contrary to what I believed upon awakening, he knows nothing of the seal. I assume he thinks my fighting came from Paul teaching me and that I fulfilled my purpose as a bred weapon. I watch him pull open the door to reveal two guards standing by outside.

"Escort her down the hill. I want her back by nightfall."

My hands have been bound as we head down the hill. The trip to my hut usually takes an hour. I am thankful for the time as we make the trip so that I can devise a plan. I cannot return to the stronghold. Once I do, I will never be let out again. I vaguely recall what happened after watching the gruesome murder of the late king. Even now, the memory brings sickness to my gut. Cyrus's father was right. They have invited hell into this place.

I don't know if Cyrus will ever find it now. The king was smart in the placement of his stronghold. There are many places to lose my scent and my trail. And it's been weeks since we left the camp with no sign of him. I don't even know if Dimitri made it out alive. If Cyrus hasn't discovered me by now, I believe he never will. My plan was to get his father out safely because I believed it would equal me having an easier life. But the hunters have ripped that possibility away from me.

Can I start a new life this deep into the war? I can find ways to get rid of the child that lives inside of me, ending any and all connection with the beast empire. Cyrus will think I died in the stronghold, and the king will be too busy with war to worry about my fate. It's the perfect time for me to disappear.

My hut slowly appears in the distance as my new plan solidifies. After taking it away from me, the human king has dropped salvation in my lap. I inhale a deep breath, clasping my chained hands together as I swing for the guard to my left. My fist connects to his face, and I use the opportunity to sprint away.

"Hey!"

I hear them shouting after me, followed by their footsteps. My adrenaline is pumping, my mind whirling like a windstorm as I make my way to the river. That is where I can lose them. I hear the running water of the river ahead of me, meaning I am on the right path. Once I reach the river, I'll be able to use the current to get swept away. They won't follow me down the river.

I push through to the clearing, the river directly in front of me. I can also hear the men gaining on me, but the river is right there. All I have to do is jump. I'm inches from stepping into the river when I notice the figure standing across it. He's kneeling with his hands cupped in the water. His white hair pulled up and away from his face. I stop dead in my tracks, my heart beating as fast as possible.

The figure seems to sense my presence, his face slowly rising to meet mine. His dark eyes land on me, and my body trembles with familiarity. I hear the hunters behind me approaching, but I can't move. Their footsteps falter next to me as they spot the beast across the river. We all stand face to face with the king of the beasts. His gaze roams over the three of us, lingering on me.

The guard next to me doesn't hesitate. He draws his blade, his trinket lighting up as he runs toward his opponent.

"No, wait!" I shout, but he doesn't listen.

Cyrus's gaze slightly narrows, and, in an instant, he vanishes from his place across the river. I watch in horror as he appears inches from the guard's face, his hand closing around his throat. He uses his brute strength to smash the guard's body into the ground, sending a tremor beneath us as dirt and rock separate to accommodate the forced entry.

"Son of a bitch!" The guard next to me reaches for his blade but doesn't get close as Cyrus's eyes meet the action. One second, the guard is standing next to me, and the next, Cyrus is standing next to me with a bloodied blade. The man's lifeless body drops, his head severed from his neck.

I take a panicked step back, looking at the king of the beasts in horror. His gaze is still focused on the lifeless body of the guard next to me. I've only ever seen Cyrus display his strength once, when he killed the servants in front of me. But this is nothing like that moment.

Cyrus's eyes finally meet mine, and the trembling doesn't stop. Tears well up in my eyes as my training immediately kicks in. I drop to my knees, pressing my head into the dirt. I feel like I can't breathe. My fingers dig into the dirt as well, and my whimpers soon fill the air, giving off how frightened I am. I hear Cyrus's soft chuckle above me. He kneels to my height, placing his finger under my chin, lifting my gaze to meet his. Those dark eyes bore into my soul with all the intensity they can give.

"Are those tears of joy to see your king?"

Chapter Thirty-Two

ANNALISE

My body craves his touch. The frazzled nerves and stress I've felt all but melt away as his hands roam over my body, bringing me to heights I've learned to expect with Cyrus. His mouth covers my beaded nipple as his tongue laves over the sensitive flesh. I arch my back, needing more. And he gives it to me. His hand moves between my legs, lighting the fire that only he can with such ease. He purrs in delight at finding me wet and wanting for him. His fingers expertly rub my clit before dipping inside of me, filling me. I open my mouth, letting my moan echo off the walls of my small hut.

I don't know if or when the hunters will come looking for their missing comrades, but Cyrus doesn't seem to care in the least. He dragged me back here and hasn't spoken a word to me from the moment his lips met mine. His hands are warm and slightly roughened from recent battles. He releases my nipple, coming up to kiss me on the lips, dipping his tongue in my mouth. Each stroke of his tongue sends me to new heights, and I find myself squirming against his fingers, trying to find release. He notices the action and chuckles softly against my lips.

"What do you want, Anna?" he murmurs.

His voice causes chills to break out across my skin. His hand threads through my hair as he cranes my neck so that he can suck on it.

"Tell me what you want, Annalise. Or I won't give it to you."

"I... I want you," I whisper.

All of my anger and shame disappear. Cyrus never keeps pleasure from me when I ask. And this time is no different. He pulls his fingers out of me, replacing it with the thick head of his cock. He doesn't waste any time as he thrusts inside of me, causing me to cry out in pain mingled with pleasure. It's been so long that my body takes a second to remember what it's like to have him inside of me. He fills me up to the point of not knowing where I begin or end. All I know is the pleasure he gives.

His arms wrap under my legs, his palms flattening against my back as he thrusts inside of me. I place my hands against his chest to steady myself, and I mentally note the soft warmth that his skin gives under my fingers. He leans closer to me, picking me up with ease. I let out a strangled gasp as more intense pleasure ripples through me. He penetrates me deeper and quicker at this angle, and I can no longer contain my moans.

"Ah, Ah, Ah!"

The intense pulse of my orgasm hits me with sudden intensity. Cyrus's eyes meet mine, and he has a small smirk on his lips as he watches me tense in pleasure, my body violently pulsing against his. His lips cover mine, and he swallows my moans, guiding me through my orgasm.

"You didn't follow instructions, Annalise."

Cyrus is standing over me, fastening his pants. He looks at me with those dark eyes and I immediately look away. Seeing Cyrus was the last thing I was expecting to happen. But now that he's here, I feel even more terrified and uncertain of my future. I don't know how to tell him about his father. I don't know how he's going to react to my being pregnant. So I stay silent and let him scold me as he always does.

"I told you to come back to me, and you traveled into the enemy's territory with a half-baked plan," he says in irritation.

"My apologies, Your Majesty," I murmur.

He looks at me from across the room, causing me to feel squeamish under his gaze.

"Didn't I tell you to drop the formalities when we are alone?" he asks.

I nod, lowering my gaze. I didn't miss this feeling he gives me. The fireplace casts a warm glow over him, adding to his intimidation. His eyes finally leave mine, and he looks around the hut, making a face.

"What exactly were you hoping to accomplish with this plan?" he asks.

I finally look back at him, my voice catching in my throat.

"I-" Tears well up in my eyes as I stare at him in fear. I'm scared. I've always been scared of Cyrus. But as I recently found out, Cyrus's only hesitation in this war was the hope that his father was alive. He frowns at my sudden change in mood.

"Speak, Annalise."

I open my mouth. I try my hardest. I really do. But I can't. I can't force it out. He comes closer to me, causing all my fear to double.

"Why did you use my seal?" he asks. His eyes search my body for distress, but he sees none. "You don't look to be hurt, and you weren't using it when those hunters were chasing you."

I'm trembling at this point. I can't get my brain to work. Or my mouth. I can't get anything to work as I look into the eyes of the king. The real king. The beasts' king.

"Speak, Annalise!" he shouts.

I immediately get off the bed, falling to my knees.

"I'm sorry, Cyrus. I tried. I swear, I tried. It wasn't enough. I couldn't find a way to free him. I couldn't save him once he was in the stronghold. I was weak. I tried to follow his orders, I—"

My body is pulled from the ground, and in an instant, my back collides with the wall. I cry out in shock, and when I open my eyes, my breathing stops. Cyrus's gaze is something I've never seen before. Not even when I first encountered him at the river of my village. The dark part of his eyes has sharpened into slits. I find myself paralyzed in fear at the proximity of this... beast.

"Who?" His voice is cold and dead. The sound alone causes my blood to run cold, and I tremble in his arms. His aura has completely changed. He isn't the same beast he was only seconds ago.

"Your father... he... he was killed... in the stronghold."

A loud crack fills the room, and I cry out in pain. Cyrus drops me, and I realize in shock that he crushed my arm. I don't know if he did it on purpose or from the shock of the news, but it doesn't matter. I clutch my arm in pain, biting my lip hard enough to draw blood. I don't dare make a sound. I don't dare remind him I am even here. He stands above me, rigid. If he weren't holding me only seconds ago, I would think he was a statue.

The temperature of the hut drops just from Cyrus's presence alone. And I regret at this moment that I didn't just jump on the hunters' swords the moment I saw Cyrus standing in that clearing. I would rather be dead than on the end of Cyrus's wrath.

"Get up," he snaps.

I try my best to stand, whimpering in pain as it jostles my arm. I turn to see him putting the rest of his armor on. His face is blank of any emotion. It terrifies me. His eyes finally meet mine, and he narrows his gaze at me. He makes his way towards me, and out of instinct, I step back. I don't get far. His hand lashes out, grabbing me and roughly pulling me in close to him.

"Do. Not. Look at me. You do not have that right, slave," he hisses.

My breathing comes out in short pants as tears silently stream down my face.

"M-my apologies... Your Majesty," I whisper.

Cyrus walks to the door of the hut, pulling it open. He doesn't say another word to me as he walks through the opening, but I know better than to make him have to call for me. I don't look back as I follow him through the mountainside.

It takes a while, but we finally reach where Cyrus left his horse. And once we head back to his camp, it takes the rest of the day, our arrival coming at nightfall.

I look around as the sounds of metal and conversation pull my attention. Cyrus hasn't said a word to me. Nor has he bothered to heal my arm. It's numb, and I can feel myself beginning to shift in and out of consciousness as I slide down from his horse. I trudge slowly behind the king, trying my best to remain awake. But the edges of my vision are dimming.

"Your Majesty, you've returned!"

I hear the familiar sound of Felix's voice. But I don't dare look up. I keep my eyes trained on the ground.

"Cyrus? What's wr—"

"How many humans have we rounded up on the trip here?" Cyrus asks.

Felix is silent for a moment before responding.

"One-hundred sixteen, Your Majesty," Felix says.

"Kill them."

"Cyrus—"

Cyrus looks at Felix, his eyes wide as he fights for control. "Since when do I have to ask twice, General?"

I feel a rough pull on my arm, and I stumble forward, collapsing in the dirt between Cyrus and Felix.

"Take her to a healer. Have them check her condition. Have her cleaned and sent to my tent," Cyrus says.

"Yes, Your Majesty."

I'm trembling as Cyrus walks away, his newfound presence already affecting the tension in the camp. I slowly look up to see Felix watching his retreating form, a small frown on his lips. He releases a breath, looking at me.

"What have you done, slave?"

Chapter Thirty-Three

ANNALISE

I've been here before. Frightened. Filled with dread. Desperate for answers or at least an indicator that everything will be okay. But as I sit in the king's war tent, staring at the table with maps covering it, I have yet to grow used to this feeling. Cyrus has abandoned all emotional ties to the world. I'm sure of it. I can still hear the screams of any human prisoners. Cyrus also didn't bother healing me himself. Or looking at me, for that matter. He resents me for what I am. I represent the people who took his father from this world.

I face the entrance of the tent when I hear voices I recognize immediately. It's Cyrus and Felix.

"I want everyone prepared to return to the kingdom at daybreak." Cyrus's voice sends a chill down my spine. The strange transformation he had when I told him the truth about his father is burned into my skull. He may look human at times, but he isn't. He's a beast.

The tent opens and I quickly step into the corner as Cyrus enters, bowing my head. I don't want to give him any reason to attack me, not after the long trip to get here. Cyrus doesn't make a sound, nor does he acknowledge me. He moves around me, approaching the table with maps stretched across it.

The sound of liquid pouring fills the silence. I tense, looking up when I hear shattering glass. Cyrus sits at the table with a savage look in his gaze. The glass that once held his wine has splintered into a million pieces in his hand.

I make my way toward him, moving to clean up the mess.

"I'll clean it up right away-Ah!"

Cyrus shoves me hard, and I don't have the reaction time to catch myself. I land on the ground, crying out in pain.

"Do not touch me, slave."

I meet his gaze in shock but immediately crawl to my knees, bending my head.

"I-I'm sorry," I whisper.

Cyrus's gaze remains on me, and I fear the direction of his thoughts. He throws what remains of the broken glass down, letting it shatter next to me as he storms around me. His fist comes down in the center of the desk that once held battle plans—the wood splinters easily beneath the force of his blow. My eyes burn as the fear of death overcomes me. Cyrus is beyond livid, and I am the nearest human, possibly the only one remaining in this camp.

Cyrus's breathing fills the room, followed by a faint laugh. When I look up, he's staring at the pile of crushed objects with a strange smile on his lips. I've never seen him so out of sorts. He's always been calm and calculating. But now, it seems like something has broken inside of him. He reaches into the pile of splintered wood, grabbing the glowing necklace out of the rubble. It's the necklace my father gave me. The trinket I had when I first arrived. I don't know what emotion to perceive right now. He's trembling before me. But I see no sadness. No despair. No defeat. Nothing.

His eyes meet mine.

The beating of my heart flutters even faster at his attention. Contrary to everyone's belief, Cyrus has shown me no favor in light of my condition. In his eyes, I am another human responsible for his father's death. I fear the only reason he's keeping me alive is that I hold information about the king's stronghold. But he's been so angry he has yet to speak with me.

He keeps his eyes on mine, pulling his blade from its place against the beam. My trembling picks up the closer he gets, and I immediately drop my gaze. The blade stabs into the ground next to me, forcing a squeal from my lips.

Cyrus chuckles above me.

"So fucking weak."

I shudder at his tone. The trinket he held lands in front of me with a dull thud as he drops it.

"So weak, in fact, that to survive this war, they make weapons from our own flesh and blood. Each time I fight a hunter, I feel such disgust. To sense the power of my people radiating from your pores is sickening," he says. I feel his fingers under my chin as he lifts my gaze to meet his. My trembling only strengthens at the sight of his eyes. They are sharp like a serpent.

"What if I decided to make weapons from your flesh and bone?" he asks as he studies me. My jaw trembles from the calming rage Cyrus exudes. He chuckles in front of me.

"It would be a fitting decoration, I guess. Seeing as you offer nothing to strengthen us," he murmurs.

He kneels so that he is directly in front of me, using the blade to balance his weight. An action so simple yet so intimidating.

"You would make a beautiful blade, Annalise." His finger runs over the top of my skin from my jaw down my throat until he rests it atop my collarbone. He tilts his head as he studies the bone structure of my body.

"Very delicate. Very light." He smiles, emphasizing his approval.

"And I would always have you with me," he chuckles, "Or rather, what's left of you."

His hand leaves my collarbone, and he traces it down my arm, causing goosebumps to break out across my skin. My eyes widen in horror as his nail visibly sharpens in front of me. The talon easily punctures my forearm, and blood seeps out, running down my flesh.

Cyrus's sharp gaze is focused on the trail of blood that runs down my arm.

"Beautiful," he whispers.

I can't fight my fear any longer, and I immediately yank my arm away from him, cradling it to my chest. He doesn't react like I expect him to. He only watches me with that terrifying expression. To my utter surprise, he stands.

"What are we to do with you now, slave?" he asks. He picks up his blade, moving it so that the tip is facing me. His amusement is gone as he glares at me. I keep my eyes focused on him, ready to accept whatever fate he decides to pass down. My life is in his hands. I have no chance of escape. No fighting chance. I'm just as helpless as the prisoners outside.

My eyes slowly travel to the blade. Its silver edge glints with malicious intent. It's the same blade he used the first day I encountered him at the river. The sharp edge has already had a taste of my flesh. Cyrus's grip on the weapon tightens, and just as I'm about to witness his decision, Felix enters the tent.

"Cyrus. The human king's scouts were spotted three miles north. They've located our camp."

Cyrus doesn't move. He finally lowers the blade before looking at Felix.

"Prepare for battle. We take the stronghold tomorrow," he says.

Felix nods, turning to exit. My body tenses as I'm about to speak out. I'm about to tell Cyrus of the weapon that killed his father. The weapon was specially designed for him as well. But I stop myself. Cyrus notices my movement, narrowing his gaze only slightly. I drop my head. I don't know where Cyrus is emotionally. He seems eager to kill me. Eager to kill humans. Eager to avenge his father.

I recall his father's words to me.

"Tell him at the most crucial times of war, it is best not to make haste."

He knew his son best. And he knew this was how his son would react to his death. He would make rash decisions in his emotional turmoil. And he trusted me to prevent it. But as I stare at the beast Cyrus has transitioned into, I see no reason to stop him. If I warn Cyrus and he comes out of this successfully, I will have handed victory to the beasts. As much as I hate the hunters, I refuse to be subjected to Cyrus's rule or will any longer. So I close my mouth, bowing my head, and become the docile slave he's trained me to be.

The rest of the night, I monitor closely where Cyrus places things. I pay attention to where he lays the trinket from my father, as well as the maps that are lying in the rubble. Cyrus's guard is completely down. He thinks he has me perfectly trained like Felix has Dimitri.

Tomorrow, when he leaves for battle, I will escape this place and never have to worry about the king of the beasts again.

Chapter Thirty-Four

CYRUS

It's a sickening feeling, loss. It feels like a dream, and then it feels like a nightmare that is impossible to awaken from. In times of peace, humanity was a race among us. They weren't equal in terms of power, but they had rights. They could live. They could even become noble. We had specific advisors for humans who would stand at the king's side. Out of greed and anger, they began a war they had no chance of winning. And they've dragged it out longer than I care to give thought to. They've become a disease. And it's time to eradicate it.

I silently fasten my armor, making sure everything is in place. I can sense her behind me. She's still asleep.

Usually, I can hear her heartbeat alone. But now I can hear two heartbeats. I never intended to get her pregnant. I'm not supposed to be fucking a human, let alone impregnating one. I could always sense when she was within her window for pregnancy. And usually, I'm good at avoiding it. But in the weeks before she left, my obsession with her grew. As did my lust. In hindsight, I should have prevented it. But I guess I should thank my foolishness. If she wasn't pregnant now, I fear my hatred for humanity might have fallen on her. And I would have killed her.

I turn to look at her sleeping form in the bed. She looks at peace. Her long lashes brush her cheeks. Her lips are slightly parted as she breathes lazily. She's beautiful. From the day I met her, I knew that. It called out to me. What started as curiosity morphed into an obsession.

I reach out, brushing her hair away from her face. Her skin is warm, her cheeks soft. She stirs slightly, a soft moan leaving her lips as she leans into my touch. I enjoy her like this. There's no restraint, no fear. Her body gives in to what it wants without fear being the drive. I release a deep breath, pulling my hand away from her face. The connection between us was doomed from the beginning. I turn away from her, grabbing my weapon from where it hangs.

I pull open the tent, taking in my army. They are ready to end this war as much as I am. And as eager to avenge their former king and loved ones captured and used by the hunters. I don't fight the smile that forms on my lips.

The time has finally come to end this.

"Cyrus. If the mountainside continues to grow this steep, we need to wait them out at the bottom. They'll have the advantage of the high ground."

I hear Felix's words. I even try my best to think about the logic behind them. But I can't.

"Advantage?" I scoff. "They killed the only advantage they had."

The words are like bitter metal coming out of my mouth. Accepting my father's death has been a slow spiral to hell. I am the king. I shouldn't dwell. I shouldn't mourn. Casualties are a part of war. But the more I think about the kind of king my father was, and the people that turned on him, the more I can't help but feel rage like no other. He didn't deserve this. Out of the entire beast kingdom, my father did not deserve such a meaningless, brutal death.

I think back to Annalise's tears as she told me the truth. The hurt I saw in her eyes at the death of my father still haunts me. She met him. She interacted with him. And even in the short time she knew him, he made an impact on her. Such an impact that she was upset about his death.

In the fog of hatred, I know Annalise is not responsible. But I also know that Annalise is a human. I hate humans. All of them. Even her. Even at this very moment, I don't know why I've tolerated her to this point. I don't know why I enjoy her presence. I don't know why I want her near me. I just know that I do. And yet, the sight of her sickens me to my core. Each time I look into her eyes, the temptation to kill her claws at my flesh like a plague.

I feel nothing for her, yet everything.

I pull at the reins of my horse, looking around the familiar area. This is where Anna and I reunited. I look across the clearing where the river separates the land. The trees still stand that she emerged from, determination in her eyes as she trudged into the water with hunters on her tail. She's the most cunning human I've ever encountered. Even when she's being obedient, I know her mind is running a mile a minute, trying to figure out what the smartest course of action should be.

I turn to Felix.

"The king's stronghold is a few miles beyond the river. Tell the men to stay on high alert from here on in. The hunters are conniving and cowardly," I say.

Felix nods, turning away from me to spread the message among the men. I climb off my horse, moving to the water's edge. My mind keeps wandering to Annalise. Her reaction to my plan was alarming. She's smart. Too smart for her own good. She knows when to speak and when to remain silent. And she's never imposed on plans involving this war. But when I announced to take the stronghold, she seemed almost desperate to conceal something from me.

I know she saw a lot in her time among the hunters. The half-breed gave us plenty of information upon his return that Annalise uncovered. I never asked her for any recent developments upon our return. Even in my grief, I didn't ask her the details of my father's death. She may be keeping something from me. Something important and crucial to this war. But there's nothing I can do now. I can only stay on high alert.

I mount my horse, continuing the journey to the stronghold. The sound of the river slowly dies as the small hut Annalise seemed to stay in comes into view. I keep my eyes trained on it as we pass.

"Thinking about the human again, Your Majesty?" Felix comes next to me as we grow closer to the stronghold.

I breathe deeply, looking up the mountainside.

"My Father always told me, in times of war, the best course of action is not to make haste. I can't help but wonder if I am making the right decision right now," I say.

Felix takes a deep breath, following my gaze up the mountain.

"I'm sorry about your father, Cyrus. I'm sorry we couldn't save him."

I shake my head.

"He knew this would happen. He knew that unless humanity changed its ways, he could no longer rule. He knew it was time for my reign. To lead us into a new era," I say.

I think back to the days before my father and I went into battle together. He was strangely open-minded about my ideas for the future. He always included the possibility of humanity not coming to terms with living the way we used to be. He always knew he wasn't the right leader for the change in attitude of those he ruled over. I can't help but wonder what was on his mind in his last days. If he ever lost hope in them.

"And what is your plan for this new era, Cyrus?" Felix asks.

I take a deep breath.

"Annalise carries my plan for this new era," I say, looking at him.

"I plan on expanding my empire. And that includes adding half-breeds to it. There are so many of them out there. So many that the hunters have bred and tortured over the years. So many are eager to belong and eradicate those who have wronged them, including yours. Whatever Anna gives birth to, it shall take over my empire someday and rule over two people. A more diverse race."

Felix smiles softly, a question forming in his head. "And the humans?"

I scoff.

"Humanity is an endangered species, as far as I'm concerned."

Felix is silent for a moment.

"And Annalise? What do you plan on doing with her once she gives birth?"

I chuckle bitterly as a village comes into view.

"I don't know."

I take in the village's state in amusement. The humans are unexpecting of our arrival. There aren't even guards here to protect them. I laugh at the sight. The king of the humans is far more cowardly than I thought. He's worse to leave so many of his people outside of his walls unprotected. We enter the village, and the sounds of life slowly grow silent as they take us in. We are the last thing they will ever see in this life.

Felix watches me, awaiting my command. A small part of me wants to cling to my father's philosophy, but as I look among the humans, I feel nothing. No compassion, no sense of mercy, nothing.

"Kill them all."

Felix pulls his blade from its sheath, holding it high in the air. The silence that once accompanied our arrival is now permeated with blood and screams. I revel in the sound of more humans dying at my discretion. Had they let my father live, they might've had a chance.

I don't bother taking part in the slaughter. My army is massive, wiping them out in minutes as we continue our path to the stronghold. I can see the top of it from this distance. And it doesn't take us long to reach the walls. It's magnificent and perfect to protect from invaders. The walls are high, with gates and balconies for the inner army to attack.

As we approach, the individual hunters standing in front of the stronghold and atop it come into view. I can already sense the large number of hunters that hold the power of powerful beasts. I can sense the power of Calista, a general who once fought among my men. I can sense the power of several generals and combat specialists, and above it all, I can sense the power of my father.

I feel the slight prickle of my flesh as anticipation for this battle begins. My teeth are throbbing, and my nails are lengthening. I can already feel myself shifting. At the center of the hunters, sitting atop his horse to receive me, is the king of the humans. His crown sits atop his head, his eyes holding little emotion.

This is the bastard that killed my father. The bastard that forced Annalise's existence into the world.

I slide from my horse as he raises his hands, addressing me.

"Welcome to my kingdom, Cyrus! Son of Magnus!"

I clench my jaw in anger. He has no right to speak my father's name.

"I am glad you came to me so that we did not have to hunt you down to kill you like we did your father!" he laughs.

I slowly pull my blade from its sheath, having little interest in hearing him speak. I look back to where he stands, ready to attack when the gate of the stronghold opens. A hunter emerges, and what I see forces the emotions I've had bottled to the surface.

My father's head sits atop a spike, branded and bludgeoned. The human king laughs at my expression, holding his hand out.

"Come, king of the beasts! Avenge your father!"

The hunters gather close to their king, their trinkets lighting up with our power as they take it in, becoming ready to battle. I feel my grip on my blade loosening as I look over my father's head, resting atop the spike that leads the hunter army.

My legs suddenly feel too weak to stand, my mind falling blank of emotion. I hear Felix next to me saying something, but I can't decipher what it is. All I feel is rage. My body begins its shift without my command, my monstrous side emerging. It's the last conscious thing I feel before the world blackens, and I am no longer in control.

Chapter Thirty-Five

ANNALISE

Cyrus has left for good. I push open the tent, looking at the empty camp. The only ones that remain are two guards stationed outside and the injured. I turn away from the entrance, making my way through the tent. Cyrus thought I was staying silent, being an obedient slave. But I wasn't.

I move to the shelf in the corner that holds all the maps. Cyrus meticulously placed them. I reach for the highest scroll, pulling it out to examine. It's a map of territories the beasts have conquered. It's also a map of the zones Cyrus has marked as dangerous for his people to travel alone. Meaning it will be filled with hunters and humans. Safe enough to travel for now. It's the path that Dimitri and I should have taken when we tried to escape.

I suck in a deep breath as I think of Dimitri. I would love to take him with me. But he is lost to me now. I know his time in the camp changed him. I know he belongs to the beasts now. He would only fight me and fear his days away from Felix. As much as I love him, I have to leave him.

I move to the small chest that sits atop a nightstand, pulling it open. The key sits neatly in its place. I grab it, making my way to the large chest on the floor at the foot of the bed. He thought I was asleep, but I wasn't. I unlock the chest, lifting it to reveal things that Cyrus likes to keep hidden, including weapons confiscated from hunter villages. I grab two blades and rummage around at the bottom of the chest. My father's trinket shines back at me. I grab it, wrapping it around my throat. If I am to survive, I must become the weapon I was bred to be. No matter what it takes or how this battle ends, I will not be on the receiving end of anyone's torture.

I make my way to the last vase in the room where Cyrus stores his money, pulling out the gold. I make sure to bring enough with me to survive once I escape. I move to the opening of the tent, looking up the mountainside one last time.

I try to feel a shred of remorse for sending him to his death, but I don't. I feel nothing. Cyrus and I have never had a connection. I risked my life to prove to him I was loyal. I could be the one human that would never betray him, but it didn't matter. In his eyes, I'm still human. And that's enough to sentence me for the others' behavior.

Before the day is over, the human king will have killed the king of the beasts. I don't know how the revelation will rock the world or change the course of the war, and frankly, I don't want to be around to find out. Another beast will rise in his place to take up the reins of this war.

I close the tent, making my way to the other side. Luckily, it's a tent. So I use my new weapons to cut open the backside. I can see the stables from here. I quietly approach the horses, pulling the furthest one out of the stable. I hoist myself up with ease, riding to the edge of the camp. I take one last look back, still feeling nothing.

"Goodbye, Cyrus."

Felix

War.

It's a vicious thing. It's bloody, cruel, and exhausting. And it doesn't care who it takes with it as long as there's death and carnage. And with war, there is always death and carnage. I tense as another blade finds its way into my flesh. It slices through me easily, the poisoned blade paralyzing my body for an instant. The instant is long enough for another hunter to attack. I take the opportunity to pull the blade's owner towards me, using his body as a shield for my new attacker.

Both men scream in pain, but I'm up immediately, crushing their throats. I try to stand but to no avail. My legs won't move. My body is covered in the blood of my enemy and my own. My muscles throb from exhaustion. I find myself fighting to stay conscious. The hunters have grown stronger. But that's no surprise. They've found ways to use the blood of the mightiest beasts ever to have roamed our kingdom. They've found ways to poison us with one attack, which is why, in my current state, I can't shift forms.

I look around the battlefield, trying my best to find Cyrus. He disappeared at the beginning of the battle, a path of dead bodies left in his wake. Half the bodies on this battlefield were caused by him alone. It is why he is king. Even if the hunters found one hundred powerful beasts to pit against us, Cyrus's strength is double that. He was more powerful than his father before his reign ended. I'm the only person who knows. Cyrus kept that hidden from the rest of the world. He wanted his father to rule until he felt Cyrus was ready for the throne. And yet, the throne was cruelly forced into Cyrus's hands.

My eyes land on Cyrus, and I feel my inner beast quiver in fear at the sight. He's almost fully transformed. His eyes have sharpened, his nails lengthened into talons, his teeth elongated, and his pores have begun to secrete a black aura that will swallow anyone whole. We are called beasts for a reason. Because we are not human. But we do not give in to our forms for a reason as well. Because if we do, we are nothing but an unholy beast.

Cyrus easily grabs an escaping hunter, ripping his body in half. He stands, opening his mouth to release a screech that could peel the flesh off of bones. I feel the chill in the air, as do the men. I use my blade to steady myself.

"Retreat!" I shout.

The order echoes over the mountainside as each of our own warns the other of the impending doom about to happen. I grit my teeth in pain, standing to face the remaining hunters. I know they feel it, too. Death has incarnated itself. And they are all going to be firsthand witnesses to that terrifying fact.

The human king takes off, breaking his own ranks. He carries the head of Magnus with him as he runs in a direction that is opposing the stronghold. Cyrus's form takes notice, his gaze narrowing. His form becomes a blur as he follows the human king. The aura he secretes easily swallows any surrounding hunters, and the sickening sound of their trapped gurgles fills the air. As Cyrus's form disappears over the hillside, immediate silence fills the air. I lift my gaze to look at the bodies.

Mangled and broken beyond repair. Their skin looks like it's been sucked of all life, their bones and flesh twisted and gaping. They never had a chance. They played with a force they didn't understand. And now, I fear nothing will be able to stop the rot of death from leaving this mountainside and devouring the world.

I take off in the direction that Cyrus and the human king disappeared in. This must be a trap. The human king abandoned his own people to lure Cyrus somewhere that was specially designed for him. I just hope I'm not too late. I sprint through the forest, following the trail of lifeless plants. I hear the sound of a waterfall beyond the crippling trees. I slowly round the corner, looking to see Cyrus's form facing the king of the humans. The king has a terrified look on his face as he holds Magnus's head out to Cyrus as an offering.

Is he trying to barter his life for the body of the King?

I look back at Cyrus's form. I can't make Cyrus out of it any longer; there is only a black cataclysm surrounding his form.

"Now!"

The human king's words pull me out of my thoughts, and I see it too late.

"Cyrus!" I shout to warn him, but it's too late.

A spear shoots from above, puncturing the black haze. Another follows suit immediately, and the aura that surrounds Cyrus dissipates. Two massive spears are protruding out of Cyrus's body. Cyrus doesn't seem to care. Even with blood pouring from his lips and his body fighting against him, he reaches for the human king, who now stands over him, smiling.

"And now, you will join your father in hell, beast."

Cyrus collapses in front of him on his knees, and the king doesn't move as he watches him slowly die. I take off, making my way toward him with my blade ready. The human king's eyes meet mine, but only for an instant. Cyrus launches up from the ground, grabbing the king around the throat. His hand crushes the king's throat with ease. He doesn't stop his momentum, and I watch in horror as Cyrus carries himself and the king off the cliff's edge.

I sprint into the clearing, trying my best to make it to the edge of the waterfall. I can still see his body. I can still grab him. I force my legs to move, my blood rushing in my ears. I hold my hand out in front of me, reaching for him, but I grab nothing—just the air. I fall to my knees, looking over the edge.

"Cyrus!"

The loud crash of water drowns my voice out against the mountainside, and I watch in horror as Cyrus's body disappears in the foam.

Chapter Thirty-Six

ANNALISE

Patience. Patience is key. My father always stressed that to me growing up. He would tell me to be patient with everything.

When waiting for the food to cook.

When my anger would grow.

Even when he discovered my growing affection for Dimitri.

And now, I understand the truth of his words. Patience is what got me here—watching, waiting, and knowing when to act. Had it not been for patience, I never would have recognized my chance at escape and taken it.

I trudge silently through the docks, keeping a tight hold on my horse's reins. The sound of people fills the air. Actual people, not beasts. They are speaking to one another. Bartering for food, supplies, clothes, anything they can take with them across the sea.

It's refreshing to hear the sounds of life. Free will. No more commands. No more meaningless deaths. No more silence unless spoken to. Just people like me living.

I pull open the map that I stole from Cyrus's camp, looking at the markings. Cyrus marked off places he considers overrun with hunters. His markings end at this dock, meaning he himself doesn't know what's across the sea. This is the last port that belongs to humans. The last one that is safe. If Dimitri and I had this map when we were traveling, we would have known what to avoid and exactly how to get here. But I can't dwell on the past anymore.

Dimitri is with the beasts now, and I am leaving.

Rumors of Cyrus's death have quickly circulated throughout the kingdom. The stories are all different. Some say the human king sacrificed himself to kill the beast. Some say the hunter army outnumbered him. Others even say he killed himself after seeing his father's corpse. But I know the truth. A weapon was created to kill him. A weapon curated from the blood of his people. A weapon that was strong enough to finally kill him.

I feel no remorse for my actions. I don't wish he could have changed; I don't wish he could have been kind to me. I feel no positive emotions for Cyrus. But one emotion is prominent. Fear. It will always be there, lurking in the back of my mind. I've only ever felt fear of Cyrus. Even in death, he'll continue to haunt me.

No one knows what the recoil of Cyrus's death is going to do. As we speak, hunters and humans alike are gathering in the beast kingdom to take it down and take the world into our own hands. I chuckle at the thought. I don't want to be here when humanity takes over. I've seen their ways of ruling. I am not impressed.

I turn away from the ocean, making my way through the market that sits near the water. Vendors call to me, offering me clothes, food, and weapons. But I have a clear vision in mind of what I need from them. I'm not like the rest of these people bartering for objects to take with me. I'm leaving this place to start over completely. I want to leave this world behind. I don't want my past to ever catch up with me. And I don't want to take anything from this world with me.

As I approach the right stand, I take in the woman that owns it. She's an older woman with graying hair. She offers me a kind smile as I approach.

"What could a beauty like you possibly be doing in a place like this?"

I can't bring myself to match her smile. I reach into my satchel, pulling out the gold I stole from Cyrus. I tell her the correct herbs I need, and her smile slowly drops when she realizes what it is I'm doing. Though I can sense her disapproval, she turns away from me to go in search of the potent herbs.

I look into the small mirror that sits on the edge of her table. I haven't really looked at myself in a long time. I stare at the haunted woman who is reflected back at me in the mirror. Her eyes are filled with despair. Her cheeks are gaunt from hunger. Her dark hair is messily splayed about her face. I curse the woman in that mirror. Something about her face drew in a monster like Cyrus. It made him lust after me. It made him desire me to the point of obsession. It made him plant his evil seed inside of me.

"Are you sure this is something you want to do?" I'm pulled out of my thoughts by the woman's voice. I look back at her, and she's watching me with a concerned expression. Her voice is soft, almost comforting. I release a bitter chuckle, placing my hand over the small burlap sack that contains the answer to the only problem remaining.

I meet her gaze before I speak.

"Fuck off."

Her eyes widen at the brashness of my words. I don't know how long I've been at Cyrus's mercy. Never able to speak my mind, always living in fear of the consequences. I narrow my gaze at her, snatching up the satchel. I silently continue my walk through the docks, making my way to the ship I know will take me away from here. There's a boy standing on top of a barrel shouting to the surrounding crowd the story of how the king of the beasts died. I slow my steps as his tale washes over me.

"The king had a plan! He trapped the beast, surrounding him with an army of trained hunters! Hunters that were prepared for this battle. The king handpicked these valiant men and women himself to fulfill a duty no weak soul could! They used the despicable power of the beasts against them!"

I feel my mind drifting as I listen to his tale. The way he describes the hunters as courageous people sickens me. I think of Dimitri's screams of pain and anguish. His face that will forever hold a brand. If there is one thing I regret, it's never being able to save Dimitri. I gave him up. Just like everything else in my past.

"And as the beast fell to his knees begging for dear life, the king struck him with a deadly blow! He cut off his head and stabbed him in the heart!"

The crowd applauds the outlandish story.

I know none of these people have ever encountered Cyrus. They would know immediately Cyrus was never one to beg. Cyrus was cruel, but he was a king in his own right. He commanded. He ruled. He let no one command him. Not even Marzia when she tried to put him in his place using me. The scars on my back prove it. He never bowed to anyone's will but his own. It makes me wonder what really happened on that mountainside.

Was he caught by surprise? Were the beasts simply outnumbered? What kind of way was the king of the beasts finally killed?

It's a mystery I'll never be able to unravel.

I continue my trek, finally seeing the ship come into view. The ship that will take me away from here. My freedom. I make my way through the crowd, handing off the reins of my horse to one of the crew. I then follow the procedures to board the boat by signing my name, paying my way, and finally boarding the ship.

My heart thunders against my chest. I never thought freedom would be possible, and yet here I am, seconds away from achieving it. I keep thinking that Cyrus is going to burst through the shrubbery at any second to drag me back or, better yet, kill me and everyone here. But he won't. He can't anymore.

I make my way to the edge of the ship, looking off into the distance. Storm clouds are rolling in. I hold out the tiny burlap sack that holds the herbs that will rid me of my condition. I recall Cyrus's father and Dimitri's reactions to my pregnancy. They both thought it was crucial that I stayed safe. They believed I was the key to something greater. But I wasn't. Cyrus was debating on killing me before he left.

A woman comes to stand next to me. I glance at her briefly. She has bruising and scars along her body. It makes me wonder what she sees when she looks at me. Her eyes meet mine and she gives me a sad smile.

"We made it, huh?" Her voice is soft, shaking with emotion.

I gasp softly when I realize tears are forming in my eyes. I don't fight them as they spill over. I look out at the clouds that are now flashing with lightning. The sails above are released, and I hear the crewmen around us shouting out orders. I grip the wooden edge of the ship tightly as the ship quakes, moving forward in the water. The ship slowly begins its journey to a new world, cutting through the water as it sails out of the port and into the open sea. I don't fight my smile.

I turn back to look at the mainland as it grows smaller. I don't know how long I stare at the docks. I keep my eyes trained on the wooden planks built above the water and the people. I keep my eyes on them until they grow smaller, resembling ants in the distance, until finally, they disappear into nothing.

I don't know what the future holds for me, but I don't stop my smile as I imagine the freedom that awaits me in a new world.

Chapter Thirty-Seven

FELIX

I make my way through the halls of the castle. The war horns blast to announce the arrival of the hunters. Today is the day. It's the day we will finally end this war.

News of Cyrus's death spread through the kingdom like wildfire, covering every corner, leaving no human out. We've been defending our walls for months from the constant barrage of hunters and humans that have been attacking, hoping to defeat us in light of our king's death. If they were smart, they would have used the time to get as far away from the empire as they could. But they aren't smart. Which is another reason the war shall end today. I tense when I feel the walls shaking from another bombardment of attacks. They're trying to break through the walls and the gate. And they will eventually. It's all a part of the plan.

I push open the doors to the war room, bowing upon entry.

"They've pushed through the last defense, Your Majesty. They will break the gate soon."

Cyrus turns away from the battle plan laid out on the table, looking at me.

"Perfect." A chill ripples down my spine at his words. I don't recognize my friend anymore. He's cold, distant, and unfeeling. His dark gaze holds no mercy or thoughts of negotiation, only death. The human king ended any chance his people had for a life among the beasts.

The weapon that was created to kill Cyrus would have succeeded if the human king hadn't been so in the dark about the true nature of beasts. Our society is built upon a hierarchy of strength. The weapon used was created from Cyrus's father's blood—a beast who was well past his prime. The only reason Cyrus hadn't taken the throne was that he wanted his father to reign for years to come. He wanted to give his father a chance to see his vision of peace come true.

Cyrus is more powerful than any of us could have ever imagined due to his mother's lineage. The only thing keeping his power at bay was the love he carried for his father. His father was the only thing standing between the humans and utter annihilation. And the human king killed him and taunted Cyrus with the remains of his body.

I recall the moment I found him at the bottom of that cliff. He was gravely injured. But for everything in him, he was still clinging to the severed head of his father. None of us know how the king was taken—none of us except for Annalise. And Cyrus has forbidden her name from ever being spoken. It's clear she knew about the weapon. She left the camp with stolen items. She knew Cyrus wouldn't be coming back. She intentionally kept that information from him. She's as much to blame for the human's cruel deaths as the human king is.

Cyrus has delayed putting his father to rest and taking the throne, all to keep the rumor of his death alive. He knew the hunters would mount a massive attack. He knew that as many humans as needed would show up trying to take our kingdom. And he's ready to end them.

"Has the battalion been shifted to the outer banks?" Cyrus asks.

I nod.

"We're waiting for your orders, Your Majesty."

Cyrus walks past me to the doors.

"Good. Let us put an end to this war."

We stand near the closed gate, listening to the sound of the battering ram smashing against it. I take note Cyrus is chuckling next to me as we stare at the effort they put into destroying something as simple as a gate. It shows the stark contrast in strength that humans have compared to the beasts.

"They are very aspirational for a race of weaklings," he growls.

He pushes past me and the guards standing around him, making his way to the gate.

"Step aside," he says as he walks.

I stare at him as he walks ahead of me, unable to tamp down the growing unease I feel. I note his pores are releasing the blackened exterior of his true form. I take a step back.

"Fall back!" I shout at the surrounding beasts.

Cyrus's true form can kill a man just by touching him. The more enraged he grows, the wider the spread. And the more people that die. It's why no one would ever challenge him. No one ever can. It's why we as a people both love and fear him. And it is why he will always undoubtedly be our king. It's dangerous for Cyrus to use this form so close to the kingdom, but he hasn't been himself since the stronghold.

I turn to my second in command.

"Anyone that makes it past Cyrus's form will be cut down here. Do not let anyone near him," I growl.

A soldier catches my eye as he scurries past, and I move away, snatching him quickly by the arm. Dimitri looks at me with wide eyes, immediately stepping back to bow.

"General," he says.

I narrow my gaze, looking back to Cyrus, who has made it to the gates.

"Do not get yourself killed," I say.

"Yes, General."

I keep my eyes focused on his face one last time before whipping away from him. I make my way toward Cyrus just as he reaches for his blade.

"Cyrus!"

He pauses, looking at me in irritation. Another ramming force hits the gate, but it barely moves.

"You're going to fight them alone?" I ask.

He narrows his gaze, looking back at the gate.

"No. I'm going to kill them." He looks at me. "Good luck, General."

It's the last thing he says before his form takes shape. I step back as the black smoke begins covering him. I keep a safe distance, watching in both awe and fear as he uses brute force to remove the bar holding the gate closed. The humans push open the gate with their battering ram but don't have a second to celebrate. Cyrus stands, watching them.

An intense silence washes over everyone immediately. The only sound is the random clink of armor. It's the last decipherable sound I hear before the screams begin.

I watch in shock and awe as Cyrus unleashes all the suffering of hell.

"No casualties. Everyone has been accounted for. We've kept their commanding officer's prisoner and have also taken in a few—"

"No prisoners." Cyrus's voice falls over the room, his tone chilling as he sits atop his throne, his attention focused on his blade with an eerie glare.

I inhale a deep breath. "Cyrus, we should—"

"No. Prisoners." Cyrus's dark gaze meets mine, a warning glimmering in his eyes.

I finally bow my head in submission. "Yes, Your Majesty."

Cyrus's era has begun, and it will be one that is in history books for decades to come. It will be an era unlike any other. I know Cyrus will lead our people to prosperity, but I also know that humanity will not make it out of this. Cyrus has never held them in high regard. Nor has he cared for them since his slave.

The rage Cyrus showed when the news of her escape was revealed is something I want to bury deep in my mind. Not only did she leave, but she also took the king's heir with her as well. We all know how humans behave. She won't keep it. Not only did she take money and specialty weapons, but she took maps as well. Maps that will let her have a safe journey to her destination. And with a new life on the horizon, there's no way she would keep the king's heir to remind her of the past they share. But I know Cyrus. And I know it's only a matter of time before he sets out for her.

Cyrus stands from his seat, walking down the throne.

"You've done well today, Felix. You and your men shall be rewarded handsomely for this victory," he says, walking past me.

"Thank you, your majesty."

"Gather troops. It's time to eradicate humans once and for all. Set out and find any camps you can within the kingdom. And kill them all," he says.

I take a step toward him. "Don't you think killing all the humans is a bit hasty?" I ask.

Cyrus is across the room in an instant, his hand around my throat. I tense as he shoves me into the nearest column, my air supply cut off instantly as he looks at me in a calculated rage.

"Since when do you love humans so much?" he asks. He glares at me with unspoken malice, something flashing behind his eyes as he finally releases me.

"Speak," he growls.

"I don't love them. I just think your hatred for the slave is clouding your judgment. I'm only advising you, Your Majesty. I meant no disrespect," I say, rubbing my throat.

Cyrus is silent for a moment before making a decision.

"Kill the hunters. Kill anyone with relation to hunters. If they are clean, leave them outside to die on their own. If they wish to survive, offer them salvation," a wicked smile finds its way onto his lips. "Brand them with my crest. Only then can they live among us," he chuckles.

He turns away from me, making his way to the doors. "That is all."

I watch as the beast I grew up with leaves the room. He has changed. In so many ways, he has changed. I no longer recognize the king he is.

I no longer see my friend in his eyes.

Epilogue

Dimitri

I've been summoned to the palace.

In the weeks since the great battle, the world has drastically changed for humans and beasts alike. I can only give thanks that the king saw half-breeds as a part of the beast society, more so than the humans. And I will forever be grateful to Anna for that. I make my way through the palace, the servants bowing to me as I walk by. The palace is a terrifying place to be these days. The king's temperament has drastically declined since returning from the battlefield.

I make it to the doors of the king's study, pausing when I hear the scream from inside.

A woman's scream.

"Dimitri?" I tense when I hear Felix's voice drift toward me. I slowly turn to face my master, bowing as he approaches. He has a look of confusion on his face as he takes me in.

"What are you doing here?" he asks.

I look up at him and back to the doors.

"I-I was summoned," I say.

Felix's gaze slightly narrows, but he steps past me to the doors. Just as he's about to push them open, the doors are pulled open, and a woman comes running out. She's holding what's left of her clothes in her hands, her eyes streaming with tears.

I thought when the king claimed victory and revenge for his father, he would be different: content. I thought he would forget about the anger he harbored for Anna's escape. But he hasn't. I don't know what it is about his feelings for humans that keep him so hooked on her. He hates humans more than anything in the world. Yet he won't forget about her. Maybe it's his inner beast that sees it as a challenge. Even his womanizing has become worse.

I fear the reason he has called us here today—namely me. I am only just becoming accepted by this society. The king never deals with anyone of my status.

Felix walks into the now open doors ahead of me, and I follow with my head down. We enter to find the king standing behind his desk, drinking from his glass. He eyes us as we approach, and we both bow.

"Your Majesty."

Felix and the king used to be best friends. But even now, Felix avoids him if he can. He's changed so much since his father's death. He is a formidable king. Even though he avoids him, I know Felix worries about his friend. He's let that be known frequently. But I fear this is who the king is now. And Felix needs to understand that as well. I hear him pouring another glass, and he makes his way to Felix, handing him the glass.

Felix takes it, walking towards the king's desk.

"I wanted to congratulate you, General, on a job well done. You've rid the world of my enemies," the king smiles.

Felix nods his head.

"Thank you," he says.

The king's gaze slips past Felix to mine.

"Now that the world has been cleared of hazards, I think it's time to reclaim what is mine," he says.

He gestures for me to approach, and I slowly make my way to where they stand. I follow the direction of Felix's gaze to the map that sits on the desk.

The king takes a sip of his drink as he watches me.

"Felix brags about your wit and strength. I think it's time I put you to good use," he says.

I slowly raise my gaze to meet his.

"Annalise stole a map from me. A very valuable map. A map that shows all the safe havens for humans," he says, stepping around me and pointing to specific areas on the map. I know these places. They were once hunter camps and safe houses.

"These are the places she could have made it to safely, according to that map. Though I doubt she hides in this kingdom."

I let out a soft gasp as he points to the port. I know Annalise. And we always spoke of escaping across the sea. And the king knows that as well.

"I know you, and she shared a bond. I know you'll know best how to track her down," he says.

The king moves around the table, coming to stand next to me. My heart is pounding in my chest at the direction of his words, the choice that is about to be handed to me. One that we both know I can't refuse. I feel Felix's gaze on me, daring me to refuse. If Felix prides himself on anything, it's his way of beating loyalty to the beast empire into me. And today is the day that loyalty is going to be tested. The king chuckles lightly, handing me a glass of wine.

I take it from him with shaky hands.

"I know you'll bring her back to me, Dimitri."

About The Author

Eris began writing dark novels in 2019. Eris was pulled into the world of dark content when deciding to write something everyone else shied away from or saw as "fucked up." It took years for Eris to hone the craft of writing into edge-of-your-seat erotic thrillers with spicy tones. Eris is a hermit and a cynic who sees the world for what it is and not what it can be. When Eris isn't writing, Eris likes to take long walks to clear their head of all the misfortune swirling around in there. Eris enjoys pushing boundaries in their books and hopes that one day this type of writing will no longer be censored and authors like Eris won't have to constantly look over their shoulders waiting to be banned from every platform. And will be given the same treatment as those who write fluff.

Coming in March 2024

ANNALISE & CYRUS'S STORY CONTINUES IN...

WRATH OF THE KING

Connect With Me

FOLLOW ME

*On Social Media
for latest news and updates*

@ERISTHEDARKAUTHOR

@ERISBELMONT

WWW.HISDARK96.WIXSITE.COM/ERISBELMONT